SARAH MLYNOWSKI

was born in Montreal and studied English literature at McGill University, where she honed her eccentric view of life through a biweekly newspaper column and as fiction editor of the literary journal. A vivacious and irrepressibly optimistic twenty-something, Sarah is also the proud owner of four pairs of black knee-high boots, numerous first-date outfits and a green belt in Tae Kwon Do. Passionate about writing, Sarah has been published in numerous literary magazines and now works for an international publisher based in Toronto. *Milkrun* is her first novel.

Sarah is currently immersed in her next novel, *Fishbowl*, to be published fall 2002.

For Elissa Harris
who always knows *just* what I mean
and lets me call her Mom.

milkrun

sarah mlynowski

**RED
DRESS
INK**
™

First edition December 2001

MILKRUN

A Worldwide Library/Red Dress Ink novel

ISBN 0-373-25012-6

Visit Red Dress Ink at www.reddressink.com

Printed in Canada

ACKNOWLEDGMENTS

With many, many, many thanks to the people
who helped me not become that-girl-who-always-
blabbed-about-one-day-maybe-in-
the-far-distant-future-writing-a-book:

Sam Bell for being the nicest editor
a North American girl could hope for
and for showing me how to make it "spot on"
(I think that means just right in British-talk).
Merjane Schoueri for being a marketer extraordinaire
and for literally giving me the shirt off her back.
Margie Miller and Tara Kelly for the perfect cover.
Randall Toye, Kathrin Menge, Natasa Hatsios,
Susan Pezzack, Julie Haroutunian and Louisa Weiss
for being bottomless pools of encouragement.
My dad for being proud of me and for trying really,
really hard to salvage chapter ten after I dropped my
laptop again. Laura Morris for her one-liners.
Bev Craig for the initial inspiration.
Robin Glube for being my Boston tour guide and
personal copywriter. Shoshana Riff for her Back Bay
road trip. Kate Henderson and Michael Hilliard
for helping me with those legal issues.
TOR Retail for their constant support
and for letting me hog the printer
while I printed out, um, reports. Bonnie Altro,
Rebecca Sohmer, Jessica Davidman,
Lisa Karachinsky, Ronit Avni, Jess Braun and
Judy Batalion for being my personal focus group,
fabulous friends and for letting me talk about my
book ad nauseam. Aviva June for giving me stuff to
write about. And of course, Todd Swidler,
because without him this book would not exist.

And yes, Mom, thanks again.

Chapter One

Jerk

Jerk. Jerk, jerk, jerk.

I can't believe what a complete jerk he is.

I am constantly debating whether or not I have a reason worthy of aggravating my boss by making a personal long distance call to Wendy in New York. All minor emergencies merit phone calls to Natalie right here in Boston: tension with a coworker, plans for the evening, boredom... But this—this complete and utter humiliation at the hands of a male, this travesty, definitely merits an emergency-Wendy phone call.

I minimize my e-mail screen in case my boss, the copyediting coordinator, walks by. Instead of seeing Jeremy's random act of devastation in the form of an e-mail from Thailand, Shauna will see *Millionaire Cowboy Dad,* the manuscript I'm supposed to be copyediting. I dial Wendy's number at work.

"Wendy speaking," she says in her investment-banker-don't-mess-with-me voice.

I hate him. I *really* hate him. "It's me," I say.

"I must be psychic. I wasn't going to pick up, but I thought it might be you."

No time for small talk right now. "Did you also have a premonition that the jerk would meet someone in Thailand and then write me to tell me about it?" I will never speak to him again. If he e-mails I will press delete. If he calls I will hang up. If he realizes he cannot live without me, jumps on the first available flight to Boston, and comes straight to my house with a diamond ring worth five months of his salary, that is, if his salary weren't nonexistent, I will slam the door in his face. (Okay...I'll probably get married. I'm not *that* crazy.)

"Shit," she says. "Who is she?"

"Don't know. Some girl he met while he was busy 'finding himself.' I don't hear from him for what, three weeks? Then he writes to tell me hi, how are you, I'm good and I'm in love."

"He actually said the L word?"

Jeremy has never even written the L word, let alone said it aloud. I think his hands and lips are genetically programmed to be incapable of combining the letters L-O-V-E.

I really, *really* hate him.

"No. He said he just wants me to know that he's seeing someone."

"But you did tell him he could see other people, right?"

"Well, yeah. But I never believed he would actually *do* it."

Unfortunately, I constantly imagine him doing it. I dream about him having orgies with groups of naked and frolicking Thai women. Instead of working on *Millionaire,* I find myself picturing him having wild, drug-induced sex with a six-foot Dutch goddess who looks like Claudia Schiffer and backpacks in stiletto heels and Capri pants. But up to now I believed that these self-inflicted tortures were manifestations of my overzealous why-would-he-want-to-travel-without-me-if-he-really-loved-me paranoia. Jeremy was supposed to come home after one month and tell me that, while he was away finding himself, he realized how much he truly loved me and that he wanted to spend the rest of his adult life ravishing my naked body with kisses, using the L word over and over.

Of course he had to go and ruin everything.

"Jackie, he's been backpacking through Asia for over two months. He's probably slept with half of Thailand by now. Let me hear the e-mail."

Will my computer malfunction if I throw up all over it?

"I can't read it out loud at work. I'll forward it to you. Hold on...one second...did you get it?" *Millionaire* returns to my screen.

"Call waiting, hold on." She puts me on hold and an elevator rendition of Chicago's "You're the Inspiration" plays in my ear. Oh God.

I know I'm about to start crying because the computer screen is slightly smudged as if it were run over by the crappy orange eraser on the back of a cheap pencil.

Must think happy thoughts. Julie Andrews dancing. Cadbury's chocolate Easter eggs. My sixteen-year-old half sister Iris believing I'm the coolest person ever. *Jackie, you look just like Sarah Jessica Parker, only prettier.*

Okay, I can kind of see again. The screen has almost returned to its previous non-orange color.

What other happy thoughts? The way Jeremy used to draw little circles on the inside of my arm with his thumb.

Shit, shit, shit.

Try again. The ninety-two percent Professor McKleen gave me on my Edgar Allan Poe essay. The day I got my braces off and my lips felt like they were sliding off my teeth and I kept smiling in the mirror. Okay. I'm all right now. Nothing to see here, folks.

Yuck. I notice that Helen, the associate editor who sits in the cubicle beside me is peeking over our wall divider. She always pops up at the exact moment I don't want her there. Like how you always get your period on prom or Valentine's or pool-party day. Whenever I'm checking out new movie sites on the Net, or sneaking in just a few minutes late, there she is. It's like some kind of superpower.

Her hair is pulled back into a frizzless tight bun, and as usual, not one hair has strayed. I think she uses glue; she looks frighteningly like Lilith from *Frasier.*

"Yes?" I ask in my I'm-very-busy-here voice.

"I'm sorry to bother you, but would you mind...um... refraining from making so much noise?" she whispers, putting her index finger up to her lips in her be-quiet motion. "I'm having concentration difficulties."

I resist the urge to tell her to kiss my butt. On my first day of work at Cupid almost two months ago, I decided I would not

allow this type of person, this presumptuous know-it-all, to get
to me. On that first day, when I told her I had gone to Penn, she
said she knew someone who had transferred there after he hadn't
been able to take the pressure at Harvard. She, of course, was a
Harvard graduate.

And then there was the time when I swear I was still willing
to give her a chance, and I peeked over her cubicle and said,
"Helen, Shauna wants to talk to you and I." Without looking
up, she answered, "Jacquelyn, it's...um...Shauna wants to talk
to you and *me.*"

And for some reason, most of the other copy editors seem to
think she's God's gift to Cupid. "Oh, Helen," they chime.
"You're the queen of commas." And "What was it like at Harvard, Helen?" Or "Tell us your theory of deconstruction and
subjectivity in Joyce's *Ulysses,* Helen." Okay, maybe I'm ex-
aggerating, but tell me, what normal person spends her lunches
reading *Paradise Lost* and *The Metaphysical History of Literary
Criticism?*

I'm sure she has a few theories on deconstruction and subjectivity that she'd be delighted to explain to me. "When I was a
freshman at Harvard, Jim, my world-renowned professor, insisted
on flying me across the country to present my original thesis..."
Blah, blah, blah. I did my M.A. in literature, too, you know,
although she never lets other people talk about themselves. A
half an M.A., actually. I completed the first year of a two-year
program. But why is a Harvard graduate working here, anyway?
She should be off editing Michael Ondaatje and discussing the
profound meanings of life—not the torrid love affair between a
robust cowboy and his virgin twenty-five-year-old bride. She obviously had lousy grades in school.

See? I'm just not letting her get to me.

"Sorry," I say, incredibly, with a straight face. "It's just that
I'm having a semicolon crisis and I'm finding it very unsettling."

"Really?" Her eyes swerve back and forth between my computer screen and my telephone. She's not sure if she should take
me seriously. "Well, I could help. I *was* a copy editor before I

was promoted to associate editor. I would consider scheduling a combined colon and semicolon meeting this afternoon. If you're serious.''

"Of course I'm serious.'' I'm amazed that people like her exist in real life. Do geeks know they're geeks? Does she wake up in the morning, look at herself in the mirror and think, "Wow, I'm such a loser''? Probably not. Does that mean that I, too, might be a complete freak and totally unaware of it? Do stupid people think they're smart? Do ugly people look in the mirror and see Cindy Crawford? Is it possible that I'm not as cute and witty as I think I am? Is that why Jeremy doesn't want me? Am I a hideous, moronic freak?

Helen taps her pen against our divider, a signal that she has decided to believe me. "All right. Since other people have voiced concerns as well, I'll schedule a discussion group.'' Her cheeks start to flush with excitement. Punctuation appears to be foreplay for Helen. "Is 3:45 a good time for you?''

Yeah, a real good time. "Sounds fantastic.''

"Excellent. I'll send out a group e-mail to all my copy editors.'' Her head finally disappears behind the cubicle wall. Like she can't just pop across the hall to tell Julie. The only copy editors who work on her series, *True Love,* are Julie and me. And I'd like to further object to her using the possessive term "my.'' We do not belong to her. Shauna is the coordinating copy editor. Shauna writes our reviews. Helen's series just happens to be one of the many we have been assigned.

"Sorry,'' Wendy's voice resurfaces on the phone. "Okay, I'm reading it now. Blah, blah, blah…'Today I did *E* again'…Why were you wasting your time with that druggie?…'Someone stole my green J-Crew shirt from the balcony'…God, what a loser!…'I'm seeing a great girl and we've been traveling together for the past month…That's *it?*''

"No, you forgot the 'I thought you might want to know' part.''

"'I thought you might want to know. Take care, Jer…' Is this a joke? Is this some kind of sick joke?''

"Unfortunately not.'' But wait! What if it is a joke? Or maybe some kind of new computer virus tapped into my wildest fears and mutated accordingly.

"And you've been sitting on your ass every weekend while he's been slutting around? Ridiculous. Do you realize you haven't met one guy since you've moved?"

Sometimes I think Wendy definitely lacks in the sympathy department. "I've met guys," I respond defensively. "I just haven't dated any of them."

"You've been pathetic."

I *have* been pathetic. I even refused to go out with Jason Priestly's look-alike, introduced to me by Natalie, because I was worried that word would somehow get to Jer and he'd feel the need to get back at me and go ahead and fall in love with someone else. And what if Jer called while I was out? I could never have brought a guy home—my room is a shrine of pictures of Jer: Jer and me at the park; Jer and me at formals; Jer's graduation; pictures of Jer, Jer, Jer. It never occurred to me that Jer wouldn't have a picture of us next to his sleeping bag, that maybe it was time for me to buy one of those funky photo boxes and do some filing.

Pathetic.

Hmm. Wait a second. "Is it possible seeing just means *seeing?* Like with his eyes?"

Pause. "No."

Sigh. Yeah that sounded lame even to me.

Pathetic.

"You're right. I'm going to start dating again. I'm going to become Crazy Dating Girl. I'm going to date every guy in Back Bay." Back Bay is the oh-so-hip, oh-so-overpriced area in Boston where I live.

The time has come.

I will date witty, hot, ridiculously rich men who will shower me with expensive jewelry, send roses to my office, and whisper how wonderful I am in my ear while massaging my I-sit-all-day-in-front-of-a-stupid-computer back. Life will be wonderful. I will wake up every morning with a smile on my face like the perma-smile women in coffee commercials.

"You're right. No more whining." But I can't go out by my-self, can I? "I don't have any friends to go out with," I whine.

Pause. "Don't you have any girlfriends?"

"Not really." Everything sucks. I hate my life. I will have to send roses to myself with an anonymous love letter and whisper sweet nothings into my own ear. "I guess I can always call Natalie."

"You must have someone else to call."

Wendy does not like Natalie. All three of us used to live on the same floor in a student dorm at Penn. Natalie calls Wendy an intellectual snob. Wendy calls Natalie a Brahmin elitist. Truth-fully, Wendy *is* an intellectual snob and Natalie *is* a bit of an elitist. I didn't even know what a Brahmin was until Wendy explained that Natalie belongs to the *upper caste* of Boston so-ciety. "It does sound kind of snooty when you say it like that," I told Wendy.

"Unfortunately, I have no one else to call." The only new people I've spoken to since I moved, besides the weirdos at work, are my fifty-year-old manicurist and my superintendent. I haven't got out of the apartment much, devoting my spare time to Sein-feld reruns and reading *Cosmo, Glamour, City Girls* and *Made-moiselle* to try to mentally collect what I refer to as the Fashion Magazine Fun Facts. These are life rules that will one day help me pinpoint all the things I did wrong in my relationship with Jeremy, make myself a better person, and allow myself to live a successful, sexy and ultimately satisfying life. Page five says ask him out, page seventy-two says wait for him to call me, page fifty says he wants an independent woman, page fifty-six says he'll walk if I don't make him feel needed... Will smoky-colored eye shadow really make me more desirable? More desirable than a Brazilian bikini wax will? What is a Brazilian bikini wax? It's all very confusing.

"So go out with Natalie tonight, but then you've got to find new friends. What about Samantha?" she asks.

Sam is my annoying roommate. She and her boyfriend are always all over each other. "I don't like her. She makes me use color-coordinated sponges in the kitchen—blue for dishes, green for pots, pink for the counter."

"That makes sense."

Maybe it makes sense to people like Wendy who open public bathroom doors with their feet because they don't want to touch the handle. Not to me. I wonder why I surround myself with such anal personalities.

Still, anal friends are better than no friends.

"Again, why do you like Natalie?" Wendy asks.

Natalie may not be the brightest star in the solar system, but she's fun. Brahmins do have some advantageous qualities. She knows the whole world and would be great at introducing me to lots of Brahmin men, if I ever let her. When I called to tell her I was moving to Boston, she had me hooked up to live with Sam in less than a week. "If you moved here I could hang out with you. Since you don't, Natalie is my only option."

Let's face it, Wendy is a bit of a snob. She is one of those A-plus girls who have no patience for stupidity. We've known each other since Mrs. Martin, our second-grade math teacher who wore the same gray turtleneck every day and smelled like Swiss cheese, sat us next to each other at the back of the class. We bonded over our love for Michael Jackson and Cabbage Patch Kids, remaining inseparable through the traumas of middle school, high school, university, and Ted Abramson. Ted Abramson actually falls somewhere in the middle school/high school range, more specifically when he broke up with me after fifth grade and asked Wendy out at her bat mitzvah, then dumped her during the summer and liked me again in eighth grade.

But we survived the Ted crisis just as we survived my accidental disposing of her retainer into the cafeteria wastebasket, even though to this day I insist she left it wrapped in tissue on top of her lunch bag and it did look like garbage. And in our junior year at university, she survived me almost killing her after she told Andrew Mackenzie, her lab partner in her calculus class—I'm still not sure why math class has a lab—that I thought his friend Jeremy was a hottie. We spotted Jeremy exactly three years ago in *Twentieth Century American Prose*, which came right before Wendy's calculus class. The farther Huck Finn floated down the river, the more smitten I became. Of course, Andrew told Jeremy. *Very* embarrassing.

I should never have forgiven her so easily.

"It's all your fault, anyway," I snap.

"What's my fault? Your not having friends? Let me remind you that you were still in school when I was offered this job, and besides, how could I possibly turn down Wall Street?"

Wendy had been offered investment banking jobs at every company she applied to—not only because of her perfect Grade Point Average at Wharton, Penn's business school, but because she had volunteered at food banks, wrote for the school paper, taught English in Africa for a summer, and worked part-time for the computer center, training students in Excel. While most people, including me, took *Space, Time, It Doesn't Matter 101*—a one hundred percent paper physics course where I was allowed to write about the physics of dating—as an option, Wendy took *Deconstructing Post-Colonial Narratives* and *Russian Formalism and Anglo-American New Criticism.* Conveniently, her optional courses were my compulsory courses, so we got to hang out a lot. I also got to skip many classes because not only did Wendy type up her notes, she also made detailed indexes and four-color pie charts.

"My entire relationship with Jeremy is your fault. You fixed us up."

"Quit whining. You shouldn't be surprised, after all the crap he's pulled."

I hate when she uses against me things I tell her. "I so don't want to get into this now, 'kay?"

"Fine. Call Natalie. Tell her you want to go meet boys. Immediately."

Doesn't Wendy have enough people to boss around at work? "Fine, I will."

"Good."

"Fine."

"Good luck, I love you, call me later," she says, and slams down the phone.

I dial Natalie's number at home. Except for university, my Brahmin friend has lived with her parents in Boston all her life.

She spends her time shopping, getting her nails done, looking for a husband, and if there's time, doing volunteer work.

One ring. Two rings. I know she's checking her Caller ID.

"Hi!" she exclaims in her high-pitched voice that sounds as though she ingested a minor amount of helium. "How are you?"

"We're going out tonight so I can flirt with everyone. Where are we going?"

"Sorry, but I can't leave my house today. I'm having a major fat day."

Natalie weighs about eighty-seven pounds. I have no patience dealing with her ridiculousness.

"How am I supposed to meet guys if I don't go out?"

"Why are you suddenly meeting guys? What happened to Jer?"

"I don't want to talk about it. It's over. I need to meet men."

"Well—"

"Please? Pleasepleasepleaseplease?"

"Uchhh, fine. I'll meet you at your place at nine. We'll go to Orgasm."

Orgasm is a very trendy martini bar about four blocks away from my apartment. Very hot men go to Orgasm.

"Perfect." I say.

"Get the vodka ready. I don't know if any of my clothes will fit me, though. I may have to borrow something of yours."

Hmm. Thanks.

Helen peaks over the divider again. "Jacquelyn…"

"Deal," I say to Natalie. I smile sweetly at Helen. "I'm really sorry, Helen. I'm feeling punctuation-overwhelmed. I'm sure you understand. See you later, Nat." I hang up the phone without looking up.

I will date. I will become the queen of dating. I will forget all about him. I will sit on patios wearing strappy sandals and skimpy sundresses, drinking Cosmopolitans and flirting with my new boyfriend. Make that plural. *Boyfriends.* Jeremy who?

Jeremy the Jerk. Jeremy who is dating a tall, leggy blonde who wears crop-tops to expose her navel ring. She's probably gorgeous and brilliant, and he sends her roses, and scatters love notes on pink heart-shaped paper around their hostel.

Jackie? Jackie who? Oh yes, that's right, that other girl I dated in university before I fell madly in love with my leggy navel-pierced blond goddess.

She must be from Holland. The Dutch are all gorgeous. He doesn't even care that we've been dating on and off since our junior year in college, and that up to about sixteen minutes ago, he was the center of my life. All I wanted was for him to ask me to come with him, but apparently, finding yourself is something that a man has to do without his girlfriend. Even a girlfriend who is so in love that she's prepared to drop everything and run away with him.

I need a new boyfriend. Somewhere in Boston there is a man who will realize how wonderful I am. There must be a ton of eligible men in the Hub. There are at least…well…I don't even know how many people there are in Boston.

Luckily, the Internet knows everything. Yay! Project. How many eligible men are there in Boston? Hmm. How many eligible men are there in Boston between the ages of twenty-five and thirty? Search: single men.

After about forty-five minutes of looking at unrelated sites— *Love Match, How to Catch a Sexy Single Man, What Men Want*—I find the U.S. Census. Fifteen minutes after that, I find information on Boston. Median rent: $581. Five hundred and eighty-one dollars? Are they paying in English pounds? Do they live in a bathroom?

Almost three million people live in Boston: 1,324,994 men, 1,450,376 women. Damn. Bad ratio.

Okay, age range…eighteen to twenty. Too young.

Twenty-one to twenty-four. Still too young.

Twenty-four to forty-four. To forty-four? That's quite a range. My dad is practically forty-four. Actually, my dad's fifty…fifty-something. I don't remember. I can't be expected to remember every detail. Hmmm. At least forty-year-old men are established. There are 210,732 people between the ages of twenty-four and forty-four. That makes about 100,000 men. I wish Wendy were here to draw me a graph.

One hundred thousand. And all I'm looking for is *one*. One man who is attractive, intelligent, still has hair (and doesn't part it on the side to cover where he doesn't have it), has an exciting and promising career (I wouldn't mind an equally exciting and promising car), never wears turtlenecks (straight men shouldn't wear turtlenecks), doesn't have back acne (a.k.a. backne), wears a nice cologne (preferably something musky), is nice to his mother (not a mama's boy), and is sensitive...no, strong...no, sensitive...definitely sensitive...but not too sensitive...would he be able to cry in front of me? He has to be able to cry...but not often...sometimes...

You have mail. Would you like to read it now?

Maybe Jeremy has realized that he is actually completely in love with me, can't live without me, and is bored with the hot Dutch bimbo.

Attn: *True Love* copy editors. The emergency semicolon meeting will take place in the production boardroom in exactly five minutes. Please be on time.
Helen

Damn.

I will have to listen to Helen ramble for an hour, and I am entirely to blame. I imagine strangling her with different types of punctuation. I imagine wrapping a nice, fat em dash around Jeremy's throat.

Jerk. Jerk, jerk, jerk.

Chapter Two

No, I'm Not a Hooker But I Sometimes Like to Look Like One

"Hello? Sam?"

Yay! No one's home. I love nothing more than walking into an empty apartment. It wasn't always this way. When I went to Penn and lived with Wendy, there was nothing I loved more than coming home to see my best friend flopped upside down on the couch watching TV, her legs thrown over the red and pink flowery pillows her grandmother had given us. "Yay! You're home," Wendy would say, and we'd make French Vanilla coffee (two Sweet 'n' Lows for me and one spoon of sugar for her), and describe our days in excruciating detail.

"And then I walked to the cafeteria and saw Crystal Werner and Mike Davis."

"They're still together?"

"Yeah, after he cheated on her. Can you imagine?"

I think it was kind of selfish of her to go off to New York and leave me all alone like this.

A red light on my phone is flashing signaling I have messages. "You have three new messages," the voice in the receiver says.

I will not think that maybe one is Jeremy. I will not hope that he has changed his mind and that as soon as I press play, I will hear, "Hi, it's me, I really miss you" in his radio-talk-show, native-New Yorker voice. I know there will be a message from him only when I least expect it. That's the sick way the world works. I can see the picture clearly: I will absentmindedly hit the play button, his name not popping into my mind even once, and "Hi, it's me, I really miss you" will hit me like the ice water showers I have to take every morning because Sam uses up all the hot water with her forty-five-minute marathons.

Look at that! I have messages! La-la-la. Whoever can they be? I'll just casually listen and not really care about who it might be.

"Hi, Sam, it's your mother. Call me back." Beep.

"Jackie! Jackie, where are you? I called you at work and you didn't answer. I'm going out now, but I *need* to talk to you. I'm having an emotional crisis. Matthew told Mandy that he likes me and I don't like him, so what do I do? Call me as soon as you get home. But I'm going out. So leave a message." Beep. Iris is always having an emotional crisis. Who's Matthew?

"Hello, Jacquelyn. It's Janie. Just calling to say hello. Call me back when you have a chance." Beep.

Damn.

Janie is my mother. When I was four, she insisted I call her by her first name. This ban had something to do with the label "mother" being part of a bourgeois ideological conspiracy to maintain the power and position of the ruling class—the parents. But by the time I was five, my father was promoted from manager of the ladies' innerwear department to the director of ladies' outerwear, and my mother began to shed some of her Marxist philosophies, discovering her inner material-girl self. But by then it was too late for me to start calling her Mom again. The imprinting was complete. I love Janie dearly, don't get me wrong, but she's a wee bit flaky.

Fern Jacquelyn Norris is my official name. I never use the name Fern. I hate the name Fern. I'm still not sure why my parents gave me such a godawful name. I think Janie must have named me while on some kind of mind-altering drug during the seventies. I've convinced Janie to call me by my middle name, but my dad seems to have a learning disability on the subject.

Once upon a time I lived with Janie and my father in a house on a street called Lazar in Danbury, Connecticut, and my best friend was a my-size pigtailed girl named Wendy. Today Wendy is a lot taller, still my best friend, and gone are her pigtails (they reappeared for a short stint in the 90s to capture that "cute" look). My dad—named Tim, but I was allowed to call him Dad—as I mentioned, made women's clothes while Janie made bracelets. She made thousands of these, some with rhinestones, some with little silver moons and stars. She sold a couple to the local boutiques, but stored most of them in old shoeboxes that she stacked like building blocks beside the bookshelf. It's a good thing that by this time she was into fashion and was buying many pairs of shoes.

When I was six, I found out that my parents, who I believed belonged to a wonderful marriage, did not like each other. This makes perfect sense to me now. Everything is always *so* clear when you look back—the right answer on the exam, the guy who liked you but who you thought was only so-so until the popular cheerleader started dating him, the blind spot you definitely should have checked before you made that sudden turn and lost your side mirror—but at the time, I found their sudden change of heart horrifying. Dad moved into a bachelor pad, and Janie and I moved into a two-bedroom apartment across town.

A few months later, Dad married Bev, a part time travel agent, and they moved into a house on Dufferin. A few months after that, Janie married Bernie, a sales guy, and we moved into his two-bedroom apartment, which was only slightly larger than our old one, on Carleton Avenue. Then when I was eight, Janie got pregnant with Iris, and the three and a half of us moved into a three bedroom on Finch. (Iris, by the way, was encouraged to call Janie "Mom.") When Iris was four, Janie decided she was sick of hearing neighbors on top of her, sick of feeling as if she lived under a bowling alley, sick of not being able to blast her Beatles CDs without the police coming and telling her to turn it down (yes, that actually happened), and that we were moving into our own house.

We moved to Kelsey Avenue, and stayed there until Janie decided she'd had enough of not being able to happily wear her Birkenstocks without fear of deer ticks and that we were moving to Boston. Thankfully, *we* didn't include me. That's when I went to Penn. They lived in Newton for four years until Janie decided to move to Virginia because "everyone should be able to walk for less than fifteen minutes and dip her toes in the ocean."

In my twenty-four years on this planet I have had, to date, fourteen different bedrooms. To reach this number, I have to include university residence, my first apartment at Penn with Wendy, my second apartment at Penn with Wendy, and my own apartment at Penn after Wendy got her investment banking job in New York. I stayed, in principle to do my M.A., but really to be with Jeremy. This list also includes the apartment my parents lived in when Janie was pregnant with me.

I don't feel like calling Janie back just yet. I prefer to lie on my couch and watch some mind-numbing television. Click. Click, click. Nothing on but boring news.

I decide to admire the black leather knee-high boots I purchased on Newbury Street on my way home from work today. Every newly single girl needs new boots. It is step one in the recovery process.

There are actually five steps to recovery. Wendy and I wrote them up in college after she broke up with…what was his name? The economics major who cheated on her with the green-braces girl…oh, yeah, Putzhead.

I find the list in my stuff-drawer, between a Valentine's Day mix tape featuring classics like "I Just Called to Say I Love You," "Lost in Love," and "Glory of Love" and two *New Kids on the Block* concert ticket stubs. I think we were planning on sending it into *Cosmo* or something. The list, written in purple ink, smells like stale Marlboros. It was during our wannabe-smokers days.

How to Recover from a Breakup

1.   Buy knee-high black leather boots.
2.   Get a new haircut. Find an extremely outrageous hair salon, where coffee is brought to you and gay men tell you that you have the most gorgeous hair they have ever seen.
3.   Call a female friend so that you can talk about how

much you miss your ex, and the friend can remind you of all the times he pissed you off, admitting that she never thought he was nice or attractive, that you could do much better, that he was cheap, that he had a strange smell, et cetera. This step is best accomplished with a mediocre friend as opposed to a best friend, in case of boyfriend reconciliation.

4.   Call male friends so that you can be reminded of how desirable you are. Do not actually fool around with these friends. You'll need them around for several months following your breakup.

5.   Buy chocolate chip cookie dough and/or a box of tremendously expensive chocolates filled with different types of pastel-colored creams, and eat the entire box.

Amazing! Five years later and the steps are still (almost) valid:

1.   *Boots.* Check.

2.   *Hair.* I need to do some careful research before attempting this step. Nothing is worse than number two ending with tears and me having to wear that Red Sox baseball hat Jeremy bought me so that I would look like a native.

3.   *Friend phone call.* Check. Well, kind of check. Considering Jeremy and I have broken up five times in three years, I have already lost all my mediocre friends, and I refuse to take chances with the ones I have left.

4.   *Male friend phone call.* This one is a bit of a problem due to my lack of maintaining or acquiring male friends since Jeremy and I started dating.

4.a.   *Make male friends.*

4.b.   *Call male friends.*

5.   *Chocolate.* Check. Having emergency cookie dough in your freezer is as crucial as having an emergency twenty in your wallet. Not that I can ever save the twenty in my wallet. I have recently modified Step 5. Eat chocolates while watching *Sex and the City* or *Ally McBeal* to remind me that there

are other attractive, successful single women out there, and that they, unlike me, are over thirty.

Steps one through five should be repeated freely until girl is over breakup. Steps one and two should be slightly altered with each revisit, by the use of sexy sandals, leather pants, a backless tanktop, highlights, perm, layers... You get the idea.

Tonight, however, there is no time for cookie dough.

I shower, in hot water for a change (I even use the yummy-smelling soap sample I was saving for Jer's return. See? I'm practically over him already), blow-dry my hair straight (it takes forever and I keep burning my fingers, but I don't care because it makes me look very chic), put on my black knee-length skirt that has a slutty slit right up the thigh, a relatively new slinky red tank top and my new boots that right now feel so worth the $150 I can't afford.

Yup. I'm pretty hot.

I find the smoky eye shadow page in *Cosmo* and try to follow the directions without poking my pupil. I will dazzle men with my hazel eyes, I will use lip liner to show off my smile, and I will smile to show off my dimples.

I am even wearing a thong for good luck.

I'm tired of waiting for things to happen to me. Time to get out there and grab life by the...well, you know. I am twenty-four, I am young, I refuse to sit around watching my butt get bigger while Jeremy runs around enjoying himself. Women are always waiting for men to come over to them, for men to ask them out, for men to kiss them.

Wait, wait, wait! The first time I waited for a kiss was when I was in middle school. It seemed as if everyone else in the world had already been French kissed (I imagined French women all walking around licking everyone), including Wendy, who had played spin-the-bottle at her cousin's birthday party. Ted and I had already been going out for two days, and we were sitting at a picnic table outside at a school dance, talking about nothing (warm out, isn't it?), experiencing that sweaty-palmed, irregularly palpitating - heart, what - happens - if - I - pass - out - I - think - we're - about - to - kiss feeling. Finally, his face just kind of fell on top of mine, and there we were, kissing. Well, not exactly kissing, since our mouths were closed and our lips just kind of bumping as if we were two people in a crowded subway who just happen to be sharing the same pole. Then suddenly we were *kissing*. Wendy's instructions surfaced in my mind: just keep your mouth open and move your tongue around. His tongue was mushy and I could taste Clorets at the back of his mouth.

Waiting never gets easier. After the first kiss, girls have to wait for their first love, and then they have to wait to lose their virginity. Or, if you're tired of searching for your endless love, you can sleep with Rick the Deadhead, who called (and probably still calls) everyone "dude" and wore (and probably still wears) tie-dye. Yup, you can screw waiting, like I did.

You know what I hate about TV and movies? People never just fool around. They either kiss or they have sex. A guy starts unbuttoning a girl's jeans and the girl says, "I'm not ready to have sex with you," and the guy says okay, and her pants stay on, and it just ends there. You never hear about any of the bases that everyone I knew went through before the idea of actually doing it even occurred to them. Well, I'm sure it *occurred* to them.

I didn't sleep with Rick right away. We went around all the bases, around and around and around, until the end of my first year at college when I finally got tired of the idea just occurring to me and decided that I wanted to *do* it already.

Our first time was on a Sunday night, on his cramped dorm bed, with *Skeletons from the Closet* playing on the stereo. By the time we got to "Truckin'," the second track, it was all over. My body felt as if it had been clawed open, as we sat on his bed smoking cigarettes. My hands smelled like rubber elastic and I remember thinking, *That's it?*

With Jeremy everything was suddenly...different. He would run his hand along my lower back and I would lose all ability to focus on anything but his fingers. He had perfect guy hands.

About twice the size of mine, they never got sweaty and they smelled like burning leaves. In a good way. He wasn't into holding hands, but he always had his arm around my shoulder, or on my back, or on my knee.

Enough of that. Change the channel in my head.

JulieAndrewsJulieAndrewsJulieAndrews.

Chocolate Easter bunnies.

Look at me, I'm Sandra Dee.

Well, not quite Sandra Dee. I'm waiting in full slut-attire for Natalie, when I hear Sam and Marc approaching the front door. Giggling. They're always giggling. They're also one of those couples who are always touching each other, making everyone around them uncomfortable.

I didn't realize when I signed the lease that I would have two roommates instead of one.

Okay fine, the truth is that I hardly ever see Marc. Sam has a TV and a bathroom in her room, and they hardly ever come out. They just have sex. A lot. And they watch *Law and Order*, which for some reason seems to be on about six times a day.

What really bugs me about Sam is her why-can't-you-clean-up-cuz-your-mess-is-really-annoying look. Like when she finds my socks on the coffee table. Or when she asks why I always leave the remnants of things in the fridge, like a milk container, a pizza box of only crusts, the pitcher of iced tea that has a rim of brown gel on the bottom but no tea. Once, she told me as she tossed my moldy half-leftover cheese sandwich in the trash can, that next time I didn't have to save her any. No, no sarcasm there.

Here's the thing: finishing something usually involves cleaning up or throwing something out, which probably also involves replacing an already full garbage bag with an empty one and then having to bring the filled one to the garbage chute—which all together spells too much work.

I have the same issues with filtered water. I never finish the pitcher. I hate having to fill it up.

I guess I haven't as yet discovered the joys of closure.

Sam gets annoyed that I make everything her responsibility. Like collecting the rent, paying the bills, watering the plants, feeding the cat...I always assume she'll take care of it because I take care of the other stuff, right? Don't ask me to define the other stuff; right now, I'm into the intangible (Jer, Jer, Jer). Luckily, Sam always ends up doing everything, because otherwise we'd have an eviction notice, brown plants, and a dead kitty.

I'm kidding about the cat. I'd remember to feed a cat. We don't even have a cat, I swear.

Sam opens the door. She and her attachment are each holding a bag of groceries.

"Look at you! Sexy stuff! What are you up to tonight?"

"I'm going to Orgasm."

Marc laughs. "Lucky you."

Sam giggles again, drops her bag of groceries, and grabs Marc around the waist. "The bar Orgasm, silly."

"I know. I was just teasing, Sessy Bear."

Marc calls Sam "Sessy Bear." I don't know why. I don't even know what it means.

"I know, Biggy Bear."

Sam calls Marc "Biggy Bear." I don't know why. I don't want to know why.

"Who are you going with?" Sam asks.

"Nat. We're going to get very drunk and meet men. You two wanna come?" Please say no.

"Sounds like fun," Marc says. "But we're going to watch 'L and O.'"

Thank God.

Sam giggles. "Is that the new name? Like SNL and KFC?"

"It's all about acronyms now, you know," Marc says. "If you're nice, Sessy Bear, maybe afterwards we'll get an ice cream from DQ."

"Is it normal that someone could be such a geek?" Sam asks me, playfully patting Biggy Bear on his behind.

"You're the geek," says her attachment.

For the second time today, I think I'm going to throw up.

After they disappear behind a thankfully closed door, I decide to prepare the instruments of our intoxication while I wait for Nat.

I take out the vodka and two shot glasses. She'll be here any second. I might as well pour while I wait.

Yay! I'm going out tonight! Although I've never been to Orgasm, I've heard many-detailed descriptions from Natalie. "It's *the* place to be seen," she once explained after I had lied about having too much work to do to go. As if I ever brought work home. They certainly aren't paying me enough for that. Paying me enough, period.

"Anyone who's anyone goes there," she said. I was slightly surprised that people besides the prom queen on TV movies actually used that expression.

Whatever. Tonight I'll be seen. If Natalie ever gets to my house, that is. Nat, where are you?

Jeremy, where are you? Long, Dutch legs come to mind.

I might as well get started and have mine. Drink, that is. Not long legs. All fantasy should be based on some degree of truth; what's the use of yearning for something that can absolutely never happen?

Ouch. That burns. The drink, that is, not the truth (although that, too, can jolt a girl if she lets it).

Damn slut and her damn Dutch navel ring.

Now Nat's shot is just sitting there, all alone, like the last lonely chocolate chip cookie in the box.

So I down it just as the downstairs buzzer rings. "I found something to wear," Nat's voice flows up through the intercom. "Come downstairs."

See? If I hadn't had those shots, they would have gone to waste.

Chapter Three

Orgasming

"Hi, hon! Shall we walk?" Natalie asks, slinging her arm through mine.

"Of course we should. It'll only take us eight minutes."

"Which way is it?"

Silly Natalie. It's not that I'm a walking compass or anything, but I pass the bar at least twice a day. So does Natalie. True, Boston's not the easiest city to navigate; streets tend to inexplicably change names from Court to State, from Winter to Summer, and then disappear altogether. I'm no stranger to getting lost-induced panic attacks (I will never find my way home, I will end up in a bad neighborhood, I will get robbed and killed and no one will notice until months later when they find my decomposed body still strapped to my ten-year-old Toyota in the river—for the love of God, why don't I have a cell phone like everyone else?), but Back Bay is pretty much a grid.

"Tonight I can have three shots," she says.

Sobriety is not Nat's concern. She is a self-admitted obsessive calorie counter. She carries a yellow spiral notebook with a picture of grapes on the cover, a purple felt pen, and a highlighter everywhere she goes. She writes down everything she eats. She even highlights her "boo-boos" (her word choice, not mine).

"You know," she continues, "one shot of vodka has sixty-two calories."

No, I don't know. Or care. This week, anyway. One hundred and twenty-four calories down. Six zillion to go.

Today, Natalie does not in fact look fat. She looks exactly the

same as she always does—very, very skinny and very, very tall.
Well, not very, *very* tall, but tall compared to me (everyone is
tall compared to me, since I measure about three inches over five
feet). Natalie is probably only five foot six, but standing next to
me I tend to think of Michael Jordan).

Actually, she looks more like Buffy the Vampire Slayer, except that Nat has brown hair. Though she'd never admit it, according to Sam, Natalie paid a visit to Dr. Harvey Gold, one of
Boston's top nose-job specialists, as a combined high school
graduation/birthday present from her parents (Nat, that is, not
Buffy). The first time I was at her house in Beacon Hill, I ex-
amined every photograph, searching for a before-picture. Of the
thirty-five frames prominently featured throughout the huge
house, not one featured her before the age of eighteen. Suspicious?

And she dresses just like Buffy (sort of). Her Dolce and Gab-
bana black tube top and tight red pants must have cost more than
my month's rent. Luckily, she's the type of person who can pull
that outfit off—financially *and* aesthetically. As for myself, I tend
to camouflage instead of highlight.

Nat volunteers at various mental health clinics. One day she
plans on doing her master's degree in psych. One day mentally
disturbed people might go to her for help. Scary. Even the remote
possibility that she actually gets in to one of these programs
terrifies me.

Eight minutes later, as promised, we arrive to find twenty fidgeting people lined up by the door, huddled under the metallic
silhouette of a woman's head thrown back in complete orgasmic
abandon.

Natalie walks to the front. "George!" she squeals to the intimidating six-foot, very bald bouncer whose wraparound sunglasses remind me of the Terminator.

"Hey, sexy," he says. Kiss, kiss. Kiss, kiss.

"George, I want you to meet Jackie. She's one of my best
friends."

"Hi," I say meekly, and into the bar we walk.

* * *

"How's the sky?" Natalie says, raising her head. That's her code phrase for "Do I have snot in my nose?"

"Clear," I answer.

"And the street?" That's the code for "Do I have anything in my teeth?" What could possibly be in her teeth escapes me, considering I'm pretty sure she doesn't eat. Her smile gleams the way I'm sure capped teeth should.

"Clean. Me?" I ask just in case. I go for the two-in-one: I smile and tilt my head simultaneously.

On our left is the coat check. I'm thankful that this late September weather has allowed me to get away without wearing any kind of overclothes. (I need to expose as much as I can get away with right from the start; Nat, on the other hand, could wear a burlap sack and still leave 'em panting.) On our right is the dance floor. Some scantily clad women—good God, do I look like *that?*—are gyrating to a thumping song I am having difficulty deciphering: *boom, boom, boom slut, boom, boom, boom, go down on me.* Lovely.

"Let's go." Straight ahead is the bar. I motion in front of me, maneuvering my way through the crowd. A waitress with way too much breast exposure asks me what I'd like.

I'd like to have your cleavage, I think but don't say. She'd think I was some sort of pervert if I did. But I really, really would like to have her cleavage. It's true I fill out a solid Victoria's Secret B-cup, and Jeremy certainly seemed happy enough ("More than a handful…" he'd say), and this waitress can't possibly be wearing more than I am, but let's face it, I'd need a serious WonderBra to achieve *that* look. But here's the thing: what happens when you take a guy home and the bra comes off? How does one explain that exactly?

I order two Lemon Drops and try to keep my eyes leveled on the busty waitress's face. I love this shot—first you lick a sugar-covered lemon, then you shoot the vodka, and finally you suck the lemon. Very fun. It's like buying a bingo lottery ticket; it not only serves its purpose, but doubles as an activity. "Ready?" I ask.

"Cheers," says Natalie.

Yay! I'm going to get drunk! I'm going to have fun! I'm already having fun. I'm having so much fun, I've practically forgotten about the jerk.

Natalie reaches into her bag and takes out her calorie notebook. I'm surprised she didn't ask for Sweet 'n' Low for her lemon. "Look, there's Andrew Mackenzie!" she says, pointing across the room and waving.

Please, please tell me, how am I supposed to forget about Jeremy when his Penn buddies are all over the place? Particularly the one who practically fixed us up.

Andrew waves back and pushes his way toward us.

"I was hoping to run into you, hon," Natalie says. "I heard you were in town. We were just talking about you."

We were?

"What were you saying?" he says, kissing her lightly on the cheek.

What *were* we saying?

"Just how sexy you are," she says, wrapping her arms around his neck.

Natalie is a terrific flirt. She may not know which way is north, but she can certainly find her way around the male species. She's not exactly the queen of originality, though. Who uses a line like "just how sexy you are"? But usually these guys just lap up anything good ol' Nat has to offer. And at this moment I'm not sure what her sudden interest in Andrew is all about, because I tried to set her up with him about a gazillion times so that Jer and I would have someone to double with. Correction: *could have had* someone to double with. Anyway, Andrew had been all for it, not that this was much of a surprise—what guy wouldn't be interested in Nat? But she claimed he wasn't her type. Too nice, she said.

"Jackie!" he says, untangling himself from Natalie's arms. "I didn't know you were in Boston."

Oh, God, oh, God. That means that Jer doesn't talk about me

to his friends! Apparently I'm so insignificant in his life that I don't even merit being mentioned. Jackass.

Or maybe Andrew and Jer aren't even talking anymore. Yes. I like that possibility better. They are *so* not talking anymore.

Andrew even kind of looks like Jer. Well, not really. They're both pretty tall (I know, I know, everyone is tall next to me). Yeah, that's pretty much it. Jer is more Ethan-Hawke-hot, scruffy-sexy (he even had that goatee thing going for a bit) while Andrew is more clean-cut, boy-next-door cute. Jeremy's hair is light brown and Andrew is a redhead. Not red-red, but blond-red highlights. Real ones though, not chemical dirty blond streaks like mine. And Andrew's eyes are brown. They're a nice brown, though, like dark chocolate, but they're not Jeremy's big baby blues. Okay fine, Andrew looks nothing like Jer, but they used to hang out, so he reminds me of him, okay?

"I got a job here," I answer.

"Where? When did you move?"

"Cupid's. A few months ago."

"Really? Are you writing?"

"No. Editing."

"Good for you. Have you met Fabio?"

I'm not sure why everyone asks me this question whenever I mention I work for Cupid.

"No, I haven't met Fabio. I don't deal with the covers that much. What have you been up to?"

"I was working in New York the past couple of years and now I'm doing my M.B.A."

"Really? Where?"

"Harvard," he says, trying to hide his smile in a I-love-being-able-to-say-I-go-to-Harvard-but-I-don't-want-to-sound-like-a-showoff kind of way.

Aha. This explains Natalie's sudden interest.

"That's fantastic," I tell him.

"It's quite incredible, Andy," Natalie coos, placing her hand on his shoulder. Andy? Since when is he Andy?

"Thanks," he says. "Do you girls want a drink?"

Natalie's attention is already distracted. Some tall guy in an Armani suit is beckoning from across the bar. "I'll be back in a minute, 'kay?" And off she goes.

"Sounds like a plan," I say. We push our way back to the bar. I wonder if I should ask him about Jeremy. No, bad plan. Even though I'm absolutely convinced the two aren't talking to each other anymore, what if he tells Jer I asked about him, and I look completely pathetic?

Ms. Cleavage asks Andrew what we want. His eyes flick to her exposed flesh and then back to me. "What's your drink of choice?"

I will not ask about Jeremy. I will not ask about Jeremy. I will not even mention Jeremy's name. "How about Lemon Drops?"

"The lady has decided," he says, placing his plastic on the counter.

Lady? "How much?" I ask.

"My treat."

"Thanks." Sounds good to me.

"Ready?"

"But of course."

Sugar...vodka...lemon...mmm.

"Ready?" he asks again.

"Yup."

Sugar...vodka...lemon...mmm.

He motions to two empty seats along the bar.

I will not ask if he's heard from Jeremy. I will not ask if he's heard from Jeremy. I will not ask if he's heard from Jeremy.

We sit down.

"So what's new with you?" he says.

"Not much," I answer. "Have you heard from Jeremy?" Damn.

"No, not since he left for Thailand. You guys still together?"

Uh-oh. Suddenly tears are dripping into my mouth and I'm tasting a weird lemon/sugar/vodka/salt concoction. I will never mention Jeremy's name again. If I absolutely have to think about him, I will use an abstract symbol, like Prince did. From now on he is "ϖ."

I cover my eyes with my hand so that maybe Andrew won't realize I'm crying. I feel like that kid in the second grade who used to cover his nose with one hand while he picked it with the other. Except we all knew what was going on.

Andrew, of course, knows what's going on. He puts his arm around me and I start to cry right into his chest. I'm probably making a huge wet stain on his gray shirt, and my mascara is going to be all over my face, making me look like as if I'm in the middle of exams and haven't slept in weeks, only periodic naps at the library between several cups of black coffee—

His chest is awfully hard.

Okay, so he's no Ethan Hawke, but he's certainly cute, and an M.B.A. from Harvard will make him even cuter. I can seduce him tonight and we could have wild, passionate animal sex and then we'll wake up smiling in each others arms and go for breakfast, strolling hand in hand along the river—

He smells very, *very* good.

He smells like ϖ.

I absolutely cannot have a wild affair with anyone who wears ϖ's cologne. You see, the whole point is to be with someone who does not remind me of ϖ, who will in fact make me forget him. For a little while, anyway. Here's the plan: ϖ will be so devastated that I have fallen for someone else, he'll realize I am his true love and ask me to get back together. And then we'll live happily ever after.

I'm not supposed to think that out loud, am I?

I know I'm supposed to want to meet someone else with whom I can have a healthy relationship, but in all reality, I would be perfectly content to use the other person to get Jeremy to want me back.

Sigh. I know. I'm hopeless.

I pull myself away from Andrew. "I'm really sorry. I should go fix myself up." A wet stain is smack in the center of his shirt.

"No problem." He scribbles something down on a matchbook. "Call me if you ever want to talk, okay?"

"Thanks." I am becoming increasingly mortified by this entire experience.

What a nice guy.

I push the washroom door open to ten women unreservedly checking themselves out in the overhead mirrors. I'm not sure what it is about ladies' rooms at bars, but women become animals. They fiddle with their breasts and wedgies, and line up their makeup like ammunition along the sink. Case in point: a woman in a short snakeskin skirt pulls a full cosmetic bag out of her purse, empties it along the porcelain, and retrieves her eyelash curler.

I look at myself in the mirror. Instead of appearing smoky, my *Cosmo* eyes look as if someone rubbed a dirty ashtray around them.

"Excuse me," I ask the snake-woman. "Any chance you have any eye-makeup remover?"

"Of course, honey," she says. (She's a lot older: hence the "honey." There is a distinct difference between "hon," which Natalie likes to use, and "honey.") "Here's a cotton ball, too, honey."

"Thanks." I practice smiling into the mirror. I smile again and again until it looks fake and evil. Maybe I'll become the bitch. Guys love the bitch.

I push my way back out the door and head back to the bar.

"One Sex on the Beach, please." Sitting on a stool, I try to stop myself from swerving back and forth with annoyance. A blow-dried blonde twirls her hair and bends over so that the suit she's talking to has to look down her shirt. The three men on the other side of me call out numbers, rating the women as they walk by. A man with sagging skin vocally calculates a nine and a half for the brunette sitting four stools down. She's wearing a long skirt with a slit up to her armpit. His face looks like a rotting peeled grape; his eyes are like raisins. When he says eight, I think he might be referring to me. I'd like to pour my drink over his head, drama-queen-like, but I decide to stare him down instead. After all, a drink's a drink, not to be wasted, but to get us wasted. I stare at him until his skin turns into dots of brown and then into specks of orange, as if I've been sitting too close to the TV.

Why am I here? Why am I not at home watching TV? It's almost eleven and I could be watching "L and O" with Sam. The blow-dried blonde's giggles sound like recorded sitcom laughter. I hate Orgasm, I hate Boston, and I hate Natalie. Where *is* Natalie?

Wait.

Is that who I think it is?

Jonathan Gradinger?

Foxy Jonathan Gradinger?

Foxy Jonathan Gradinger who grew up in Danbury and played Danny Zukoe in our high school's rendition of *Grease* when he was a foxy senior and I was an eager freshman? I sat in the front row for three nights straight because he was such a fox. Jonathan Gradinger's picture, cut out from the playbill, was taped to the inside of my locker, right up there beside my poster of Kirk Cameron. My five-section binder was covered with sprawls of Jackie Gradinger, Jacquelyn Gradinger, Fern Gradinger, Fern Jacqueline Gradinger, and Fern Jacquelyn Norris Gradinger. I knew Jonathan's schedule by heart and would casually happen to be walking behind him on the fourth floor staircase between second and third period, just as he was going from chemistry to trig. So what if my English class was in the basement? Thankfully he had been way too cool to notice some crazed groupie trailing after him.

It's getting hot in here. My chills are multiplying! *Grease* lyrics hurl through my head. I sip my Sex on the Beach and think of lightning.

From the back it looks like him. He's wearing a button-down shirt that looks like the type of shirt Jonathan Gradinger the fox would wear.

I'd know the back of that head anywhere.

He just needs to turn a bit to the left…a bit more…a *little* bit more…why is that wench distracting him? He's walking away! Stop! Stop!

I try sending him telepathic messages. "Turn around. Turn around right now. Turn around right now, foxy Jonathan Gradinger. Fall madly in love with me."

My telepathy is not working. Drastic measures are called for.

I accidentally let go of my glass. Better to waste a drink than an opportunity.

Smash.

It *is* him. It's foxy Jonathan Gradinger from our senior/freshman year! And he's looking at me! He's looking right at *me!*

Okay, I know. Everyone's looking at me. I think Raisin-Eyes has demoted me to a six.

"Are you all right?" the breasted bartender asks.

"Yeah, fine. I'm sorry about that. I really don't know how this happened." Yes, I do. I know exactly how this happened. And I know that it worked, because Jonathan Gradinger is coming over.

Omigod.

He's coming over.

I've never actually spoken to Jonathan Gradinger.

What can I say to Jonathan Gradinger?

I need a drink. Where's my drink?

Oh, yeah. Damn.

Breathe. Calm. Damn. Think calm thoughts. Hot bath with vanilla-smelling bubbles. The two-hour massage I used to get from Iris in exchange for two dollars in coins (but look how much silver it is!). A couch, my duvet, the *cchhhh* of background TV…

Mmm. I'm getting…*mmm*…sleeeepy.

"Hey," a very foxy voice pleasantly intrudes upon my reverie. "I recognize you. Are you from Danbury?"

Jonathan Gradinger is talking to me.

Jonathan Gradinger is talking to me.

Jonathan Gradinger is *talking* to me.

Jonathan Gradinger is talking to *me*.

Wendy is not going to believe this.

Calm. I can do this.

"Shfjkd sjsydhd jksav jasdadgaj dghykg."

"Excuse me?" he asks, which is a perfectly logical question considering I'm not sure what I just said. Or what I was even trying to say.

"Hi." One syllable at a time. No problem. "Yeah." There, I've said two words to Jonathan Gradinger. I now have something to tell my grandchildren.

"Did you go to Stapley High?" he asks.

More? Oh, my—he wants to have a *conversation*.

"Yeah." I nod. I'm doing it! I'm conversing!

"Were you in my grade?" He's running his hand through his gorgeous, thick hair—thin hair now, actually. What happened to his gorgeous, thick hair?

"ActuallyIwasafewgradesbehindyou." If I don't think and just say all my words in one motion, gosh darnit, I think I can do this.

"Wait a second," he says and smiles his still very foxy smile. "I remember you. Weren't you that girl who used to follow me around? Jackie something?"

Oh. My. God. He knows my name. Danny Zukoe knows my name.

I nod. I can't speak. My tongue has been sewn to the roof of my mouth.

"Do you want a drink?" he asks.

Jonathan Gradinger is offering to buy me a drink. I nod again. Actually, I don't think I actually stopped nodding. It's not that I expect myself to suddenly sound like a loquaciously articulate *Dawson's Creek* character, but this is getting old.

"It appears," he looks at the floor, "that you like Sex On the Beach."

"Especially if it's with you," I say. Just kidding, I didn't really say that. I continue nodding.

"So, how are you liking Boston?"

"Now that I'm talking to you, I'm liking it a lot." Wait—this time I really did say that. That *so* wasn't supposed to be out loud. But what's this? He's laughing! He thinks I'm being funny. He thinks I'm flirting with him. I *am* flirting with him. I'm flirting with Jonathan Gradinger.

"Actually, I do like it here," I say seriously. "What about you?" Okay maybe not a witty or sexy response, but two full sentences, one that requires a response. Give me a break here.

"I've been here awhile already. I like it. I'm used to it. "

"When did you move here?" That makes two questions. I'm on a roll.

"About eight years ago."

"You're practically a Brahmin by now." Another joke!

He laughs. Yay! "Not quite. I haven't moved up to Beacon Hill just yet."

Pause. One second lapse. Two second lapse. Uh-oh. What do I do now? Wait, I've got an idea. "So, what are you doing in Boston?" The ultimate crowd pleaser—giving men the opportunity to talk about themselves.

"I'm a doctor."

Reee-lly.

"What kind of doctor?" A pediatrician? An ER resident? A heart surgeon?

"A podiatrist."

"A what?"

"A foot doctor."

I know that. I'm an editor. Someone who cares for and treats the human foot. "That must be…interesting." C'mon, what else was I supposed to say? How about that athlete's foot? At least I have nice feet—they're a size $6^1/_2$ and very cute, if I do say so myself. My pedicurist even says they're a pleasure to work with, although she's probably just buttering me up for an extra tip, which is ridiculous because she owns her own place. You're not supposed to tip the owner, everyone knows that, but I once saw a fake-nailed snob leave a four-dollar tip for a twenty-dollar mani-cure and then I had to leave four dollars, too, and now every time I go I have to leave twenty-four dollars instead of twenty. As far as I'm concerned, she should say, "Don't be silly! Take your four dollars! You're insulting me! I'm the owner," but instead she just takes it. It's all so absurd.

Anyway.

"So I guess you went to med school here?"

"Tufts. What about you?"

"I'm an editor."

"Really? Where?"

"Cupid's"

"Cupid's?"

"We publish romance novels."

"Oh, my mom reads those! Do you know Fabio?"

I giggle my oh-that's-so-clever-and-original flirty-laugh (I've been friends with Nat for long enough) and pat him on the shoulder. "Unfortunately not. Do you?"

"He's actually a patient of mine. He has really nice feet."

"You're kidding, right?" I ask.

"Right. But you know what they say about people with nice feet."

"What?"

"Nice shoes."

Can I handle feet jokes? I do the laugh again.

"You have quite a pair of shoes on," he says, looking down.

"Thanks. Fresh purchase. Single-girl boots. "

"Why is that?"

"Because they're notice-me boots."

"I'm noticing."

He's noticing?

"Good." I smile demurely.

"You've certainly grown up."

"You haven't seen me since I had pink braces and crimped hair."

"You look great, Jackie."

"Thanks. So do you." You're a hottie. A total hottie with a

little less hair and a little more love handles...but still very, very hot.

"So you're not dating anyone?" he asks.

That's what I've been trying to tell you. "No. What about you?"

"Single as charged." His hand is suddenly on my shoulder. Hello there.

"Jackie! Jackie!" Nat is yelling in the background. I'm not sure how I hear her over the thumping *boom, boom, getting laid, boom boom,* but I do. And it's very distracting. Her arms are flying over her head now.

"Can I have your number?" At last. The magic words have escaped his lips.

"Sure." I feel a bit like Cinderella, although my fresh-purchase single-girl shoes are definitely a lot funkier than glass slippers. Although I have always wanted a pair of those, too. I ask Ms. Cleavage for matches, and reach into my purse for a pen. She gives me the evil eye but no matches.

He takes the pen from my hand, and little tingles kind of like little ants, the black kind not the poisonous red ones, scramble up my arm. "Shoot."

I recite my number, and good God, he writes it across his hand.

"Jackie! Jackie! Jackie!"

"I have to go," I say, motioning to Natalie. He sees her. This is good. It looks as if I have friends.

"Great," he says. "I'll call you."

Please do.

I spend the rest of the evening being introduced to anyone who's anyone, but mostly posing so that Jonathan Gradinger can see how sexy I am. I'm also watching him carefully to see that he doesn't smudge my number up against any potential rivals. Mind you, I'm being very discreet; no more overt stalking for me.

Will he call? It's Friday, so maybe he'll call tomorrow. Maybe tonight? Maybe he'll call me the second he gets home. Maybe he'll say he can't sleep until he hears the soft, inviting lilt in my voice.

"Having fun?" Natalie whispers, as much as one can whisper over the music. We sit at a table with the Armani guy and three of his friends. One of them keeps talking to me with a thick French accent. I keep nodding, not really understanding anything he says. The only words I can make out are, "More drink, yes?"

Definitely yes. What a wonderful night. I am going to have the most perfect boyfriend in the whole world. He'll want to get married, and because he's a doctor I probably won't have to start with the *No dear, that's not the clitoris* thing, and he'll want to get married, and he's brilliant and the rest of my high school class is going to kill themselves with envy, and he'll want to get married. I particularly like the envy part of this whole fantasy. Hmm...snotty Sherri Burns thought she was so cool. *Oh, look at me, I'm the only freshman cool enough to get cast as a pink lady; oh, look at me, I'm so cute; oh, look at me, I'm going to wear my pink lady jacket every single day.*

I can't wait 'til she hears about us. I'm sure she had a thing for my Jonathan, but what does it matter now? I can be big about the whole thing. Maybe I'll call her tonight and let her know about my engagement, although I don't even know where she lives. Maybe I should plan a reunion; it's been at least eight years since we graduated. I'll just let it slip out: "I'll be coming with my fiancé. You might remember him, Jonathan Gradinger?" Maybe I'll wear pink.

Or I could send a picture of us to the Stapley alumni Internet site. I'll just have to remember to bring a camera on our date.

I like that idea better.

"Tomorrow, we're going to hit The G-Spot, 'kay?" Natalie says, grabbing my hand. I assume she's talking about a bar.

"Sounds good." I answer, wondering if I can get away with wearing this outfit again.

Chapter Four

Why Bother Getting Up?

My first thought this morning is about Jonathan Gradinger. It is not about ϖ.

Therefore I am officially over him.

Actually, my first real thought is *djjfhskakd*—why, oh, why, is my phone ringing at 9:15 on a Saturday morning? Someone had better be on fire. Secretly, it's only six minutes past nine. I set my huge clock (oversize so that I can see it without my contacts in) nine minutes fast in the hope that somehow this deception will make me on time.

"Hellooo?" I say.

"Fern!" It's my dad. "Are you still in bed?"

"No." I always say I'm awake when I'm asleep. Don't know why.

"But you're wasting the day!"

"I'm awake." Eyes…heavy. Mouth…can't open.

"Good. What's new?"

Uh. "I forget."

"Do you want to call us back when you wake up?"

"No, now's good. Nothing's new." Okay, okay. I'm sitting up. I'm awake. I'm going to have dark circles under my eyes and I'm practically out of concealer and no man will fall in love with me and it'll all be your fault.

"If nothing's new, why have you been too busy to call us back?"

Whoops. It's not that I ignore them on purpose. I am just

constantly forgetting that they exist and that I should call them. "I've been busy at work."

"Work is good. What have you been editing?"

"A book."

"A book about what?"

Did he wake me up to learn more about *Millionaire Cowboy Dad?* How come he's not a millionaire daddy? "A romance, Dad. Same story as every other story."

"What's that?"

"Girl meets boy. Girl loves boy. Boy screws over girl."

"That's the story?"

I must really not be paying attention if that's what I just told my father. Why is he calling me so early? This I don't ask either, afraid to risk another lecture on how the early bird gets the worm. "No, that's not the whole story. Boy apologizes and they get married and live happily ever after."

"That's nice, dear. But you know what they say, all work and no play makes for a dull life. And what about you? What's happening with the boys? Are you still seeing Jeffery?"

"No, Dad. He's screwing girls in Thailand right now." I don't really say that. I don't want to give him a heart attack; he thinks I'm still a virgin. "It's Jeremy. And no, I'm playing the field right now."

"No rush, dear, no rush."

Most parents would be bugging you to start thinking about getting married, or at least tell you to find a boyfriend by the time you're twenty-four, but not my dad. He still thinks I'm fifteen. Whenever he goes on business trips, he still buys me those "Welcome to (insert name of visited state here)" T-shirts in children's sizes. Janie, on the other hand, constantly reminds me that she does, in fact, "want to be called Gramma someday." If I ever do have kids, I might insist they call her Janie. Just to annoy her.

"What's new with you, Dad?"

"I joined a new jogging group."

"That's good. How's work?"

"Good. I'm only working four days a week now."

"How come?"

"I want some time for myself. Life's not a dress rehearsal, you know. I have to live for the moment. I can't waste all my time working."

Definitely Bev's influence. I may have even heard her use the exact phrase "Life's not a dress rehearsal," followed by "We only have one life to live." My dad used to be a workaholic, especially after the divorce. Since Bev got him into psychoanalysis, he's become more of the how-does-it-make-you-feel and listen-to-me-recite-clichés type of guy.

I hear Bev's voice in the background. "Tim, is that Fern? Can I talk to her?"

"Bev wants to say hello. Love you, 'bye." He passes off the phone.

It's far too early in the morning to talk to Bev. It's not that I don't like her. I do, really. I just have a few minor issues with her. Bev is a fanatic; she's addicted to talk shows. Specifically *Oprah*. And instead of working like a modern woman in the twenty-first century, her calling herself a part-time travel agent is a euphemism for "she plans her own vacations." When she's not traveling, she spends all her time watching *Oprah*, doing Oprah makeovers, and cooking low fat meals from Oprah's recipe book. Verbs like share and discover are too often combined in her speech pattern with nouns like soul and self.

"Hi, Fern. How's your spirit?"

"My spirit's fine, thanks. How's yours?"

"Wonderful, wonderful. Quite phenomenal. How's therapy going?"

"Great." Bev has convinced my father to give me seventy-five dollars a week for one-hour therapy sessions. She's convinced that kids never get over divorce and that my sudden move to Boston might throw me over the edge. The money has been very therapeutic so far; I've bought new sunglasses and my hooker boots, and I'm saving up for a CD player for my car.

"So what have you learned about yourself this week?"

"Not much," I answer. It's way too early for psychoanalytical babble. "What's up with you?"

"Oh, the usual. Power walking. Writing in my gratitude journal."

I refuse to ask her what a gratitude journal is.

"And I just read the most amazing book last week," she says. "I'm sure you'd love it."

"What is it?"

"Oh, um...um. It's about an underprivileged girl who was a victim of incest. Gosh, I don't remember the name, but the story hit home."

I don't quite see the relation between the unidentified novel's protagonist and my Manhattan-born stepmother, who spends Saturday at the hairdresser, Sunday at the manicurist, and Monday through Friday at the mall when not watching *Oprah*. However, we've never quite reached the level of intimacy that would allow me to point that out. "Let me know the name of the book when you remember it, and I'll buy it, okay? I gotta go now. "

"Okay, 'bye. Remember your spirit."

"Of course." I hang up the phone and fall back asleep.

When I wake up at 1:30, I have my first coherent thought. It's 1 A.B. (After Breakup), and I have already kindled a relationship with my future husband.

I may have a date. Soon.

Yay!

With Jonathan Gradinger. The thing is, once we get married, I'll have to stop referring to him by his full name. I'd sound like a character in a Jane Austen novel: "Good morning, Mr. Gradinger. Please pass the newspaper, Mr. Gradinger."

Why hasn't he called yet?

I'll admit I'm being a bit crazy. According to *Swingers,* he has to wait at least three days. Or is it five days? How am I going to wait five days?

I must call Wendy.

I dial her number at work. How pathetic is that? It's Saturday afternoon and I don't even bother trying her apartment.

"Wendy speaking."

"Hi!"

"Hello," she says. I hear her rummaging through some papers. "So? How was it?"

"Wonderful. I'm completely over Jeremy."

"Sure you are," she says. Do I detect sarcasm?

"I am. I ran into my future husband."

"That's good. Do I get to be the maid of honor?"

"No. You can be a bridesmaid. Iris made me swear she'd be the maid of honor. But you can plan the bachelorette party."

"Seems fair. But you still have to be *my* maid of honor. If I ever have time to date again, that is." Wendy has been unwillingly practicing abstinence since she started her job.

"Of course I'll be your maid of honor! I've already written my maid of honor speech," I tell her. Well, not all of it. But sometimes really funny things happen, and if I don't write them down right away, I'll never remember everything I should have said and then…fine. I'm a geek.

"I'm sure you have. So, who's the future Mr. Norris?"

I pause for effect. "Jonathan Gradinger."

"What?"

"You heard me."

"My God! Where did you see him? Are you sure it wasn't a dream?"

"Yes, I'm sure." It wasn't a dream. I'm pretty sure it wasn't a dream. Was it a dream? I look around my room for evidence of the Orgasm excursion. My black skirt is lying on the floor where I dropped it last night. I grab it. It smells like smoke and Sex on the Beach. *P-hew.*

"How did that happen?" she asks.

"He saw me at the bar." I leave out how that came about. "We talked. He asked me for my number."

"That's amazing! Is he still a fox?"

"Of course. Maybe not *the* fox, but still foxy."

"Has he called yet?"

"Not yet."

"Oh."

Oh? What does she mean, oh? "He wouldn't have, Wen. What guy calls the next morning? He'll probably call tomorrow night. At 8:30. After *The Simpsons.*"

"Not if he wants to go out tonight."

"He's not going to ask mc out for tonight."

"Why not?"

"Because then he would look desperate. Trust me, Wen, that's not the way the game is played." Dear sweet Wendy. Dear sweet, naive Wendy.

"How do you know how the game is played? You've been on the dating scene for one day."

Hey, I can remember L.B.J. (Life Before Jer). I did have a life, you know. "He'll call me on Sunday and ask me out for Tuesday, so he can see me on Tuesday and ask me out for next Saturday. See?"

"I see. Where do you think he'll take you?"

"On Tuesday or Saturday?"

Wendy doesn't answer. I can tell that all this is getting a little too complicated for her. Not dating in over a year has started to melt her brain.

"Sherri Burns is going to die," she says.

"I know! Isn't it wonderful?"

"Would she ever find out? Besides by reading the wedding announcement in *The Times,* of course."

"I was thinking of taking a picture on our date and posting it on the Stapley Internet site."

"Not a bad plan. Uh-oh. I have a meeting. Gotta go."

"A meeting? Who else is in the office on Saturday?"

"Who's not in the office?"

"Poor you. You sure you don't want a normal job?"

"I am far from sure. We'll chat later."

"'Bye."

What should I do now? Probably get up. It's already two.

"Hello?" I call from my bed. "Anyone home?"

"Hi!" Sam hollers. "I'm cleaning the bathroom." I'm pretty

sure she cleans her bathroom every day. I've seen her sneak into the bathroom with disinfectant after a guest uses it. She's just as psycho with the fridge. She has a bit of an expiry fetish. She spills out her milk exactly three days after it's been opened. It doesn't matter what the expiry date says, either. For some reason I can't seem to convince her that the expiry date refers to the date you buy the stuff, not when you have to throw it out. "You're not really going to eat that?" she asked me yesterday, staring in disgust at my six-day-old package of sliced turkey. Um...I was. If I did things Sam's way, everything I own would be in the trash can or down the toilet.

I throw off my duvet and slide my feet onto the floor. The cold floor. Where are my slippers? Do I have slippers? No, I do not have slippers. Why don't I have slippers? Where are my socks?

I slip on some shorts. Not even Sam wants to see my Granny panties. I walk into her room. "Morning."

"Afternoon," she says. She is using some sort of contraption to scrub the tiles. "Late night?"

"Yeah. Very fun."

"Good. I'm almost done. You can borrow my supplies if you want to clean your bathroom."

I'm not sure, but I think that's a hint. Oh, well, I have nothing else to do today, anyway. And my bathroom is pretty gross. The last time I cleaned it was...let me think. Have I ever cleaned it? "Thanks. I'll do it right after breakfast. I mean lunch."

I make myself a sandwich. A pretty lame sandwich because now that I have no turkey left, all I have left is lettuce. Okay, I'll clean the bathroom right after lunch and an hour of TV.

What's on? Click, click. A *Cheers* rerun! That Diane. So literary. I always kind of hoped she and Frasier would stay together. Lilith/Helen didn't deserve him. As soon as I got to Boston, my first excursion was to the Cheers bar. Quite disappointing. No one screamed "Jack!" when I walked in. Okay. Three o'clock. Time to clean. But *Blind Date* is on. I love that show. Maybe I'll just watch until the first commercial...

It's five o'clock and I haven't moved. My butt feels asleep. I really should get up. Sam left all the cleaning supplies on my bathroom floor.

Why hasn't he called yet?

Six-thirty. I'm hungry. Macaroni and cheese? I have no milk left. I hate when it's too margariney. I order a pizza. Extra pepperoni. What am I going to do tonight? Natalie mentioned The G-Spot. I should call her. At the next commercial.

Seven-fifteen. I'm still hungry. Where's my pizza? What happened to thirty minutes, fast and free? I dial Natalie's number.

"Hi, Jack," she answers.

"What's up?"

"Not much. I'm just getting dressed."

"Where are you going?"

"For dinner. With E-reek."

"Who's Eric?"

"E-reek. The guy I was talking to last night."

Wait a second. A guy she met yesterday has already called? "The guy in the Armani?"

"That's him. He called this morning. I think he might be royalty, but I'm not sure."

I ignore her latter comment and focus on the more surprising element of her declaration. "He called this morning?"

"Yup."

This morning? "And he asked you out and you said yes? For tonight?"

"Yeah. Should I have said no? He actually asked me last night, and I said we'll see, but he called me at eleven to confirm, so I said, Why not?"

Why not? What am I supposed to do tonight? "Didn't we have plans?"

"Oh...did we? I didn't think you'd care."

"Well, I do," knowing quite well that if the situation were reversed, I'd do the same. Fashion Magazine Fun Fact # 1: let no man come between two best friends. And let no man come between two mediocre friends unless he's really hot. I mean, let's face it; why else would you go to a bar with a mediocre girlfriend on a Saturday night in the first place? To discuss politics? So, when a guy like my Jonathan calls, you expect your friend to be understanding, even if you don't like it when she does it to you. Not that someone as cool as my Jonathan Gradinger would call so soon.

"You don't want me to cancel, do you?"

Yes, I do. "No, go. Have fun."

"You can still go to The G-Spot."

Who goes to The G-Spot alone? I'd have to wait in line for three hours by myself. And then I'd have to talk to myself at the bar. "No. It's okay. I'm tired, anyway." Someone knocks on my door. "The pizza's here. Gotta go."

"Swear you're not mad?"

I'm mad. "I'm not mad."

"Good. Love ya, hon! Have fun!"

I was only going to eat half the pizza and save the rest for Monday's lunch, but now that I don't have to wear anything tight tonight, I'm going to eat the whole thing and stuff myself with misery. I hate my life. I'm spending an entire Saturday in front of the TV. Jeremy doesn't love me. Jonathan Gradinger doesn't want me. Natalie's guy called the next day.

Sam walks into the living room. If she asks me if I've cleaned the bathroom yet, I'm going to take the pizza and rub it all over her toilet.

"What's up?" she says.

"Nothing."

"What are you doing tonight?"

"Nothing."

"Wanna come see the new James Bond movie with us tonight?"

"No." Actually, I do want to go see the new James Bond movie with them tonight. "Well, maybe."

"Come on! Why not? You haven't moved in six hours."

"Since when is a movie aerobic? Are we going to be fighting crime along with Jimmie?"

"At least you'll have to get off the couch to walk to the car."

This is true. Although at this particular moment it seems like more work than it's worth. "Okay, I'll come."

Standing in the shower, I try to ignore the greenish-brown circles of dirt that sporadically appear on my tub. Tomorrow I'm *definitely* cleaning.

Marc pulls up at a quarter to nine. He rolls down the window of his brand-new two-door Civic, and Sam plants a kiss on his lips. If they're going to be smooching all night, I'm sitting by myself.

I maneuver my way into the backseat, through the seat belt that is doubling as a limbo stick, recalling an earlier conversation overheard through paper-thin walls. "We weren't arguing—we were discussing," Sam told me later.

Sam: "Two-doors? We're not sixteen."

Marc: "A four-door? What am I, thirty-five?"

This went on all night—two doors or four, four doors or two— the same old thing over and over, keeping me awake (I was forced to sit in a rigid position, with my ear cupped to the wall) until I went to my desk to write Honda a letter begging the company to please produce a three-door vehicle so that Sam and Marc would just shut up already.

I step on a crumpled old burger bag on the floor of the back seat. It smells like rotten vegetables. Sam lets him get away with that?

"We should take your car for a wash," Sam says, sniffing. She picks up an old Big Mac carton with her thumb and index finger as if she's holding a soiled diaper, and folds it into a compact rectangle.

"Yes, Mom," Marc says, and turns on the radio. There's only so much nagging even he can take, I suppose. I wonder if he's ever tempted to smear stale McDonald's fry grease on her toilet seat?

"Don't be rude," she says.

I'm feeling a bit like their kid in the backseat. "Are we there yet?" I ask.

"Soon," he says.

We pull into the twenty-four-theater multiplex parking lot, which is already crammed with at least a thousand cars. Apparently, we're not the only ones with a let's-go-to-the-movies-and-see-the-stars idea. Don't any of these people have a real life? We pull into a tight spot at the back of the lot.

"Couldn't you have let us off in front?" Sam asks.

"Sorry," Marc says. "I forgot."

A front drop-off would have been nice. Some sort of trolley would have been even nicer. Couldn't you have built us a trolley, Marc?

Not a bad business proposal, actually. A trolley that runs up and down the parking lot, picking and dropping off passengers like at Disney World. But people would constantly want to get on and off, the train would have to stop every few seconds, and it would take longer to get a lift back to the car than to actually walk.

"Hurry up, girls, we're already late," Marc tells us. Tells me actually, because I'm the one slowing us down. I'm a slow walker. Is it my fault that short people have short legs?

If he had dropped us off at the front door, like a gentleman, we'd have tickets by now.

The multicomplex looms in the distance like Cinderella's castle. Three-D cartoon animals impressively swirl over the entranceway. The theme-park adventure continues with giant bats, which would have terrified a younger, less mature version of me, that hang threateningly from the ceiling. We buy tickets and then join the popcorn line. Sam and Marc buy jujubes and two diet Cokes. Puh-lease! Not buying popcorn at the theater is like going to a baseball game and not buying a hot dog. Why else do you go to a baseball game?

"We'll get seats," Sam says, and they disappear hand in hand.

"One small popcorn with extra butter and a small Orange Crush, please," I tell the eyebrow-pierced teenager with bleached-blond hair.

"Would you like to upgrade to a large, ma'am? Then you get free refills."

Ma'am? Ma'am?? "No thanks." The smalls are already giant size.

"It's only an extra thirty-five cents," the pierced kid says.

"Well...okay." For an extra thirty-five cents, why not?

"Would you like to upgrade your popcorn to a large, ma'am? It's only an extra sixty-five cents."

"No thanks."

"You get free refills, ma'am."

I'm not sure when exactly I'm going to refill, considering that the movie is starting in about thirty seconds. But free is free. I can do the refill right after the movie. I can bring a snack to work.

The pierced kid hands me two huge cartons, a drink about the size of a two-gallon container of orange juice, and a popcorn the size of a water cooler.

Oooh! Sour berries! I love sour berries! "Can I have those, too?"

"Here you go, ma'am. That will be $15.50." Fifteen-fifty? Why is my snack twice the price of the movie?

Uh-oh. I have to pee. This is good. Maybe if I go now, I won't have to go in the middle of the movie. One can always hope. Only now I feel kind of like a kid in a snowsuit. How can I carry the tub of popcorn, a pack of sour berries, a gallon of soda, and a separate straw into the cubicle without spilling everywhere?

The first life-lesson Jeremy taught me was that I should never put my straw in my drink at a movie theater until after I sit down, in case of leakage. Seems like a simple enough strategy, except you'd be amazed at how many times I'd left the theater with orange stains on my jeans before I started dating him.

The last life-lesson I learned from him was to never date a backstabbing selfish bastard.

I can hold it in.

The theater is dark, and the please-turn-off-your-cell-phone-because-it'll-really-piss-everyone-off-if-it-rings   announcement flashes across the screen.

How the hell am I going to find them in here?

I walk down the aisle and peer. I feel like I'm looking for Waldo.

No.

No.

No.

I arrive at the screen amid a chorus of "Hey, sit down!" and "Get out of the way!" and "What's the matter with you?" God forbid they should miss the ads. So where are Sam and Marc? They're probably sitting in the back. I must have passed them.

They're not in the back. I turn around again, and make my way back toward the screen.

Sam waves from the front row. "Sorry, I forgot my glasses," she whispers. "Hope you don't mind."

I wonder if it's rude to sit by myself, in the middle of the theater like a normal person. What if a potential date is in the theater and sees me sitting by myself and concludes that I'm a complete misanthrope who has to go to the movies alone on a Saturday night to try to pick up men, or maybe not even to pick up men but just to get out of a cat-infested apartment for a few measly hours? What then?

I sit down next to her in the front row. I tilt my head eighty degrees and try to get comfortable.

This isn't going to work.

"I'm going to find a seat in the middle," I whisper to Sam. I'm a big girl. I can sit at a movie by myself. I scout for an empty seat. I spot one next to a blond girl about ten rows back and push my way through.

"Hey, sit down!"

"Get out of the way!"

"What's the matter with you?"

I slide into a seat, trying to make room for my industrial-size purchases.

Jeremy and I always sat on the aisle. Correction: Jeremy always sat on the aisle. He liked the leg room. Of course he never asked if *I* wanted to sit in the aisle seat. *I* always sat near the weirdo who left his arm on the seat rest. *I* was always the one who had to feel the weirdo's arm hair brush against my skin. Let me ask you this: if there's only one armrest between the two of you, why does the other person always assume it's his right to take it?

Oh, well. At least the girl next to me is giving me a lot of space. She's snuggling with her date. I can't see his face, but she's all blond and shiny and I'm really trying not to hate her.

I have to pee. I really should have gone before the movie started.

Wow. Pierce Brosnan is really hot. Natalie says he's too pretty, too good-looking. What does this mean exactly, too good-looking? She says she could never go out with a guy prettier than she is. She says she hates going to a restaurant and everyone looks at the guy instead of her. Such problems I should have.

Look at that bod. Maybe I should suggest we do spy books at work.

I really have to go to the bathroom.

I try crossing and uncrossing my legs. I'm not sure why, but I drink more of my Orange Crush.

Maybe I can convince the marketing people at work to put Pierce on the cover of our new spy books. Of course, I won't be invited to the shoot, but Pierce will hate the fake-blond bimbo chosen to model with him. I, of course, will happen to be passing through the room, and he'll ask "What about her?" in his husky-British voice. "Her?" Helen will say (although she is only an associate editor, not a senior editor, so she won't have a fat chance of being there, either). "But she's just a copy editor!" The whole scene will unfold with perfect timing and I'll say, "Me?" And he'll nod enthusiastically, beckoning me with his wonderfully strong hands, and I'll join his pose. And while the wind machine blows my hair, he'll turn to me and say, "Will you be my next Bond girl?" And I'll play a DNA expert who runs around the hospital in a tight white tank top and silver stretch pants.

Oh, God. It's a waterfall scene. This isn't going to work.

I have to use the washroom. Now.

"Excuse me, excuse me, excuse me..."

"Hey, sit down!"

"Get out of the way!"

"What's the matter with you?"

I sprint to the ladies' room and run into an empty stall. I carefully place a paper toilet cover on the seat. I'm not Sam, but I'm not crazy.

And then just when I'm minding my own business...swoosh.

What is wrong with these automatic bathrooms? Why do they flush while I'm still using them? How can I be a Bond girl when I can't even figure out how to work a toilet?

I sneak back into the theater ("Hey, sit down!" "Get out of the way!" "What's the matter with you?") and despite the temptation, I don't ask the blonde what I missed. After all, she might think I want to be friends with her, which probably wouldn't be so bad since she probably can get any guy she wants and therefore has great castoffs. Forget that; I don't want her to think I'm friendless *as well* as annoying—or, God forbid, desperate.

When the credits start to role, I leap up to make a quick exit to beat the refill line. Granted, I barely even ate a quarter of it. But I paid for a refill and dammit, I'm going to get it.

"Jackie?"

I turn to the seat next to me and see Andrew Mackenzie's lightly freckled arm curled around the blonde.

I am never sitting by myself at a movie ever again.

The blonde is checking me out, most likely thinking, So this is what a person who has no friends looks like.

"Hey! Andrew. I know it looks like I'm here by myself, but I'm not. I'm here with friends. Really. But they're sitting in the front row, and it was hurting my neck..." They both stare at me, expressionless.

Andrew is going to tell Jeremy I went to see a movie by myself on a Saturday night. I might as well just throw myself in front of Marc's two-door Civic.

"How are you?" he asks. Smiling, he motions for me to exit into the aisle.

"No, really. I'm *not* here by myself." I'm not exiting *anything* until Marc and Sam walk by so I can prove that I am not here alone.

"Jackie, this is Jessica. Jessica, Jackie." I shake her perfectly French-manicured hand. She looks like a Jessica. She looks like how I used to picture Jessica Wakefield, the Sweet Valley Twin.

Who is this Jessica? And why didn't he mention a girlfriend? Not that I gave him much of an opportunity at Orgasm to talk about himself.

Sam and Marc are already near the doors. Damn. They went around the other side.

"Nice to see you, and nice to meet you. I have to go," I say, choosing not to prolong the misery. I hurry out of the theater.

At least there's no line at the popcorn counter.

No line because it's closed. What a rip-off. This sucks. I'm the worst Bond girl ever.

"I'll get the car, girls," Marc says.

"Oh, you're so sweet, Marc."

"That's Bear. Biggy Bear."

Never mind. I don't want to be a Bond girl, anyway. I hate silver stretch pants.

No message. Not that I'm expecting one, but you never know. He wouldn't call on a Saturday night. If he does, it would mean that he thinks I'm home, meaning he thinks I have nothing better to do but stay and wait for his call. And why would he be home on a Saturday night, anyway?

Thank God he didn't call. I don't go out with losers.

I wash up. The green mold around the drain is starting to scare me. I really have to clean the bathroom. Where are the supplies? Why did Sam take them away? Tomorrow for sure I'll do it. I'll even set the alarm. For nine. Okay, nine-thirty. Ten.

*   *   *

Brrring… It's 9:57. Secretly, 9:48. I still have three more minutes. I am not answering. Go away, Dad. I unplug the phone and turn off the alarm.

Shit. It's 12:40. I've got to clean the bathroom. But wait, I have a message. It wasn't Dad who called; the Caller ID says *Anonymous.* What inconsiderate fool calls at 9:57 on a Sunday morning?

''Jackie, this is Jonathan Gradinger calling. My number is 555-2854. Call me back when you get a chance. Call me back when you get a chance.''

Chapter Five

Run Your Fingers Through Your Own Damn Hair

Yay! He called. Yay! Yay! Yay! Thank goodness I didn't pick up when I was asleep. I might have said something awful. I might have told him how foxy he was. Why did he call so early? He must really like me. I mean *really* like me. He thought of me as soon as he woke up. Assuming he wakes up at around 9:30, which is pretty probable considering that's a usual wake-up time. Or maybe he woke up at eight, thought about me, decided to go for a run to diffuse the energy building up in his loins, and when he couldn't take it any longer, called me.

Omigod. What if he wants to go out tonight? Or what if he wants to go out today? What if as soon as I call him back he asks me if he can come by and pick me up for lunch, and what if once he comes inside he has to use the bathroom? I've got to clean it *now* and only after I clean it, can I call him back.

I walk into the bathroom. Strands of my hair have woven themselves into a blanket on the tiled floor. "Sam!" I holler, close to tears. "Help! I don't know how to do this!"

In a jumping-jack five-second flash, in comes Sam, fully equipped with liquid cleaner, yellow gloves, and some sort of brush I'm pretty sure is supposed to go in the toilet but I'm not a hundred percent.

"Why don't I have one of those?" I ask.

"They don't come with the toilet, my dirty friend, they're sold separately. Like batteries."

"Got it. Thank you, thank you, thank you."

"I'm not cleaning it for you. I'm just showing you how."

"Oh."

A half hour, a half bottle, and two rolls of paper towels later, I am satisfied.

Now I can call him back. Maybe he's planning an afternoon picnic with champagne and strawberries and cut-up tuna sandwiches. But first I have to make myself presentable. Right now, my frizzies are pointed in many obtuse angles. I feel like Pippi Longstocking. I shower, blow-dry my hair, and squeeze out what's left of my concealer. And a little lipstick. I put on my bathrobe. I don't want to get dressed if I don't know where we're going. Duh.

I listen to his message again: "Jackie, this is Jonathan Gradinger calling. My number is 555-2854. Call me back when you get a chance. Call me back when you get a chance."

I'm not sure why he says that last part twice. His message reminds me of the ones Wendy's grandmother used to leave when Wendy and I were at Penn together: "Vendy, this is your bubbe calling. Your bubbe called. Call your bubbe. Call your bubbe."

I write down his number. I dial.

"Hi," his sexy voice says. Omigod. I'm talking to Jonathan Gradinger.

"Hi, Jonathan?"

"This is Jonathan Gradinger. I can't get to the phone right now. Please leave your name and number and I'll call you back as soon as I can. So leave your name and number and I'll call you back as soon as I can. Have a great day." Again with the double statements. That should tell me a little something, but do I have foreshadowing on my mind? No, foreplay is more like it. At this point all I can think of is, omigod, I'm talking to Jonathan Gradinger's answering machine! Forty-eight hours ago I never would have believed that I'd be leaving him a message. If some psychic had read my palm and told me that in a few days I'd have Jonathan Gradinger's home phone number—so much more intimate that a cell phone—I would never have believed it.

Wait a minute. How do I know it's his home number?

Beep. I have to leave a message. Beep.

My mind is blank. I have no idea what to say. Beetlejuice, beetlejuice? I stare at the receiver and hang up.

My fault. I should have known to be prepared. Where's my red felt pen? Okay, let's keep it simple.

Hello, Jonathan. This is Jacquelyn.

Too formal.

Hi, Jon, it's Jack.

Too close. We're not even phone-acquainted yet. And what if he thinks I'm a guy?

Fifteen minutes pass and I'm still struggling.

"Your bathroom looks great! I'm impressed!" Sam calls out, interrupting my concentration. "Jackie, where are you?"

"In my room."

"What are you doing?" She enters tentatively, as if expecting something alive to jump out of my overfilled laundry basket and attack her.

"Composing." I outline the situation for her.

"Okay," she says. "How about this. Hi, Jonathan, it's Jackie returning your message. Give me a call when you have a chance."

"Oh, that's brilliant. What comes after 'message' again? Say it slowly so I can write it down."

"You're a nut."

"Never mind. I remember."

"Don't forget to block your number."

"Why?"

"What if he has call display? You already hung up once. It'll look funny if it says your name twice with only one message."

"Soooo clever! You'd be single-girl *extraordinaire*."

"Thanks, but no thanks."

I pre-dial the code to withhold my number, then re-dial Jonathan's. Sam holds my other hand for moral support.

"Hi. This is Jonathan Gradinger. I can't get to the phone right now. Please leave your name and number and I'll call you back as soon as I can. So leave your name and number and I'll call you back as soon as I can. Have a great day.''

Trying to make my voice sound as natural as possible, I read my scrawled message and carefully place the phone back on the receiver.

Now all I have to do is wait.

Hmm, hmm, hmm.

How am I going to wait all day?

How is he supposed to pick me up for our picnic and see my clean bathroom if he doesn't call me back?

''What should I do all day, Sam? What are you doing all day?''

''Correcting some homework.''

''You give homework to fourth-graders? That's mean.''

''I have to give a little homework.''

''Wanna go shopping?''

''I can't. I'm broke.''

''Yeah, so am I. So what's your point?''

''I find window-shopping depressing.''

Oh. Oh, well. I'll just watch TV then. Jonathan will call back soon.

Six o'clock. No Jonathan.

Seven o'clock. I'm sure he's just out for the afternoon.

Eight o'clock. He just got home now. He's turning on the TV. Getting ready to watch a new episode of *The Simpsons.*

It's the last scene. Any minute now.

It's over. Any second now the phone is going to ring. Any second now. C'mon, phone, don't be shy.

It's eleven and I'm not waiting anymore. I detest Jonathan Gradinger; he obviously met someone else tonight, fell in love, and forgot all about me. No one will ever love me again. My days will consist of work, my nights will consist of TV, and I will spend Saturday nights from here on at the movies—alone.

And so I go to bed—alone.

The next day at work I try to proofread a manuscript, but every time I get to the end of a paragraph I call in for my messages. "No new messages," the anal recorded bitch says.

I get home feeling pathetic. But what's this? From the doorway I see the flashing red light. I leave my shoes on—I mustn't waste any time!—even though I know Sam will shoot me. Please don't be Janie, please don't be Janie, please don't be— "Hi, Jackie, this is Jonathan Gradinger again. Give me a shout back. My work number is 555-9478. My work number is 555-9478."

No waiting this time, no bathroom cleaning, and no red ink preparation. I don't care if my bed isn't made, I'm calling him back *now*.

"Dartmouth Clinic," a woman says.

"Hi, can I speak to Dr. Gradinger please?"

"Whom shall I say is calling?"

"Jackie." I'm still not crazy about the repeating everything on the answering machine thing. Half the point of the recorded message is so you can listen to it again if you need to. Or again and again and again like I might want to do with this one.

"Jackie who?" Okay this woman obviously wants a piece of my Jonathan. Maybe she's already had a piece of him. Maybe that's where he was last night.

"Hello?" she asks somewhat impatiently.

"Norris. He knows who I am. He called me. I'm calling him back."

"One second please."

I'm on hold. What type of date will he propose? You can tell a lot about a guy from the type of date he suggests. Dinner means he's not afraid to jump right into it.

"Jackie?" he says in his foxy, sexy voice.

Coffee means he's a coward. "Jonathan! Hi."

"Great to hear from you."

On the other hand, it could mean he's sensitive. "Great to hear from *you*."

He laughs. "I told you I'd call."

"I know." Drinks would be best. So trendy.

"How was the rest of your weekend?" he asks.

"Good, thanks. Yours?"

"Great."

Great? Why great? What made it great *exactly?*

"What are you doing Thursday night?"

"Nothing, why?" *Why?* I can't believe I asked him *why.* Sometimes the stupidity that comes out of my mouth even amazes me.

"I was hoping you'd come see *The Apartment* with me."

This I am not expecting. Tickets to *The Apartment* are a gazillion dollars apiece, never mind completely sold out.

"I'd love to."

"Perfect. The show starts at eight. I'll pick you up around six-thirty and we'll grab a bite somewhere, okay?"

"Sounds perfect."

"I'll call you on Wednesday to finalize everything."

"Okay."

"Great. Have a good week."

"You, too."

I stare at the dead receiver in my hand and place it down gently in its cradle. I remove my shoes and leave them near the door so that Sam won't find out that I wore them into the house.

Yay!

I'm pretty sure taking me to a play symbolizes more commitment than drinks do.

Omigod. I'm practically engaged.

"I think it's a little sketchy," Wendy says. "He bought the tickets before he asked you?"

"He's trying to make a good first impression."

"Or maybe he was supposed to take someone else."

"Or he wanted to impress me."

"So he just assumed you'd want to go with him? What if you couldn't make it? Would he ask someone else? The tickets are two hundred dollars!"

"He's a doctor. What's two hundred dollars to a doctor?"

"He's a podiatrist, not a real doctor. He works with feet! Anyway, don't you think he's going to expect a little something in return for his two hundred dollars?''

"He doesn't think I'm a prostitute, Wen.''

"Whatever. I'd be leery.''

"Thanks for the encouragement. I'm going to call someone now who's not Scrooge.''

"'Bye.''

"'Bye.''

I hang up the receiver. Three days 'til true love! What will I wear? Should I dress like the girl-next-door-Sandra-Bullock type, or like the I'm-not-wearing-any-underwear-Sharon-Stone type?

It's only three days A.B. and I already have a date. Have dating regulations changed since I last played the game?

Do I mention the Prozac right away?

Just kidding. I'm not on Prozac—yet.

Do I invite him in for coffee and Letterman? Letterman and sex? Coffee and Letterman *and* sex?

Can I make the first move, or should I play hard to get? What about Fashion Magazine Fun Fact # 2: women are supposed to keep the first date impersonal and vague so that the man longs to know more, more, *more* about the mysterious woman sitting across from him. In other words, she must be the Fonz.

I'm feeling the pressure here, a culmination of years of contradictory First Date training regulations. I try to remember my first date with Jeremy.

Try to remember? My, now that's a good sign.

On our first date, he took me to the Motley Hotel, to the dining room, that is, not to an actual room. He ordered a bottle of wine, after asking me what kind I preferred. I said white since red stains your teeth and you end up looking as if you haven't been to the dentist in years, as if you're in serious need of tooth bleaching. (I'll admit I'm a bit crazy when it comes to teeth. I had braces for three and a half years in high school, which I'm sure is the longest braces-run anyone ever had. When they finally came off, the whole damn orthodontist's office cheered, and I vowed to never, ever mistreat the pearly straight darlings—which to this day means no smoking, no red wine, no curry, and no red spaghetti sauce. And I still wear my retainer once a week on Sunday, and will continue to do so until the day I get married, which is the date my ortho proposed, not a self-inflicted time frame.)

Jeremy noticed me ogling the brushetta. I love brushetta, and without even blinking an eye, he ordered it for me. When the bill came, and I made the fake reach; you know, the oh-look-the-bill-is-here-I-guess-I'll-reach-into-my-purse-and-take-out-my-money gesture, but he pulled out his Amex and said, "No, it's my pleasure." I, of course, silently breathed a sigh of relief because if I'd paid for even half of this dinner, I would have been eating macaroni and cheese for at least a month. So I smiled and said, "Okay, but next time it's on me," which was an absolutely brilliant thing to say, since it implied a second date.

A second date at McDonald's, if I'm paying.

And I swear, I didn't fool around with him after the expensive dinner. I said thank you, I had a nice time, and then kissed him on the cheek. And then the clincher—my answering machine broke. He told me later that he'd called and left a message, which I didn't get, but this I didn't tell him. He must have thought I was too busy/very cool/didn't really care, when in reality I was being my old pathetic let's-analyze-the-date-in-excruciating-detail self. (Does he think I'm a pig because I eyed the brushetta? A cheapskate for my fake reach? Did he see through my cheesy next-time-it's-on-me comment?) When it occurred to me that not one person had called in three days, not even Janie, I realized my answering machine had to be broken. So I immediately invested in one of those funky virtual machines that exist only in your phones.

My next problem was that I had no idea if he had called or not. I figured since our date had been on a Saturday, and it was already Thursday, chances are if he was at all interested he would have called and tried to leave a message. I decided to risk it and call him. He said that he was wondering what had happened to me. He'd left not one but *two* messages. Suddenly inspired, I told him I was sorry I hadn't called him back yet, but I'd been really busy. He said no problem, so how does it sound?

I said it sounded great, having no idea what *it* was.

It was a movie. *It* was for Friday night.

An hour earlier I had promised Wendy I'd go to a party with her on Friday night, after putting her off all week in case Jeremy would actually call. "I already have plans for Friday." Damn. Damn. Damn. (Can't break plans with your best friend for a guy, Fashion Magazine Fun Fact # 1.)

"Saturday then? Are you free Saturday?"

"Saturday sounds good," I said, realizing that I had managed to play by the Fashion Magazine Fun Facts without even trying, and by God they had worked! I had heard he was a player, but obviously my newly acquired attitude (albeit acquired totally by accident) was driving him to his knees.

If only I'd remained aloof and really not cared, the whole "Jeremy" episode in my life could have been avoided. Or I could have at least pretended to be aloof so that he'd have stayed on his knees. But virtual machines inside your phone *never* break down.

On my first date with Jeremy I wore basic black pants and a tight maroon sweater. This first date with Jonathan calls for something radical. My knee-highs are the only Sharon-Stone-like item of clothing I own, and Jeremy's already seen me in those. I mean *Jonathan*'s already seen me in them. *Jonathan*. In any case, hooker boots would be somewhat inappropriate for a play.

I must consult *Cosmo*.

I must go shopping.

On Tuesday I get my Visa bill.

Oh. *Oh*.

There won't be any new first date outfit after all. I know. I'll wear my black pants and maroon sweater, the outfit I wore on my first date with Jeremy.

On Wednesday I realize I can't wear that outfit; I would be jinxing the date before it even started. Okay, I'll compromise.

I'll buy half an outfit. I'll go buy a new sweater to go with the black pants. They're really great pants. My ass looks very small. They're kind of boot-cut but not too flared, and they cost as much as it cost to fix my teeth.

On Thursday I leave work early to prepare. My new red sweater, looks, um…almost exactly like my old one, but newer. The black pants are spread out on my bed like paper-doll clothes. Time to primp.

My phone rings just as I'm applying mascara to my eyelash-curled lashes.

''Hi!'' It's Natalie. ''So what are you wearing?''

''My black pants and a new red sweater.''

''Oh.''

''What do you mean, 'oh'?'' What is ''oh''?

''Well, it's just that…never mind. It's too late.''

''What? What!''

''Well, he'll probably be wearing a suit. It's at the Wang Center for the Performing Arts, right? My parents went last week, and my dad wore a tux.''

A tux? ''I'm not wearing a prom dress.'' Hysteria is rising in my voice.

''Not a prom dress, but definitely a dress. Don't you have one of those black dresses that are perfect for any occasion?''

Silence.

''Do you want to borrow one of mine?''

Natalie has about nine of those perfect-for-any-occasion dresses. Nine of those perfectly too small any-occasion dresses. I'm about to cry. Tears are about to overflow. I am going to look blotchy and red and my mascara will run down my cheeks like spilled ink.

''I have to go,'' I murmur and hang up. What will I do? What will I do? ''Damn! Damn! Damn!'' I scream.

Suddenly Sam, my fairy godmother, walks into my room. ''What's wrong? Did he cancel?''

''No, he didn't cancel.'' Sob.

''What happened then?''

"I can't wear this. I need to be wearing a perfect-for-any-occasion black dress. But I don't have any." I am breathing carefully, as if I'm in labor.

"Do you want to borrow something from me?"

Yay! I'm going to the ball. I'm not sure why borrowing from Sam has never occurred to me before. Maybe because I've never had anywhere to go before.

I nod, too choked up to speak.

"I have a couple of ideas. How long do we have?"

I look at my watch. "Nineteen minutes."

"Okay. Go put on panty hose and black heels."

I comply. Six outfits later, I'm looking quite Gwyneth, in Sam's gray tube top dress and silk black shawl.

"Let me fix your hair," she says, and swooshes it over my head into some sort of up-back-twist that makes me look very grown-up.

Twenty-four years old and only now do I feel grown-up.

And then the buzzer rings.

"Hello?"

"Hi, it's Jon."

"Hi, Jon. I'll buzz you up."

"Hold on," Sam says, running after me with hairspray. She sprays it all over my head, and pretty much all over my face.

"At least my eyebrows will stay in place."

"Where's your purse?"

I think of my big chunky one, and know instinctively that Calvin Klein here won't approve.

"Here, I have one for you." She reaches into a drawer and pulls out a small beaded black bag. "Take this. Pack a lipstick, an extra pair of hose—and a change of underwear and a tooth-brush just in case." She whispers the last part.

"Are you crazy?" I whisper back. "A toothbrush won't fit in here."

There's a knock at the door. I smile at my reflection in the mirror.

"Who is it?" I ask, and then feel like an idiot. I open the door before he can answer. He's wearing a dark gray James Bond suit, a white shirt, and silver tie. I'm very, *very,* glad I changed.

We have great seats. So far no major runs in the stocking of my date. Only minor ones. We're kind of balancing smack in the middle of perfect and almost-perfect.

He opens the car door for me—a navy-blue BMW. Mmm. Yummy expensive, leather smell. This is good.

"Is Dave Matthews okay?" he asks, motioning to the CD player.

Whatever. "I love Dave," I answer.

"Me, too," he says. "Are you a real fan, or a I-like-the-song-'Crash' fan?"

I don't know any other Dave songs by name. "'Crash' fan."

"Oh." This is not good.

"You look beautiful tonight, in case I haven't mentioned that earlier," he says after opening the car door for me when we arrive at the theater. This is a double good.

Just outside the entrance, a woman left over from the sixties approaches. She's holding a large wicker basket filled with red roses.

"No thanks," Jon says, barely even looking at her.

This is not good. Okay, fine, I know the whole rose thing is a little cheddary, but just once I'd like a guy to feel so over-whelmed by me that when he sees the rose person, he instinc-tively has to buy me one immediately. Double bad because Jon looks right through the woman, as if she isn't there.

Inside the theater, I shift around in my seat so that my stomach doesn't do that two-bulge thing it does when I'm sitting still. Sam's dress is a little tight across my tummy. Thank God for control-top panty hose.

Jon is sitting with his right leg crossed over his left, his hands folded in his lap.

"I can't wait to see this," I say. "It's gotten a ton of press for giving a public voice to homeless people."

"It *is* wonderful," he says.

"Oh? You've seen it?"

"Twice. And I listen to the CD all the time."

"Oh."

He picks up my hand. His hand is cold. He looks into my eyes.

"Don't you know you're my defrost button?" he sings in his low, foxy voice.

"Huh?" I'm not sure what he's singing, but he can be singing in Japanese for all I care. His high school rendition of "Summer Nights" comes floating back me. How could I have forgotten how awesome his voice is?

"Won't you run your fingers through my hair."

Excuse me? "Sorry?"

"Those are lyrics from the play."

"Oh."

"It's starting." He doesn't let go of my hand. I think I'm in love.

And I really am in love.

Until the Defrost song.

When the actors start singing, "Defrost" Jon starts to hum. And then his tune suddenly explodes into a song. Out loud. A loud song. At the play. He starts singing, out loud, at the Wang Center for the Performing Arts.

He lifts my hand that he never lets go of, and pretends it's a microphone: *"Your breasts melt my hands."* All right, one line I can handle as long as he stops. *Right now.*

He shuts up for a second. There is a God.

And then he comes back with a vengeance.

As a duet.

His boy voice: *"Why won't you wear your leather pants?"*

His girl voice: *"I'd rather do a lap dance."*

Omigod.

The gray-haired woman in the seat in front of us turns to give him the evil eye.

He doesn't notice.

The man in the tux on the other side of him looks at him as if Jon's face has grown warts.

The couple behind us starts to snicker.

People are laughing, not at the play, not with us. They're laughing *at* us.

Girl voice: *"Do you like it when I'm naughty?"*

Boy voice: *"Sometimes it's good to be bad."*

Bad. Very bad.

"What a great tune," he says when the song is over. "And my favorite song is still coming up in the second act. I know all the words to that one, too."

Very, very bad.

Mercifully, he remains still for the remainder of the act, except for random moments when he bursts into ill-timed applause. I run into the washroom to hide during intermission.

The lights dim, signifying the start of the second act. The play resumes, and I am forced to leave my retreat. As soon as we sit down, he reclaims my hand, drawing a circle in my palm. And another. And another. He squeezes and tightens his hold.

Okay, so he's affectionate. A little too tight a grip, mind you, but he's still Jonathan Gradinger. As long as he never sings in public again, as long as he never sings anywhere again, we can live a long, happy life together.

I return the hand squeeze. Ms. Jackie Gradinger. Mrs. Jonathan Gradinger.

Suddenly our hands that were nicely placed on the seat rest between us become separated. Circles are being drawn on my thigh.

Whoa.

Slow down, cowboy.

His thumb is getting dangerously closer to my, um, "femininity," as Cupid authors would call it.

I don't think so.

On the stage, one of the characters is dying. A song is in progress.

Why doesn't he sing along with it? Sing, Jonathan, sing!

I pull his antsy hand back toward my knee.

He starts kissing my ear.

The gray-haired woman is sobbing quietly. Her shoulders heave.

"You're so sexy," he slobbers into my ear.

Please. "Watch the play."

"I've seen the play," he whispers. "I'd rather watch you."

Then you should have invited me to dinner like a normal guy.

He starts kissing my neck.

I squirm out of his grasp.

He puts his hand back on my thigh.

On stage they're singing about true love.

"True love/Fits like a Lycra glove," Jonathan signs along.

If only Jon was wearing cement mittens, maybe he'd keep his hands to himself. True love? What the hell is that?

We continue to play tug-of-war for the rest of the show. When I push away his hand, he goes for my neck. When I move my head, he goes back to my thigh. This asshole deserves an Oscar for Persistence, if not for Worst Date.

After the show, he holds the door open for me, then takes my arm as we walk out of the theater, once again the perfect gentleman. Maybe I won't annul the marriage just yet.

"Did you enjoy the play?" he asks.

"Very much," I reply.

We step down the stairway onto the cobbled street, and he puts his arm around my waste. "The problems people face are incredible—homelessless, poverty, drug abuse. It's a tragedy, really," he explains.

A man in ragged jeans and a dirty green sweatshirt blocks our path. "Spare some change?" he asks.

Jon ignores him.

He is so going to have to invest in a huge three-carat to make up for this night. I slowly, purposefully take out a ten, and stick it in the guy's jar.

I want to give him only five, but I only have a ten. It's not as if you can ask a homeless guy for change, and I *really* want to make my point.

"Aren't you noble," Jonathan comments snidely.

We make small talk in the car.

"I heard that they reduced ticket prices of *The Apartment* in New York to make it more accessible," I say. Wendy told me that.

"Why would they do that?"

All righty then.

He pulls up in front of my house and puts the car into park. "Let's sit outside for a minute."

"Okay," I say. Now I know as well as the next woman that this really means "Let's fool around." Okay, I admit it, I'm fickle. At this point, I still haven't decided to completely discard him. On the plus side, he *is* Jonathan Gradinger, *Dr.* Jonathan Gradinger. He has a BMW, he's hot, he's older, and he still has most of his hair. On the minus side, he's a creep who will never see the irony of spending two hundred dollars on a play about homeless people.

This time he does not open the car door for me. We sit on a bench outside my apartment building. Suddenly I feel a wetness soaking through my legs. Unfortunately, it isn't the I-really-want-to-fool-around kind of wetness. It's a wet bench. Damn. Sam will kill me if I stain her gray tube dress.

When I try to stand up, Jonathan throws his lips at my face.

I say throw in the literal sense. Jonathan does not kiss me. I will not degrade the verb "to kiss" by using it to describe his affront.

His upper lip is nowhere near mine, his tongue getting in the way of everything, and I'm not quite sure what is going on with his bottom lip.

I push him away. "I have to go." Sigh. I'm going to have to give him back the three-carat ring.

"But it's early!"

Thankfully it's Thursday and I can use work as an excuse. "I have an early meeting." I decide to not be a bitch; after all, he's still Jonathan Gradinger. He may have some hot friends. "Thanks for the play."

"My pleasure. I'm sorry you have to get up early. I was really enjoying myself."

I'm sure you were. "Good night," I say, taking out my keys and unlocking the front door.

It turned colder, that's where it ends. I wish I could tell him that *we'd still be friends.* But he's no Danny Zukoe.

A pervert I can handle. A lack of sensitivity we can workshop. But a bad kisser? I don't think so.

At least I know why he's still single.

Chapter Six

Surge Your Manhood Somewhere Else

"She had never felt such strong stirrings. As he pressed his hard, ripped chest against her, her nipples tightened. She realized she didn't want to wait any longer. She was wet and ready. She pushed aside her white panties and shifted herself on top of him. With a single deep thrust, he filled her with his surging manhood."

It's hard to concentrate on where to put commas when my work reminds me of where other stuff should go. Although after the week I had, the idea of sex completely grosses me out. First Creepo-Jon on Thursday, and then Supercreep on Friday. Coffee will help me concentrate.

I manipulate my way through the maze of cubicles to the dingy kitchen, and open the cupboard to grab my... My mug's gone.

I should check in the dishwasher, a last-minute desperate measure since I know my cup's not there; my washing technique extends to occasionally rinsing it out in the sink.

Where *do* they keep the dishwasher?

Aha!

No. No. No! My mug's not there.

Why would someone take my mug? Actually, it's Sam's mug, but she hasn't noticed it's missing yet, so theoretically it's mine. It has a cute polar bear on it, and it's mine, mine, mine, and now some office thug has stolen it. Maybe once I find it, I should lace it with a laxative. That way, I'll find out who could do such a vile act by the number of visits she makes to the bathroom. Now

I have to go and take someone else's mug. I really, *really* hate when this happens.

"Morning, Jackie," says Julie, the other *True Love* copy editor. Although she's very serious, she's one of the few copy editors I actually don't hate—she's not one of Helen's groupies.

"Morning, Julie. How are you?"

"Good, you?"

"Good, good."

"Jackie, I've been meaning to ask you something." Her arms are crossed in front of her chest, puffing her black blazer.

Here I am expecting, "Do you capitalize after a colon?" Or even better (since this would solicit my professional opinion and therefore affirm the notion that I have one), "Do you prefer an em dash or an en dash?" Instead, she says, "Can I fix you up with my brother?"

"Huh? Your brother?"

"Yeah, I think you're his type."

I'm not sure exactly how she's come to this decision since *I* don't even know what type I am. But she nods with affirmation, so I ask, "What type am I, exactly?"

"Small, curly hair, cute, outgoing, smart." And to think I always had so much trouble defining myself in magazine quizzes.

"How do you know he's *my* type?" Does this mean my type is short with curly hair like me? Or is my type skinny and bony like Julie?—assuming, of course, that her brother looks like her. At this point I am extremely hopeful; if she can define my type, it will certainly save me a lot of time on bad dates in the future.

"You don't think my brother Tim would be your type?" she says, huffed. "He's a great guy."

Fashion Magazine Fun Fact # 3: stay clear of guys described as great. "He's a great guy" is the masculine equivalent of "She's got a great personality."

As much as I was considering it before (which was virtually nil due to the fact I never even knew that Julie had a brother—in fact, it always surprises me whenever a person I've been acquainted with for a while suddenly emerges as having a *life,* this

reaction probably sprouting from too much editing of paper-
people), the chance that I will ever date Julie's short, curly haired
bony brother with the great personality has now dwindled into
nonexistence.

It's not that I have anything against short, curly haired, bony
guys with great personalities, particularly if they're my type, but
I will not, let me emphasize *not,* date a guy who has the same
name as my dad. Too weird. Too Freudian. How could I whisper
his name in his ear? How could I scream his name in ecstasy?
In anger, maybe—that is, scream his name, not whisper in his
ear. Not that I'm ever angry at my dad. I'm only angry at my
mom, sometimes, though I can never figure out why. No Freud
there, either.

"Actually," I tell Julie, "I just started seeing someone."

Liar, liar, pants on fire.

Time for my second cup. Coffee breaks remind me of recess,
except there aren't any cute guys at work to pretend to ignore.
There aren't even any not-so-cute guys. Of the two hundred Cupid employees, one hundred and sixty-seven are women. Thirty-
five of these women are pregnant. Weekly Lamaze classes are
conducted on the third floor.

This pathetic female-male ratio unfortunately results in a low
potential for making male friendships. So where else am I supposed to make male friends so that they can fix me up with their
friends? It's not like I can saunter up to a guy at a bar and say,
"Hi, wanna be my friend?" Andrew would actually be an excellent male friend, but I haven't seen him since the movie fiasco.
I thought maybe he'd be at Orgasm on Friday, but no, he was
probably off frolicking with his Sweet Valley Twin.

Friday night…

Instead of talking to Andrew, I had to spend the entire night
avoiding E-reek. It turns out he's not royalty at all, just some
Euro guy with a lot of money. Natalie was not impressed. She
insisted we ignore him, which drove him crazy, so he kept sending over fancy vodka shots, which Nat kept refusing, which I

kept drinking. Well, someone had to. Obviously Nat's indifference threw E-reek into a seizure of love, once again proving the bitch theory, Fashion Magazine Fun Fact # 4: men want you more when you don't want them. (This fact is different from fact number two where you're supposed to remain aloof in order to snare your man; fact number four warns you of the possibility that overcoolness on your part might lead to potential stalkers.) Take Jonathan, for instance. We went out only once, six days ago, and already he's called seven times. I've had four hang-ups and three messages.

Saturday: "Hey, love. (Love? Aren't we a little too familiar, here?) It's Jon calling. Call me. Call me."

Sunday: "Hello, dear. (Dear? What am I, over forty?) It's me. It's me. Just calling to see how your weekend was. Call me back. Call me back."

Tuesday: "Hi, sexy. (Sexy's good, but from him? Ew...) Want to catch a flick this weekend? Call me back soon. Call me back soon."

I know I should be a big girl and call him back to tell him I'm not interested, but then I'll have to listen to him...twice. However, if I ignore him enough, eventually he'll go away. His messages remind me of a Doublemint commercial.

Thank God for call display.

Well, at least he wasn't at Orgasm. After six rounds of E-reek's courtship, in my hazy state of mind I might have let it slip that I thought he was a creep. Or I might have gone home with him. I'm talking about Jonathan, of course. Not E-reek. Although in my condition, who knows?

I did spot one bleached-blond hottie, a definite potential boyfriend, or at least a potential let's-get-it-on guy. He was wearing New York rimmed dark glasses and one of those ski sweaters with a beige stripe running across the chest, which are still sexy despite them being so 1996. He sat on a bar stool talking to two other guys, and I decided to try my look-over-right-now telepathic powers on the off chance they might work.

Like I said, it was an off chance.

At about two, Nat and I decided to call it quits and head home. Her Jetta was parked in my lot again, since I live so close. We chatted noisily as we headed through the side streets to my house. About three minutes into our walk I noticed a guy in a jean jacket and jeans lurking about a half a block behind us.

"...I know E-reek's cute," Nat was saying, "but I could barely understand anything he said. Maybe if he could make me a princess, or at least an heir to something, but..."

A block later, the guy was still behind us.

"Nat," I whispered, "there's a guy behind us that's really creeping me out. At the corner let's switch to the other side of the street."

"Is it Jon?"

"No, he's more of a telephone stalker, not a physical one. I don't know who this guy is."

I could see her face turning white even under her perfectly applied MAC foundation. We crossed.

"Okay, now let's pretend we're tying our shoes."

"We don't have laces," she whispered. True, I thought, staring at my knee-highs. Why wasn't I wearing a solid pair of Sketchers? Why, why?

We fidgeted with the heels of our boots.

One, two, three, four, five, six, seven, eight, nine, ten.

I figured that by ten he would be gone. But no, he was crossing the street.

"Shit," Nat whispered. She motioned to the nearest building. "Let's pretend we live there," she mouthed. "I can't run in these things."

We moved as fast as our boots would allow, the sound of our heels cracking against the sidewalk. When we reached the white high-rise, Natalie opened the glass door and marched inside. I picked up the phone, struggling to decide on a number to dial.

"Dial something already!" Natalie hissed. I dialed one-two-three-four-five, hoping someone nice lived at my old Hotmail account code.

"He's going to walk by any second," Natalie moaned.

Why isn't it ringing? Please ring!

Suddenly, the stalker walked past the door. He peered inside, then continued down the street.

"That was crazy," Nat said as we stared into the empty blackness. Empty for a second, anyway. Because suddenly Supercreep reappeared in front of us, this time with his pale blue jeans around his knees, holding what I'm assuming was his surging manhood. "Do you believe?" Nat cried.

I whipped my head away, and grabbed the phone again. This time I tried my answering machine code: five-four-three-two-one. I know, I know, I'm not the most original.

Ring, ring.

"Don't look! Don't look!" Natalie whispered frantically, but I could see his reflection in the inside door, and he was just...going at it.

Ring, ring.

"I don't believe this is happening," I whispered. "We have to do something."

Suddenly he "finished," did up his pants, and walked away.

"Hellooooo?" said a very groggy, very annoyed voice from the nice people who lived at my answering machine. I hung up.

"Ew..." I said, pointing to the gift he had left us in the form of a white lump on the sidewalk.

"I think I'm going to be sick," Nat said.

We waited until we saw a harmless-looking couple walk by, and then ran hysterically into the street to beg them to walk with us home.

Nat slept on my couch because she was too freaked to drive home alone. "What if he creeps into my car and attacks me while I'm driving? What then?"

We woke up Marc and Sam, forcing Marc to look out the window to make sure he wasn't outside.

"You guys should never have walked home alone," Marc criticized.

"So it's our fault?" I asked. "It's our fault that some guy's a perv?"

Marc shrugged. "I only meant that you should be more careful. Did you at least get a good look?"

"Don't be disgusting. I didn't want to look down there."

"I meant at his face. You know, to identify him."

"Oh. No, I didn't."

"Maybe I should carry some sort of weapon," Natalie piped up. "Like Mace. Or a gun. Something that would really scare a guy away."

"Do you think this is Texas?" I commented. "We can't just go around shooting people."

"You should have just ran outside and told the guy you wanted to get married, that you're looking for a serious commitment. That always seems to scare them off," Sam answered, shooting a sarcastic smile at her boyfriend. We all ignored her.

"Do you at least remember what he was wearing?" Marc asked.

"Yeah, a jean jacket and jeans." Natalie said. "Do you believe? You're not supposed to wear a jean jacket and jeans together. What a fashion faux pas."

Then we ignored *her*. Then she actually had a half-decent idea—to take a self-defense course. So, yesterday at work, I spent half the day on the Net researching our options. It seems that most classes are all female and are led by male martial arts teachers. I could learn all kinds of cool moves like how to kick a guy where it hurts and poke his eyes out, without offending the teacher.

Because I spent so much of yesterday surfing the Net, I have fallen more than slightly behind in my work. It's just so hard to focus. I've started to see commas in my sleep, like when you play too much Tetris and start to mentally insert your pencil holder into that space between your bulletin board and the wall. Today I will work through lunch on this week's manuscript, *For the Love of a Cowboy*.

I take a bite of my sandwich and read on.

"The sensation made him cry out. He lowered his head and ran his hands over her peaked nipples. He'd never wanted a woman the way he wanted Julie. He caught her hips, wrapping her long silky legs tightly around his waist, and drove himself deep within her hot wetness. She was tight and slick. With every stroke, his thrusts became deeper, harder, faster, and she moaned. He no longer cared what his family had said. Now that he had this woman, he knew he could never let her go.''

"Oh, Ronan!" I cry out through sticky lips that have been partially glued to my teeth with peanut butter, as Julie digs her nails into her lover's smooth back. I continue reading.

"He left one of his hands on her soft, supple breasts and used his other one to pull her head toward him. He crushed his lips over hers and drove his tongue deep into her mouth. With every rocking motion, he moved fuller and deeper inside of her, joining them, moving them closer and closer to a tidal wave of pleasure…''

My ringing phone interrupts me. Oops, I forgot to edit. But who can pay attention to condoms (oops again, Freudian slip—I mean commas) when it's getting so damn hot in here? Then again, Julie's not paying attention to condoms, either. Hopefully she's on the pill.

"Jackie speaking," I say.

"Darling, it's me." Am I Darling? "Me" is Jonathan Gradinger. How did he get this number?

"Hi, Jon," I say in my most I'm-really-busy-here-so-I'm-going-to-have-to-get-off-the-phone-shortly voice. "How are you?"

"Good, good. You? Been busy?"

"Yeah, busy. Sorry I haven't got back to you. You know, work."

"Yeah, ever since last week's walkathon, I've been swamped with podiatric emergencies."

"What walkathon?"

"Some women marching at night because they don't feel safe after dark or something. Some feminist crap."

It's official. I hate him. "Actually, I'm looking to find a good self-defense course."

"You mean like karate?"

"No, I mean self-defense."

"Just kick the guy in the balls, and he'll stop bugging you."
Something I should practise on you, lover-boy.

"Anyway, I was wondering if you wanted to catch a flick tonight."

"Sorry, Jon, I'm going to be stuck here late tonight. I have no idea what time I'll get out."

"No problem. I'll wait up for you. We don't have to see a movie. We can do something else."

"I really don't want to make you wait. Tonight's just not a good night." Just what else do you have in mind, lover-boy?

"Okay. We'll do something tomorrow then."

This guy is like a yeast infection that just won't go away.

"I really don't think it's a good idea, Jon. Actually, I'm still kind of hung up on someone." I can't believe I just used Jerk-Face as an excuse. At least Jer is still good for something.

"You didn't mention anyone."

"I know. I'm sorry. I was involved with someone before I moved here and I'm just not over him yet." See, that part is true. I'm not lying. It's not something I would have admitted if I had liked Jonathan, but whatever. It sounds a lot better than saying, "It's not you, it's me."

"What happened?"

"He was supposed to move here with me, but it didn't work out."

"Okay, no problem. I understand. Call me if you ever change your mind."

"Definitely." Definitely *not*. I know I'm probably breaking his heart, but what else can I do? Fashion Magazine Fun Fact # 5: it's better to be cruel at the beginning than to string him along.

"So, Jackie, since you won't go out with me, do you have any friends you can fix me up with?"

I've come to a conclusion: all guys are assholes. Particularly the ones I date.

But even this asshole has nothing on Jeremy.

Jeremy was supposed to mov ...
ished one year of a master's prog...
undergraduate school. It's not that...
took a year off after high school, a...
semester instead of five in university s...
in school politics. He was vice preside...
Wendy and I spent days making his can...
vorite being a bristol board of three-dimens... bricks
with the slogan "Jeremy for VP, Not Just A ... brick in the
Wall." He was a Pink Floyd fan, what can I say? I glued his
picture to each board; he looked so cute until someone decided
to color in one tooth black on each poster.

"I told you I shouldn't be smiling," he said.

So self-centered, that boy.

Like when he would pick out extra marshmallows from the
Lucky Charms box for his bowl. He never did grasp the concept
that more marshmallows for him meant less for me.

Or when I sat with him at the dentist's office for three hours
when he had a cavity, because I know how much he hates going
to the dentist. ("They take pleasure in my pain," he'd say.) But
when we had that condom-breaking scare, the precursor to me
going on the pill, did he offer to come with me to the gyno?
Nope. I had to drag Wendy.

And now that we're on the subject of Jeremy's overwhelming
self-centeredness, allow me to describe the Boston fiasco. Picture
this: your long-term boyfriend gets into a philosophy master's
program at Boston University. He tells you the city has a million
opportunities, terrific jobs, wonderful people, and asks you to go
with him. You agree to make the move, not because of the opportunities or jobs but because of the people, namely him.

You drop out of your own master's program—you were becoming disillusioned with academics anyway, you told yourself.
You agree to get your own apartment because you know he's not
"ready" yet. You agree despite your mother's warning that a girl
shouldn't follow a boy around the country without a ring on her
finger. You think your mother's ridiculous—you're only twenty-

...ng to get married. So you look for editorial
...ou were an editor at your college newspaper, and
...you don't want to go into academia and you don't
...to be a teacher and you're not really sure what else you
can do with an English lit degree.

Cupid offers you a job that comes with full benefits and an
intensive two-week copyediting course. You know correcting
grammar isn't what you want to do with your life, but since the
only thing you currently feel worth doing is being with Jer, you
take the job. So you call your old college friend, Natalie, who
introduces you to Sam. You sign a lease. And your boyfriend is
still looking for a place. And looking.

And then one day while you're packing your books in the
cardboard boxes from the liquor store (you were just finishing
the nineteenth century; you always organize your books chronologically, not by author), the so-called love of your life rings
the bell. How sweet, you think. He's brought you supper. And
he has brought you supper, Thai noodles and egg rolls. But he's
also brought a plane ticket. One plane ticket. *His* plane ticket.
His plane ticket to Thailand.

He says he has to find himself, and has deferred his acceptance
into the master's program until the winter semester. You wonder
when he got lost in the first place, but this you don't ask. He
circles his hand along your back and tells you that you'll be fine
without him, that it's only for a few months. You start crying
and ask how he could do this to you, and he says it has nothing
to do with you. And that's just the point.

Then you suggest an idea: you'll go, too. You haven't taken
time off in a while, and you've certainly earned a vacation.
You'll take out a loan. You'll even learn to eat with chopsticks.
But he isn't looking at you anymore; he's looking past you at
the print of Francesco Hayex's *The Kiss* hanging on your wall.
The print he bought you for your birthday. The Romantic painting's dusty red color of the Robin Hood-like hero matched with
your duvet, and at the time you thought the fact that he'd picked
such a romantic painting, one featuring a hero gallantly kissing

a woman, instead of any other picture he could have bought, meant something.

"This is something I have to do alone," he says. You cringe. Suddenly, you start to cry again, and he's kissing your cheeks. His hands are under your shirt, and somehow you find yourself in bed with him even though you think you might hate him.

And then you're helping him shop for backpacks, travel pillows, and *Let's Go* books, and you're trying to smile and be supportive, and he kisses you as you stand in line in front of the cash register. And then the night before you move, he's helping you finish packing, and you're sitting on a duffel bag filled with your shoes, and he says, "We have to talk about something." And suddenly you want him to shut up, shut up, *shut the fuck up,* but he tells you he wants you to see other people while he's gone.

Translation: he wants to screw Thai women.

"We're breaking up?" you ask, but he insists that you're not, that you're just seeing other people, and you wonder what he'll do if you say no. But you don't say no; you don't say anything at all.

The next morning, you say goodbye and tell him to e-mail.

The most ironic part of my life right now, is the juxtaposition of my love life against the love lives of my alter egos, my heroines. They've all found their soul mates. Where is my everlasting love? Where is my Prince Charming? Where is my incredibly handsome, brilliant, stoic romantic hero?

Jeremy is not him. He's too busy screwing Thailand. And possibly, Holland.

Jon is not him either. Heroes must be good kissers.

Enough! Back to Ronan and Julie.

My screensaver pops up and three handsome, topless heroes in cowboy hats smile devilishly. Lovingly. Look at those hairless, buffed chests! Where have buffed chests been all my life?

I need a man who's rugged. A man who smells like sweat. A man who could kill someone with his bare hands. A man who *would* kill if he had to. Not that I'd want him to, of course, but a man who would if he had to would definitely be a plus.

That's what I need now. A fling with a rock-hard hero. Arms like a he-man. Legs of a hunk. An alpha male. No more of this philosophy bullshit. And no more dating guys whose names start with the letter J.

Now where can I find this strapping, young lad? A construction site? A rodeo? Home Depot? What was it Jonathan had mentioned? Karate? Suddenly it comes to me as clear as filtered water. Forget self-defense! I'll enroll in a martial arts class; at least Jonathan will have been good for something other than fuel for a "It-Happened-To-Me" magazine column.

I look up "Boston" and "martial arts" on the Net. Fourteen matches. Karate, judo, Tae Kwon Do, origami… Origami? I click on Tae Kwon Do. It sounds kind of like Tae Bo, something I once tried. Okay, I didn't actually try it; I bought the video. Fine, rented the video. Whatever.

Ten muscled, dark-haired gods in crisp white uniforms spring onto my screen, performing perfect sidekicks, and *Only $500* flashes across the console. Only $500? Excellent! Of course, this doesn't include the costume, the cost of each belt as you progress, the testing fee per level so that you can achieve these higher belts, not to mention the designer bricks you get to break, or the required café latte after each lesson.

Nevertheless, I will get to:

1. Meet very hot men.
2. Learn how to protect myself so that men dressed in fashion faux pas cannot use me as a sexual object on street corners (unless I choose to be used as a sexual object on a specific street corner).
3. Get a great body that is much, much better than Jeremy's Dutch bimbo's body—and if Jeremy ever comes back, I can beat the crap out of him.

Right after work, I'm joining the gym.

"We want you!" the screen flashes. And I want you, I think. All of you.

"How's your lunch?" Helen's nasal voice asks. She pops up from behind her cubicle wall, interrupting the "wax on/wax off" hand-motions in my head.

"Oh, fine. Thanks."

Her eyes drop to my desk, onto my borrowed coffee cup. "So you're the one who stole my mug this morning! I was wondering who the culprit was. I don't mind you borrowing it, but next time, please ask."

Helen's mug? Ew. Helen cooties.

Chapter Seven

More Beef

Okay, so I didn't go Wednesday right after work, but it wasn't because of laziness, I swear. It was because I now have a new life game plan: think ahead. Instead of running straight over as I'd normally do, I called first to arrange an appointment. See how organized I can be when I put my mind to something? The teacher, Master NanChu, told me to come Saturday morning at eleven for a trial class. Yay, a free class! Wait a minute—why do I need a trial class? What if he doesn't like me? Can he refuse me?

I'm going to look just like the *Flashdance* girl in the ''She's A Maniac'' workout scene. Luckily I have an adorable pair of Calvin Klein black workout shorts and a matching tank top I bought at an outlet mall last winter.

Tomorrow is Saturday, so I can't stay out late tonight. Not too late, anyway. If I have to be at the Tae Kwon Do studio at eleven, then I'll have to leave my house by 10:30, which means I have to get up at ten. Wait—I should probably eat before I go. You're supposed to wait at least an hour after you eat before going swimming; it's probably the same for martial arts. Okay, I have to be finished eating by 9:45, which means I have to start eating at 9:30, which means I have to get up at 9:15. Maybe 9:25, considering there's no point in showering if I'm only going to get all gross.

But first things first. Tonight I'm off to Orgasm with Natalie. As soon as she gets here, that is. I've been waiting in the lobby forever, teetering in my new boots, which I'm wearing under pants because even though no one can see them, they make me feel quite sexy.

Finally a BMW comes to a screeching halt on the circular driveway. The driver has shiny, toothpaste-commercial teeth and glossy long black hair, and waving frantically next to her is Natalie. I open the car door and climb into the backseat.

Natalie introduces us, glancing at me in the rearview mirror. "Jackie, this is Amber."

Amber? Is she an 80s pop singer? A porn star? "Hi, Amber, nice to meet you."

Amber's arm raises slightly in acknowledgment. Her nails are *so* fake, and I'm not too sure about the expanse across her chest, either. I bet she has a miserable handshake; her wrist is about the size of a chopstick. My dad always says you can judge a person by his or her handshake.

"So how do you know Nat, Amber?"

"School."

I assume not college. She's got the word bimbo written all over her slinky frame. "High school?"

"No, junior high." Her voice is low and scratchy, and she sounds a bit like Grover from *Sesame Street*.

"Amber lives around the corner from me," Natalie says, trying to cover for Amber's lame conversational skills. Not that she's doing any better.

"Fun." Pause. Now it's time for you to ask me something, Amber darling.

Silence.

All right. My turn again. "What are you doing in Boston?"

"I live here."

Yeah, I figure that, dimwit. I was asking if you have a job or if you go to school, but I now suspect that you sit on your skinny ass filing your fake nails all day except for when you meet your friends for a lunch of celery sticks.

Since the stalker episode, Natalie refuses to walk anywhere. "Where are we going to park?" I throw out the question to apparently deaf ears. "Park? Hello? Car? Anyone?" Am I in some type of absurd Beckett play? An episode of *Twilight Zone*?

Natalie turns to face me. "Amber parks at the fire station."

"The fire station! Who do you know at the fire station?"

No answer.

"Is your dad a fireman or something?"

"No, he's a surgeon."

Well, *excuse* me. At least I know how to elicit a response: imply civil servant lineage. "So does that mean *you're* the fireman?"

"No, I'm a dentist."

I certainly didn't see that coming. Apparently she's not a bimbo—just a bitch. It actually makes a bit of sense, since it's so painful to be around her.

The fire station is directly behind Orgasm. Six men, firemen I'm guessing (a brilliant assumption, I know), are smoking in the driveway's corner. There's something very wrong with this picture; I mean, fireman shouldn't smoke, right? What would Smokey the Bear say? Amber pulls into an empty spot beside a fire truck and cuts her engine. "Flirt back with Fred, 'kay?"

Fred? Who's Fred?

Amber steps out of the car, and I realize that the toothpaste description extends even further; she actually *looks* like a tube of Crest—a used tube. Like when I roll the bottom to squeeze the rest out of the top. Well, not exactly. I twist and wring to get the final drops out. Sam rolls. In any case, any toothpaste left in Amber's body has been squeezed upward, and is now spilling over her shirt in the form of cleavage. I'm *definitely* thinking boob job. A very perky boob job.

Come to think of it, her nose looks a little too perky, too.

A short, very built Asian man walks toward us.

"Hi, Fred." Amber runs her arm down his forearm. "Miss me?"

"The love of my life! I thought you forgot all about me."

"Forget about you? Impossible." She kisses Fred—get this—on the lips.

Is he a boyfriend? A civil servant Romeo?

"Remember me, Fred?" Natalie says in a pouty voice.

"Of course I remember you! How could anyone forget such a beautiful face?" Now he kisses her, also on the lips.

Do I have to kiss him, too? "Hi, boys!" Amber squeals to the other firemen, saving me.

All the Smokey Bears hoot hello. Fred, who is easily my dad's age, stomps on his cigarette and asks, "Here to entertain us?"

"Not tonight, hon," Amber says. "We're off to Orgasm."

"Need any help?" he asks. Ew. Is this really worth a parking spot?

"Another time. I assume it's okay that we park here." Amber does not ask. She informs.

"Who could say no to three hotties like you?"

"Thanks, I really appreciate it." She kisses him again. On the lips.

Natalie kisses him again. On the lips.

I wave.

The hostess says hello to me; apparently I've graduated to regular-patron status. It's Amber, though, who knows the hostess' name and gets us a table near the bar. According to the bitch looks from two girls in pleather, this appears to be a huge score. Amber and Natalie grab the seats facing the bar, leaving me staring at the window. Unless all the guys in this bar all have a back fetish, I might as well be invisible.

The buxom waitress comes over to our table. "What can I get you girls?"

"A Manhattan," Amber says.

I really want to ask what a Manhattan is, but I know it'll sound like a stupid question.

"Same for me," Natalie says.

"Me, too, please." Okay, so I'm a suck. But Amber seems like the kind of girl who knows what to order in places like Orgasm.

"Do you believe!" Natalie squeals. "I think I just saw Darlene

Powell. No, it couldn't be her. I ran into her at Saks last week and she looked like shit. She had pockets under her eyes the size of her shopping bags…''

I focus on their eyes, which continually flicker around the room. It's as if Natalie and Amber are stage actors who have been instructed to face the audience instead of each other.

The waitress places three very chic red drinks in Martini glasses on our table. ''Cheers,'' we say, clicking glasses.

Mmm. Quite good. Very alcoholy. At least you're good for something, Tiffany. Debbie. Amber. Whatever.

''Did you see Debbie's ring?'' Natalie asks while jotting down some numbers in her calorie notebook.

Amber runs her fingers through her mane. ''You call that pebble a stone? How embarrassing for her.''

I can't handle this ridiculousness. ''I'll be back soon,'' I tell the gossiping duo. I'll do a once-around stroll through the bar.

Obstacle number one: stroll is a misnomer. Elbow/squeeze stepping in the Lilliputian gaps that divide women's bare skin from too touchy men would be a more accurate term. My height disability only adds to the situation; I can't see over anyone's head.

Problem number two: every elbow/squeeze step sends a tidal wave of my drink over the glass rim. Whose decision was it to make glasses in this stupid V shape anyway?

Finally I maneuver my way through half the bar. The end looms in the distance like a pot of gold or a two-for-one sweater sale. What if my soul mate is waiting at the end of the bar? And what if he'll only be standing in that same spot for the next four minutes? If I don't happen to bump into him within this time frame, the moment will be lost forever and I'll be forced to roam the earth alone for the rest of eternity.

Oh, my, it's Stripe-Boy! The cute bleached blonde with the New York rimmed glasses from last week! He's sitting by himself on a stool in the corner, and here I am, trapped in the age-old eleventh-grade math question: if I always have to cross the halfway point before reaching the endpoint, how is it possible to ever reach my destination, since every halfway point is a destination, and every destination has a halfway point? See where I'm headed with this? If the distance between a girl and the end of a bar is say, twenty feet, she has to pass the halfway point at ten feet before she can reach the end of the bar, but first she has to pass the halfway point of that, which is at five feet, and so on, and so on... Good God, there will always be another half point, and I will never reach my damn soul mate, oh, Stripe-Boy, you adorable, unattainable goal!

Which might be a good thing because Jon Gradinger is currently standing smack in the middle of a halfway point with his elbow against the bar, wearing a black turtleneck, which simply reinforces my I-won't-date-guys-who-wear-turtlenecks rule. What guy wears a turtleneck to a bar? What guy wears a turtleneck? I turn around and walk back through the three halfway points I survived getting here.

And while we're on the subject, why is Stripe-Boy obsessed with stripes? A dysfunction from his childhood? Maybe he's the kind of guy who linearly plans for his future. Like me. Didn't I plan ahead by calling Master NanChu in advance? Stripe-Boy probably already has a ten-year plan. To meet a nice girl. Me. To fall in love with a nice girl. Me. To propose to—

A splash of red hair surfaces at another halfway point. Andrew? Thank God. Now I get to talk to someone I know while simultaneously proving to all skeptics (mainly Andrew himself) that I do in fact have friends.

Quite the social butterfly, that Andrew. Always doing the scene. I elbow-squeeze my way toward him. Push. Elbow. Push. Someone pats my butt.

Andrew smiles when he sees me. "Hey, Jack." A gentle arm wraps around my waist.

Destination complete. Math theory proven false.

"I thought I spotted you in the distance. Are you here alone?" he asks.

I smack him lightly on the arm. "No, I am *not* here alone. Natalie is sitting right over—"

"I'm kidding." He takes a sip of his beer. "I'm sure you don't go out alone every night." He smiles, his eyes crinkling into half moons.

"So, who's the blonde?"

"Blonde? Where?" he looks around the bar in a mock search. I swat him on the arm.

"Jessica. The Sweet Valley Twin. At the movie."

"What's a Sweet Valley Twin?"

"Don't they teach you anything at Harvard?"

"Apparently not."

"When do you study, anyway? You're Mr. Scene."

"I don't know about Mr. Scene—I've only left my apartment four times all year."

"Yeah, sure. And three times in the past two weeks." What is he, a socialite in denial?

"The more important question is, Where have *you* been all year?"

"Around." Around my apartment.

A brunette who's had one too many knocks against him, and he bumps against my leg. "I only go out when Ben drags me out," he says, apparently oblivious to our body contact.

Hmm. He's standing quite close here. Does he realize how close he's standing? Is he standing this close on purpose?

You know when someone's standing so close you can feel them even though you're not actually touching?

"Who's Ben?" I ask, after clearing my throat.

"My roommate. You didn't meet him last week? Now *he's* who you'd call Mr. Scene." The brunette disappears, and Andrew returns to his previous not-quite-close stance.

"Is he cute?"

"Cute? I can't tell if another guy is cute."

"Bullshit. I can tell if another girl is cute."

"What girl do you think is cute?"

"Forget it. I'm not allowing for any lesbian fantasies until you at least tell me if this Ben character is single." Brunette? Brunette? Come back, brunette! Come back, come back wherever you are!

"Ben!" He calls over a built blonde in a collared shirt. "Are you single tonight?" he screams over the music.

I smack him again.

"Why do you keep beating me up?"

"Because you're bitable...beatable." Good God.

"Every time you hit me, you lose more of your drink to the floor...Ben!" He raises his glass to the husky blond guy who has approached us at the bar.

Single-Tonight looks me up and down, and drawls, "Hel-looo."

"Ben, Jackie. Jackie, Ben."

He pulls my hand toward his lips and kisses it. "It's a pleasure to meet you," he says, not letting go. "Would you like a drink?"

"Why don't you give the lady back her hand and go buy us some shots," Andrew says.

"But her skin is so soft." He brushes his lips against my knuckles. Very soft lips. Who is this guy again?

"Forget it, she's off-limits."

Off-limits? Does Andrew like me? Do I comment on this? Should I let it go? Do I like Andrew?

Ben nibbles on my fingers and I start to laugh. He releases my hand, smiles, and returns to wherever he came from.

I ask straight out, "Why are you ruining my chances with an obviously available swinging single?"

"Because Jer would never forgive me if I let you go out with Ben."

Jer? *Jer?* "Jer?"

"I just meant—"

"—that the only reason you're talking to me is to make sure I sit here and virginally wait for Jer's return while he fucks everything he sees." My voice is suddenly loud. Why is he bringing Jer up? Is he an idiot? Or just a completely insensitive prick? Here I am, for at least fifteen minutes not thinking about Jer, and he has to go ahead and ruin everything.

"Whoa! I definitely didn't mean it like that. Sleep with anyone you want. But as your friend, and as an old friend of your ex, I can't recommend in good conscience that you go home, to my apartment no less, with a guy who screws a minimum of three girls a week and drinks a minimum of one bottle of vodka a day."

"Oh." Oops.

"Unless you like playboy lushes."

"Not particularly." I sniff my kissed hand. It smells like Scotch.

"In that case, you're forgiven for your outburst. At least you didn't smack me again."

"Here you go, gorgeous," Ben says, passing me two shots of some indefinable liquid.

"What is this, exactly?" I ask.

"Don't worry, sweet thing." He pinches my cheek with a sticky hand. "To Andrew's hot friend," he says, raising his shot with his other hand.

"I can definitely drink to that." I look him straight in the eyes. What can I say? Patronizing, playboy, lush…in spite of Andrew's warnings, I find myself tempted—but not too tempted.

"Cheers," Andrew says, and we shoot the first of the indefinable burning liquid.

Ben lifts the second shot in the air and toasts, "To getting laid. Tonight."

I nearly choke on the burning residue in my throat.

"Want to come home with me tonight, Andrew's hot friend?"

I pause for a moment in mock contemplation. "No."

Ben shrugs, shoots, and returns to the bar.

"Based on the sounds that come from his bedroom, I think you might be missing out," Andrew says.

"I doubt it. What you probably hear is him puking into his wastebasket. Or the sound of his crying when he finds out he can't perform, given his altered state."

"You sure you don't want to reconsider? He's not a bad guy, despite his extreme sketchiness."

"A minute ago, you were against the idea. Now you're my pimp?"

"What are friends for?"

Friends? Interesting concept. "You'd be amazed how difficult it is to make male friends in a new city," I confide. "For some reason, approaching a stranger and asking him if he'll change your lightbulbs gives him the wrong idea. Is there something phallic about lightbulbs that I'm missing here?"

"That's the barter system—manual labor for sex. How many lightbulbs are we talking about exactly?"

"Just a couple dozen." Maybe this could work. What did Sally's Harry mean when he said that men and women couldn't be friends? "And there's also this bookshelf or wall-unit thing I've been meaning to put together—"

"Let me get this straight. I slave over your apartment and get nothing in return?"

You can have anything you want in return. "You get my undying friendship. And dinner."

"You can cook?" he asks. "What can you make?"

Cook? God no. "I have Star-Search-caliber pizza-ordering talent," I answer, my back halfway turned to leave and return to Nat. "And I make great reservations."

I must sit. My feet are in bad shape. Why are all the cutest boots always so damn uncomfortable? Oh joy, there's a free seat next to Natalie. I'm about to sit down, when I realize that Stripe-Boy is sitting in Amber's seat.

"I'm back," I say. He's cute. His bleached blond hair gives him a bit of a boy-band look, but his dark-rimmed glasses add on a few years.

"Where were you?" Natalie asks. "Come sit."

"I was talking to Andrew."

"Andrew? He's here? Where?"

I point around the corner.

"Who's he with?" she asks.

"Some guy. Ben."

"Ben Mason?"

"I don't know."

"Tall? Cute? Blond?"

"Yeah."

"Drunk?"

"Bingo."

"That boy is always drunk," Stripe-Boy pipes in.

Natalie looks at Stripe-Boy, then at me. "I'll be back," she says, which translated means, I'll be gone for the rest of the night, so hopefully you two will have something to talk about. "Amber doesn't want us to lose the table," she adds just before leaving, "so don't go anywhere."

Go anywhere? Is she kidding? "Hi, I'm Jackie." Not a fine jumpstart, but a start nonetheless.

"Damon," he says, sticking out his hand. I shake it. Firm handshake. Strong personality. Dad would approve.

"Tell me about yourself, Damon." The liquid courage sets in.

He swirls his drink with his small hand. "I'm a writer."

Oh, my. This is obviously fate. "I'm an editor." Our eyes meet over the unspoken, unedited words between us. "What are you writing?"

"A novel."

"Your first?"

"Yeah."

"What about?"

"A boy's coming of age in Boston."

Omigod, I swear I'm not just saying this, but if I were ever going to write a novel, that's what I'd write about. Okay, not about a boy coming of age; my comprehension of the male mind doesn't go that deep. In fact, ever since Jer, I often find myself wondering if the male psyche has any depth at all. So I'd probably write about a girl becoming a woman, in a Judy Blume-style. And I'd probably set the book in Connecticut. The only place I'm familiar enough to write about in Boston is this sleazy bar, and the bathroom here is no place for a nice girl to get her period for the first time.

His lips curve into a Jack Nicholson devilish smile. "So how did you get to be an editor?"

"I majored in English lit. Then I did half of my M.A."

"What did you specialize in?"

"My undergrad was a general lit degree. For my M.A. I concentrated on both the romantic and realist periods in American literature." I was supposed to choose one area for my thesis, but I put the program on hold after my first year when I blindly followed Jer to Boston. At least the "on hold" part was what I told myself. "I'm assuming you majored in English lit, too?"

He smiles. "Is there anything else?"

I've never dated a lit guy. Nope, there were no stripe-boys in my Spenser's *Faerie Queen* class; for some reason my classes were unusually proportioned with cool women and nerd boys. I'm not talking about the *good* kind of nerd who is able to woo a girl over cups of espresso at two in the morning in a small café, using his profound understanding of the universe as bait. The good kind of nerd, when asked to name something that will impress you, might answer, "My idea of euphoria is reading Karl Marx, naked, on a beach in Mexico." The kind of nerd who sat in my lit classes made little holes in the dry skin on his hands with the tip of his pencil, and when asked to name something that would impress you, said, "I have a big pencil," and would really mean pencil. Not penis. Pencil.

"And you? What did you specialize in?" If he says poetry, the search is over. I'll give my high black boots to the charity shop and accept him as my destiny. Who can argue with destiny?

"I jumped around a lot. I tried to concentrate on lyric poetry."

Omigod, omigod. Fifty years from now we'll be sitting on a porch swing in the sunset. I'll be helping him with his latest manuscript. Maybe in a house hidden by a hill. Maybe in a little shack like in *Little House on the Prairie*, only with indoor plumbing and a computer and a ceramic-topped stove—and a piano. Definitely a piano (maybe I should start taking lessons now). I'll be there playing the piano; he'll be there paying the bills. And we'll collect things like ashtrays and art.

I have déjà vu. Oh, never mind. Those are lyrics from *Annie.*

"So what do you edit?" he asks.

"Ummm...manuscripts."

"What kind of manuscripts?"

"Women's fiction."

"Feminist fiction? Today's up-and-coming Woolf? Chopin?"

Not quite. "I work for Cupid."

"Romance novels?" He laughs. "Henry James would roll over in his grave. Say, would you like a drink?"

"A Manhattan, definitely."

"Manhattan? A sophisticated drink."

Love that Amber. "I'm a sophisticated girl."

"I'll have to hurry back then."

"Please do."

This is going perfectly according to my new life plan. I've already met my soul mate, and it's only taken forty-eight minutes.

He returns—of course he returns; he's unexplainably drawn to me—with two Manhattans. "Good. You're still here."

As if I'd go anywhere without him now that we've mated literally (which is not to be confused with literally mated—not yet anyway). "I want to hear more about your writing," I say between sips. I stare down at my drink, a sinking feeling settling in my stomach. What if my teeth turn red from this drink? I'll have to swallow the drink very carefully without swishing any of the liquid around in my mouth. I wish I could use a straw. "Where have you been published?"

"*Heat, Other People's Money, Playboy...* A few others. I've mostly published short stories, but I've done some interviews, too. I used to write..."

I drown out the rest of the conversation because I'm stuck on the *Playboy* portion. "*Playboy?* What did you write for *Playboy?*"

"A short story."

"Really? I'd love to read it."

"You read erotica?"

Read erotica? I'm the queen of erotica. Without me, erotica

would be full of superfluous commas and run-on sentences. "I work for Cupid, remember?"

"That's true. What are you doing tomorrow night?"

Now *that* was sudden. Or not that sudden considering I've been waiting twenty-four years for this soul-meeting moment. I pretend to think about it. "What exactly did you have in mind?"

"I'd like to take you out for a drink."

Finally, the kind of nerd who eventually woos you over cups of espresso/alcoholic beverages at two in the morning in a small café/sleazy bar! "That would be nice. Assuming of course, that your interest in seeing me doesn't stem from my declaration that I work in porn." I'm joking of course; surely he must feel the cosmic pull as well.

"Partly. But mostly because I can see my friend waving at me. I think he wants to leave. I want to make sure I see you again."

A very good reason. Not only is he sensitive (mandatory emotion for a writer), he's also smart.

He walks up to the bar to get a pen and a piece of paper, and I see the bartender smirk and mouth, "You scored digits?" How immature.

I write down my number in what I hope appears to be a sexy scrawl. And then I write Jackie in big letters underneath, just in case. Soul mate or no soul mate, my name was the first thing I said to him, and it's possible he wasn't overcome with destiny just at that moment.

And now, here I am sitting at a prime table, all by myself. Okay, I know I'll probably get attitude from Amber the Tooth Fairy, but I am not going to sit here alone for three hours. The bar is not quite as crowded at this hour, so I only have to elbow my way through, without the squeeze.

"Hey," I say to Natalie, who is standing by the bar with Ben.

"Hi," she says. "Did you have a nice chat with Damon? You guys do the same thing, sort of."

"Yeah. He seems nice. He asked me out."

"Really? I thought he was still with Suzanne."

"I guess not. Who's Suzanne?"

"He had this older girlfriend for a while."

"Guess that's over. Is he nice?"

"As a matter of fact, he's supernice."

Yay! Go me. My soul mate is supernice!

"Who's supernice? Me?" Ben asks, exhaling a puff of vinegary Scotch breath.

"Damon."

"Damon who?"

"Damon…" Damn. That's probably one of those things I'm supposed to remember. Did he even tell me his last name? I can't recall. I've never been very good at remembering details like that, or birthdays, or where I put plane tickets. But the plane ticket thing only happened once, I swear. And I'm still pretty sure the return portion fell down under my seat on the plane. Stuff does fall down. Just ask Janie. She's always complaining that her butt has fallen down. And her face. Last night she called me up, hysterical, complaining that her size three pants don't fit anymore—she had to buy a size five. Cry me a river, won't you. In any case, the very fact that I've only lost one plane ticket in my entire flying career is actually pretty impressive when you think about it. Twice, maybe, if you count the time Janie told me she had sent me a ticket for June 6, 7:00 p.m., but was actually for June 7, 6:00 p.m. If she hadn't sounded so sure of herself, I would have checked the date. Really.

"Damon Strenner." Natalie saves the day.

Jackie Strenner has a nice, smooth ring to it.

Ben snorts. "You're going out with Damon Strenner? That guy is such a loser."

Natalie rolls her eyes. "In the past twenty minutes you've called three guys losers. Tell me, is there any guy in this bar, besides you of course, who is not a loser?"

Ben tilts his head as if he's just been asked a trick question. "Yeah," he says, finally. "Andrew."

"You've got to name a guy you haven't been best friends with since you were two."

Since they were two? Tell me more! "How did you know Andrew when he was two?"

"Our parents are (hiccup) friends."

Uh-oh. He's starting to slur. Is that a hand on my back? Is that *his* hand on my back? Is that his hand reaching lower and lower down my back?

"Where *is* Andrew?" I ask, trying to squirm my way away from his hand.

"Don't know," Ben answers, swerving slightly. "I saw Jess. I guess they took off."

"Who's Jess?" Natalie says, her interest suddenly peaked.

"His lady-friend."

Jessica the Sweet Valley Twin. Does lady friend mean girl-friend? Almost-girlfriend? Sex buddy?

Ben's hand is now on my butt. I tell Natalie it's time to go.

Back at the apartment forty-five minutes later, I find Sam sitting on the couch, wrapped in her afghan. The TV is blaring an episode of *Beautiful Bride*, and Sam is in a trancelike state.

"Hello?" I call. "You alive?"

She mumbles some sort of response.

I peel off the pinching boots. "Do we have anything to eat?"

"Cereal."

That'll do. I pour a small amount into a bowl with milk. Cereal is seriously underrated. Why should it be only eaten in the morning? It's tasty, low fat, and with milk represents two major food groups. The trick is getting the ratio just right so that the cereal doesn't get soggy.

I crawl onto the couch beside her. "What happened?"

"I hate him."

What's this? Trouble in Sessie land? Uh-oh, here come the tears. "Talk to me," I say, reaching to the coffee table for a tissue. "This is what roommates are for. To listen to boyfriend complaints." Never mind that I am currently between boyfriends (not literally, unfortunately) and that I have no one to complain about. It does occur to me, however, that I've never heard Sam mention another girlfriend. "Who do you normally talk to when you're pissed at Marc?"

"What do you mean? I talk to Marc."

Wow. This girl needs some serious go-girl therapy. "No one else?"

"My mom."

Dear God. "You haven't had any girlfriends since you and Marc started dating, have you? When was that?"

"Five years ago." She is still staring at the television. A brunette is having her horrifically ugly dress shortened. "Natalie's my friend."

"And the last time you spoke to Natalie was…"

Sam suddenly looks at me in shock. "You're right. You're one hundred percent right. I have no friends, and I have a boyfriend who's never going to marry me."

Marry you? Who's talking about marriage?

"I'm already twenty-five and I'm going to be an old maid."

"I have news for you, unless they find a way to rebuild your hymen, you can never be on old maid. Besides, you're far closer to getting married than anyone else I know."

"My mother had me when she was twenty-four. That's a whole year younger than I am now! She got married when she was twenty-one."

"Yeah, so did mine, and look how well that turned out."

Sam rambles on as if she doesn't hear a word I say. "Don't you see? I'll date Marc until I'm twenty-nine and he still won't want to get married and my biological clock will be ticking and I'll have to break up with him and no one else will want me."

Biological clock? I don't even own a watch. This type of issue is way beyond the range of my radar system.

"Okay. First you've got to stop watching *Beautiful Bride*." I click off the remote. "Second, give me the CliffsNotes version of your relationship so that I can understand the problem. From the beginning. How you met."

"Okay." Sob. "I met Marc at the library. He always studied

across the table from me. One day he slipped a note in my child psychology textbook—''

''Why'd you take child psychology? To understand men?''

''No, to understand children.''

''Makes sense.''

''Anyway, the note said, 'Hi, do you want to take a dinner break?' Of course I said yes and—''

''You wrote back yes or you told him yes?''

''I told him yes.''

''How did you know who he was?''

''Because he sat across the table from me at the library.''

''But you knew *he* had written the letter?''

''Of course I knew.''

''What did you say?''

''I looked up and he was staring at me and I said, 'I'd love to have dinner with you,' and he said great.''

''Technically he might not have written the note.''

''Of course he wrote the note!''

''But how do you know?''

''I just do. You're being ridiculous. Do you want to hear or not?''

''Fine. Sorry. Continue.''

''We went out for dinner and then he asked me out again for that weekend, and we've dated ever since.''

''That's the story?''

''That's the story.''

''It would have been much more interesting if someone else had written the note.''

''Get over it. Now the problem is it's time to move things to the next level.''

Huh? Next level? ''Are you telling me you guys haven't slept together yet?'' Maybe her old maid theory isn't so far-fetched after all.

''Of course we've slept together. There are *other* next levels, you know.''

Other next levels? "Sorry, no guy has ever mentioned any other next levels to me."

"We've been together for five years now, and I think it's time to move in together."

Is she crazy? Has she completely lost her mind? "That's a terrible plan."

"Why?" she asks nervously. "You don't believe in living with a guy before marriage?"

"Of course I do. I just don't believe in leaving your roommate in the middle of the year with a two-bedroom apartment lease." I look down at my bowl and sigh.

"What?"

"I have too much milk left. I need more cereal."

She ignores me as I get up to reconfigure the bowl's ratio. "I wouldn't stick you with the rent. We'd look for someone else to room with you, or I'd wait until September first when our year lease is up."

Technically it was a thirteen month lease and not only a year since I had sublet her former roommate's final month, and then started my own at the beginning of September, but Sam was obviously trying to downplay our relationship to alleviate her guilty conscience.

What does she expect me to do? I don't know anyone else who I want to live with who is looking for a place to live. I barely know anyone I don't want to live with who isn't looking for a place to live.

"I haven't asked him yet," Sam continues after a noisy honk into the tissue. "But I drop about a million hints a day."

"What kind of hints?"

"Like last year when Angie was moving out, I asked Marc what I should do, and he said, 'Why don't you put an ad in the classifieds?' He was supposed to say, 'It's time for us to move in together.'"

"You're upset about something he said a year ago?"

"No, I'm upset about something he said tonight. I met him for Chinese food after work. He said, 'Why don't you sleep over?' and I said, 'Okay, I just need to get some stuff from my apartment,' and he said, 'You know, you should really keep a toothbrush and some extra stuff...in your car.' In my car!''

''In your car!''

''In my car! Not in his apartment, but in my car. I ask you, is this normal? As if I'm some kind of nomad. I wasn't about to stay over at his place after that kind of comment.''

''But why is *Beautiful Bride* on at two in the morning?''

''It's a tape.''

''Maybe he's a commitment-phobe.''

''Just my luck. How do I know?''

Luckily I have the answer to that question at my fingertips. Diagnosing commitment-phobia is one of my specialties. ''What does he put in his mouth?''

''Why?''

''This month's *City Girls* says you can tell if a guy's a commitment-phobe by what he puts in his mouth. Hold on, I'll get it.'' I run into my room and grab the magazine. ''So what type of breath freshener does he use?''

''Breath freshener?''

''Yeah—gum, mints or those dissolving squares?''

''He loves those dissolving things. What does that say about him?''

Uh-oh. ''It says he's bound to pull a disappearing act.''

''Oh, come on!''

''What is your man more likely to order as an entrée? Lemon chicken, ravioli, or rib eye.''

''Um...ravioli.''

I shake my head. ''No good. That means that, 'One is never enough.'''

''Meaning?''

Isn't it obvious? ''Meaning he can't commit to one girl.''

Desperation is clouding over Sam's normally cheerful brown eyes. ''What should he eat then?''

''Rib eye.''

I continue reading. '''A man who orders rib eye is willing to invest in your relationship. And when the going gets tough, he sticks around.'''

"Who eats rib eye?"

"Obviously not Marc."

"What is rib eye?"

"It's the prime cut of the rib steak. You should buy him some."

"I don't want to feed him, I just want him to want to move in with me."

"Good luck. But wait 'til September, okay?"

When I finally crawl into bed, it's 3:30. Good Lord, I have to wake up at 9:30 to go to Tae Kwon Do! I am *determined* to go to Tae Kwon Do. Okay, maybe I'll skip breakfast and get up at ten. No, I've got to eat something. Maybe I can pick up something on the way there. Something fast.

Rib eye, anyone?

Chapter Eight

Ball of Crap

I try not to inhale the stale stench of feet emanating from the blue floor mats. Glancing over at the cluster of shoes near the door, I begin to make my way toward a group of people stretching in white uniforms and colored belts. "Don't move!" a deep male voice resonates, freezing me to my spot.

"Why not?" I look up at a very built, very sexy, very Italian-looking stud whose deep tan/naturally golden skin contrasts brilliantly with his white Tae Kwon Do uniform and black belt. My knees feel kind of on the weak side. I might need him to carry me to the dressing room.

"You can't come into the *dojo* with your shoes on," this perfect specimen says.

Now look what I've gone and done. I've only been here two and a half minutes and already I've insulted the sex-god. "Sorry."

He smiles. Uh-oh. Is that a crooked tooth? Does a crooked tooth give a man character and increase his sex appeal?

No, it does not. He's definitely sexier with his mouth closed.

"No problem. I just thought I'd show you the ropes. I'm Lorenzo."

Shh...don't talk, sweet pea. "I'm Jackie. I really appreciate your help." I'm feeling a strange sense of déjà vu. He looks familiar. Maybe he's from Connecticut? No, he's got way too much sex appeal for Connecticut. Maybe he's an actor? I know that face...those pectorals...

"Jackie?"

"Yes?"

"Your shoes are still on."

"Right." Penn? No, he looks at least thirty. Orgasm? No, I repeat, he looks at least thirty...

"When you're ready, go to the Master's office. He's expecting you."

Master NanChu is a six-foot, sixty-something Korean man. He bows a bald head to me as I enter. I bow back.

"Sit, sit," he says. Is that a photograph of Master NanChu and Sylvester Stallone framed on the wall? Is that Chris O'Donnell? Master NanChu watches me ogle. "You like Chris? He's a good boy. I train stars for movies in Hollywood."

Is that Tom Cruise? That's Tom Cruise! He knows Tom Cruise? Can he introduce me to Tom Cruise? Maybe he trained him for *Mission: Impossible.* Maybe if I'm really good, I mean really, *really* good, Master NanChu will recommend me for a stunt woman's role. I can learn the short girl's killer karate chop in no time. Look how fast I learned to punctuate, and Helen always says my commas have a lot of punch.

"So, why are you interested in Tae Kwon Do?"

Back to business. "I'd like to learn a martial art so I can protect myself."

"Good. Very good."

"And get into shape, of course."

"Good. Very good."

And meet hot men.

We talk for a few minutes about Boston, and he sends me back to the *dojo.* "We will talk again after class. If you enjoy class, you will sign up, right?"

A little pushy, aren't we? But am I really going to argue with someone who knows Tom Cruise? I don't think so.

"Just leave your socks in the changing room."

Here I go. Off to a whole new me. I thank him and head to the changing room, closing his door behind me. Off to take off my socks. Take off my socks? He never said anything on the phone about taking off my socks. I can't take off my socks—I haven't had a pedicure since June. This is catastrophic. I knock on Master NanChu's office door.

"Sir?"

"Yes?"

"Can I leave my socks on?"

"Too dangerous. You'll slip."

"Oh. Okay. Thanks." Damn.

I spend the next sixty minutes trying to figure out what the hell is going on. Korean numbers and punches are being thrown all over the place. But even though I'm pretty sure my stomach is going to explode from running (the Starbucks mochaccino before class was not one of my better ideas) and I'm completely incapable of using the proper arm ("Your left arm, ma'am, left! Not *that* left arm, your *other* left arm!"), I am too busy loving the gender ratio here to care. Twenty hot, muscled men versus two three-hundred-pound women. And me. Yay! I'm not sure why other single, attractive girls haven't come up with this plan, but...who cares? More men for me. This place just drips with testosterone. I tried to convince Nat to join me, since it was kind of her idea to begin with, but she said her personal trainer didn't allow her to work out anywhere else.

Lorenzo leads the workout. "Hanna, twul, zed, ned, dasso...horse stance *jekiah!*" I'm not sure what he's saying, but it sure sounds sexy.

I must be doing something ridiculous-looking, because Lorenzo keeps coming over to fix my positioning. Or maybe he just wants to come over and *fix my positioning*, if you get my drift. Such dark, thick hair. Such tanned, soft skin. Such...what is that? It's...it's...B.O.! Ew.

I'm being unfair. I can't want a guy who's going to sweat, and expect him to smell like aftershave. He's still a hottie. Or he will be, post shower. But now I'd much prefer if he moved a little over...just a little more...to the other side of the room. There we go. Okay, now he's hot again.

Hmm. I can see the navy underwear through the white uniform of the man in front. Note to self: must buy more white underwear.

Punch. Snap-kick. Twist. Oddly, all the grown men can bend lower than I can.

"Okay, watch Lorenzo do proper push-ups," Master NanChu says. Lorenzo drops to the floor. Up. Down. Up. Down. Up. Down. "Watch how his pelvis tilts toward the floor."

Up shoulders. Up big, manly, shapely shoulders. Up pelvis. Up big, manly shapely pelvis.

Oh, to be the floor.

Post shower.

When I get home at 12:30, I have very smelly feet, and five hundred and sixty dollars less in my bank account. Five hundred for a year's worth of classes, and sixty for that adorable white costume that I've still got on because it's so darn cute.

Sam is wrapped in her afghan, watching *Beautiful Bride* again. Photo albums have been strewn all over the couch. "You smell," she says.

"Thanks, so do you. Did you sleep on the couch? Did anyone call for me?"

"No and no. Why? Who should call?" her voice sounds like a flat bottle of diet Coke I might have accidentally left on the counter.

"I met a boy at the bar. He said he'd call."

"Just because a guy says he's going to call doesn't mean he's going to call. *City Girls* says that a guy says he's going to call only because it's an easy way to end a conversation. Who is he?"

"Damon Strenner." Since when does Sam read *City Girls?*

"I know him. He's cute. I thought he had a girlfriend."

"Guess not." Enough with the girlfriend thing already. He's obviously gotten over it; can't everyone else? My *Cosmopolitan, Mademoiselle, Glamour* and *City Girls* magazines are spread out all over the floor, looking far too well-worn. "You're memorizing this stuff?" I plop down on the floor beside, and begin leafing through pages.

"They're full of useful information. I've learned all about tantric sex. If I ever have sex again, I'm going to try The Pretzel."

"And The Pretzel is what exactly?" I ask.

"The woman's on top with her legs wrapped around and under the guy's knees, and his arms are loosely looped around her back."

"Sounds like work."

"It has four barbells out of five. That means it's pretty difficult. I want to try The Diving Board, too."

I don't even want to know how that works. A thought occurs to me. "Do you know your and Marc's combined first initials are S and M?"

"So?"

What a great Halloween costume for them—they can throw on some leather clothing, sew red letters S and M onto their chests, and handcuff themselves together. However, I'm not clear whether "so" means she's unaware of what S & M is or if she knows but doesn't care. I drop the subject.

"Look how happy we were," she whines, tossing the flowered photo album onto my lap. On the right side of the page are three pictures of the then-happy couple on a Florida beach, and one of her sitting on a hotel bed. Each picture boasts a typed label: *Sam at the Hyatt, Marc and Sam on the Sand, Marc and Sam in the Water,* et cetera. The left side of the page is a collage of airline tickets, museum ticket stubs, menus, and bus tickets. She's the type of person who probably kept the wrapper from their first-time condom.

Marc and Sam certainly look happy in the photos. In one picture Sam is lying on a hotel bed, wrapped in a white afghan, smiling and holding a glass of wine. In fact, in all the pictures, even the ones of her in the water, Sam is smiling and holding a glass of wine. Wait a second… "Sam, is that *your* afghan in the picture?"

"Um…yes." She runs her hand along the white afghan draped over her legs.

"You bring your own linen to hotels?" Is it possible? Can anyone be this nuts?

She refuses to make eye contact. "Do you know what kind of disease lives on hotel comforters? There's cum stains, there's dried blood, there's—"

"Do you bring your own pillows, too?"

"Pillowcases. Don't you watch *20/20*?"

"You have to lighten up. No one will want to marry anyone who's this crazy."

And then she goes ahead and starts crying.

I was *so* kidding. Some people have no sense of humor.

Damon calls at three o'clock. I can hear the phone ringing, but I can't see it anywhere. It's got to be somewhere on the floor of my room...I see sweaters, a crumpled sheet, yesterday's thong...

"Hi, there," he says after I finally find the phone cradled between two cups of my strapless bra.

"Hi." He called! He called! He said he was going to call and he called he called he called!

"Are we still on for tonight?"

He feels the cosmic pull. The current runs straight from his stripe to my soul. "Certainly."

"Great. Where should I meet you?"

Meet me? Where should I pick you up? is what he's supposed to say. What kind of soul mate wants to meet me somewhere? "I don't know. Where do you want to go?"

"Where do you live?"

"Back Bay."

"Me, too. Why don't we meet at Marlborough and Dartmouth?"

"Marlborough and Dartmouth?" On the corner? He wants to meet me on the corner? Am I a prostitute? What if some pervert pulls me into his moving car? What if the getting-his-jollies-supercreep from last week is waiting there for me?

"Is that okay?"

No. It is *not*. Who meets his soul mate on the corner? What if he doesn't show? What if I'm stuck there for hours waiting, checking my watch every two minutes? To make the time pass I'll have to play little games with myself like trying to remember the names of all the guys I've ever wanted to sleep with.

"I guess." I guess you're not my soul mate, you inconsiderate jackass. "What time should I meet you?"

"How's 9:30?"

"Fine." If he's not at the corner by 9:33, I'm out of there.

"See you there."

Unless I decide not to show up because of these completely despicable dating conditions. "Damon?"

"Yeah?"

"What number can I reach you at? In case something comes up?" In case I find some self-respect and tell you to go to straight to hell instead of to a street corner.

He pauses. Hello? What's the problem? I'm being nice here, trying to get your number in case I decide to ditch you so that I won't leave you standing on the corner and counting cars all night.

After a long pause, he rattles off his number.

"I'll see you later then." I slam down the phone. A two-minute conversation and we're already in a fight.

"Was that Damon?" Sam hollers from the living room.

"Yes. See, he called! We're going out tonight!" I scream back through my bedroom wall.

"What time?"

"At 9:30! Why? Do you want to have dinner together?"

"No! I'm going out with Marc! But *City Girls* says you can tell how serious a guy is about you by what time he calls the date for! If he calls the date for after nine, he just wants to get into your pants!"

That's not good. However, I refuse to give in to Sam's pessimism. "Unlike some people, I'm not looking to get married! And I like guys going into my pants!"

"I don't need to get married, just engaged! He's picking you up here at 9:30?"

"Yeah!" No need to fill her in on the *exact* details.

Suddenly I am stricken with panic. What does one wear on an arty date? "What does one wear on an arty date?" I shout through the walls. "Sam? Samantha!"

"There's no need to yell," she says, appearing in my doorway. "I'm not deaf, you know."

"Do you have any striped shirts?" I ask.

"Stripes?" Sam answers. "Why stripes?"

"He likes stripes. I've seen him twice and both times he was wearing stripes."

"But what if he's wearing stripes again? You'll look like Bert and Ernie."

"I'll wear a vertical stripe."

"You'll look like a tic-tac-toe board."

"Straight or curly?"

"Your stripe?"

"No, my hair! Funky or demure?"

Demure wins. After my shower, the ritual begins. First the towel-dry. Then the comb-through. Next the frizz-control. And finally, one inch of hair at a time, I slowly make my way around my head with the blow dryer and the family-size round brush. I hear Sam's voice over the hum. "What?" I holler. *"What?"*

No answer. I hate that. It's like when someone calls and you're about to pee and you have to pull up your pants all over again and make a dash for the phone and then the person just hangs up.

Thirty minutes later, my hair is beautifully, unnaturally straight.

I stroll into the living room like a runway model. Sam is spreading peanut butter on a celery stick.

"I tried to tell you not to bother with your hair. It's raining."

Damn.

"Tonight's the night," she says, handing me a well-coated stick.

"What night?" I think I left my umbrella in the office. I hate it when I do that. Why do I always do that? What's wrong with me? Why is my umbrella never where it's supposed to be?

"Ultimatum night."

Uh-oh. At this particular moment, Sam's potential troubles obviously run far deeper than umbrellas. "That's a very bad plan."

"No, it's *not*. Candice says you have to say it like it is. And here's how it is—I want to be with someone I can plan the future with. If he can't be that guy, then I have to find someone else who is."

"Are you ready to accept his response if he doesn't say what you want to hear? Who's Candice?"

"The *City Girls* writer."

"I think you're making a mistake."

"I'm doing it." She spreads more peanut butter on another stick.

I've created a monster.

At 9:30 Damon is sitting on a bench at the corner. He's wearing a gray shirt with a green horizontal stripe. His closet must look like some sort of geometric line graph.

"Hey," he says and kisses me on the cheek, which would have been really nice if I didn't at that second notice he's wearing jeans. Jeans! Who wears jeans on a first date? He may as well have shown up with his hands down his pants, scratching himself. Was he wearing jeans at Orgasm? I was too distracted by his stripe to notice.

At least it's stopped raining.

"Hi," I say. "So where are we going?"

"I don't know. Where do you want to go?" Am I going to have to play the eighth-grade what-do-you-want-to-do-no-what-do-you-want-to-do game? This is a date. *He* asked *me* on this date. *He* is supposed to have some sort of plan beyond a street corner encounter. Besides, whatever happened to the sexy French café where he's supposed to reveal the secrets of the universe? Of course! That's why he's wearing jeans! Oh, God, does this mean I was supposed to wear jeans, too, but because I'm not, he figured I wouldn't want to go and that's why he's playing this stupid eighth-grade-what-do-you-want-to-do game?

"How about the Rose? It's just down the street," he says. Unknowingly, he just saved himself as forever being referred to in all my dating-war-stories, past and future, as the insisted-on-meeting-me-on-a-street-corner-and-wore-jeans-and-to-top-it-all-off-couldn't-come-up-with-a-place-to-go boy.

It's a cute bar, the Rose. The ceilings are so low, a taller date would have to bend his head. It's empty except for us and one other couple at the back, and we can hear the conversations of the bartender and the waitress. The wooden tables are high and round, and look kind of like the waxed end tables in my apartment. Except on Sam's tables I can see my face; on these I see fingerprints. We slide into two metal chairs at the front of the bar.

We talk about what a cute bar it is.

I start fidgeting. Why doesn't the waitress come to our table? It's not like she's doing anything else.

"What's wrong?" he asks.

I feel like I'm sitting on a foldout chair in the school gym, writing a final exam. "These seats aren't very comfortable," I say. Translation: you better find us a new table.

"I guess the waitress isn't coming. Let me go get some drinks. What do you want?"

Nothing you've got to offer, baby. So far, I am not very impressed with Stripe-Boy. "White wine, please," I say, and he scurries away. I watch as he talks to the bartender, waving his arms in the air. He looks like a stick-drawing in a flip cartoon book. I am so not going to offer to pay for this drink; I know he'd let me for sure.

"Let's go outside," he says. He's holding a carafe of house wine. "Supposedly the chairs are more comfortable out there."

That's so sweet. Maybe I'm being a little harsh on the guy.

The patio has about ten small metal tables lit with candles. We're the only ones here. We take the table in the back, under a small tin roof. I'm about to sit down when he says, "Wait—make sure your chair's not wet."

That's also sweet. I'm definitely being too harsh on the guy. Maybe he just hasn't dated that much. Maybe he doesn't realize he's not supposed to wear jeans on a first date, French café or not, and especially not to a place like the Rose. Maybe he doesn't realize that he was supposed to pick me up at my house. Are my standards too high, even for today's enlightened male? Is there such a thing as an enlightened male?

My chair is wet. He wipes it with a napkin.

"Do you mind if I smoke?" he asks, pulling out a pack of Marlboros.

"No," I say. I never quite got the hang of smoking. I tried a few times as a teenager, but it always made me cough. Too bad, really. Smokers always seem to have something to do with their hands.

He pulls out a cigarette and lights it in the candle in front of him. He pours us each a glass of wine. I tell him I love Boston's ice cream, and he tells me he's lactose intolerant. I tell him my mother is lactose intolerant and she can never have any milk or cheese. I used to use her soy milk in my cereal; it tasted as if I'd dumped a spoon of sugar into regular milk. He tells me he drinks regular milk and just takes lots of pills. The pills cost fifteen dollars a bottle; almost all he earns gets spent on those damn little milk-busters. Then we talk about cheese—we both agree it's not cheddar unless it's old. Then he says that after-dinner coffee should only be drunk with Baileys and I tell him that photographs are better in black and white.

The patio is crowded now, well, not exactly crowded, but at least three other tables are occupied. See, Sam? Lots of couples go out at 9:30. Our voices are getting louder, not only because we're straining to be heard over the new voices on the patio, but because we're three-quarters of the way through the bottle of wine. We talk about relationships and ex's. I ask him about his, he tells me how he just recently got out of a relationship, I tell him the same, and we talk about transition. Suddenly rain is pitter-pattering on the tin roof, and the couples at the other tables pick up their glasses and disappear inside.

"Where do you live?" I ask him.

"Around the corner." Is that a statement or an invitation? "In the Platinum Towers."

"Wow."

"We have rent control."

"We? You have a roommate?"

"Oh. Yeah."

Our heads are tilted toward each other and our eyes keep locking. There's a magnetic pull around our hands. I tell him that I like his glasses, that I can never find a pair that fits my face, and that I wear contacts. I try his on to see how they fit. They smell like aftershave and wet smoke.

"How do I look?" I ask, and he says gorgeous.

And I say, "Men don't make passes at girls who wear glasses."

And he says, "Says who?"

I pass him back his glasses and our hands touch and omigod he's not letting go. If I were a Cupid heroine I'd say I have shivers going up my spine, but they're really going down, and my head feels dizzy. Is this the chemistry that Julie is always moaning about? Julie the character, that is, not Julie the editor. How can I tell the difference between chemistry and wine? Is there a difference? Should I just stay drunk my whole life?

"Dorothy Parker says," I tell him.

"Ah, good old Dorothy? Wasn't she a drunk?" He's still holding my hand.

I start to giggle. "And what's wrong with that?" His fingers gently caress the inside of my palm the way Matt Roland did in the sixth grade. He told me that the palm caress means a guy wants sex, and I punched him in the arm.

"Let's play *Author,*" Damon says.

"Author?"

"Yeah. I jumble the name of a book, and you get to guess the author."

"Okay, shoot."

"David Copped a Feel."

"Too easy."

"Okay, here's another. *The Old Man Has*

I start to giggle. "Stupid game. Who's you

"I can't pick just one. Who said this?" he

eyes and recites, "'Let us roll all our strength,

ness, up into one ball; And tear our pleasures with rough strife

through the iron gates of life.'"

I've never been good at "Name That Tune" or "Name This Poem," or naming anything at all. Hmm. There was a reason I chose to specialize in the nineteenth century. The sixteenth? seventeenth? eighteenth? centuries all sound the same to me. "John Donne?"

"No, but close. Andrew Marvell. 'To His Coy Mistress.'"

I kind of remember the poem from one of my survey classes. A guy tries to convince his lady friend to sleep with him by telling her that she should enjoy her life while she's still young and beautiful, because eventually she'll be dead and then it will be too late.

I know I shouldn't do this. Every rule my mother has ever taught me, every one of my Fashion Magazine Fun Facts are shrieking *No! No! No!* in a teenage-horror movie-type scream. But it's been four months since… That's more than one hundred and twenty days. But how can this develop into the soul-mate relationship it's supposed to if I sleep with him right away? A real heroine would never sleep with a guy on the first date. The sexual tension would have to build to at least the ninth chapter, where it would cumulate into a "ball of sweetness." If in a moment of passion she does cave in and sleeps with him right off, she usually gets pregnant, and refuses to see him. The next time she sees him is two years later when she accidentally runs into him at the video store. And of course, she's with her little darling boy, Adam, who has the same mysterious smile as his father. And of course, she's never forgotten Adam's father.

No! No! No!

Screw coy; tonight I'm feeling brave.

I lean across the table and kiss him. And not just one of those wimpy, feel-my-lips-against-yours kiss. I'm talking about the kind of kiss that would wake Sleeping Beauty from her coma.

...dred years later he says, "Let's get out of here."

...we run through the rain, he doesn't let go of my hand. We're ...dels in a Maybelline ad, dancing through the drops. I bet his ...partment is a real art-boy apartment, decorated with long black bookshelves, a *Reservoir Dogs* poster and ashtrays shaped like naked women.

"Where do you live?" he asks.

Where do *I* live? We can't go to my house! My bed is unmade, and hanging over the edge of my laundry basket is something unidentifiable. So I kiss him, a wet kiss mixed with rain. "Let's go to your place. Don't you live right around here?"

He kisses me back. "Yes, but I want to see your place."

I think of Sam and her ultimatum. My place might be a very bad scene. I kiss him again. "And I want to see your place."

Putting his arm around me, he directs me right past the Platinum Towers. Maybe his apartment is messy, too. Maybe he's doesn't want me to think he's a pig. How cute that he doesn't realize that I won't care. "We can't go to my place," he says.

"Why not?" What guy would choose not having sex instead of letting a girl see his messy apartment?

"Because."

And suddenly, I have an epiphany. I may have allowed my women's intuition to fall into cruise control, but now it's back in standard transmission.

I push his arm off my shoulder. "You live with your girl-friend." Now I know how he can afford to live in such a place. She probably supports him while he "freelances."

"I already told you, I'm looking for my own place. But a free-lance salary isn't that great—"

"Go to hell."

"Can't we go to your place?"

"No. I won't sleep with someone else's boyfriend."

"I wasn't going to sleep with you." He tries to replace his arm around my shoulder.

Excuse me? What does he mean, he wasn't going to sleep with me? "What were you going to do? Recite poetry all night?"

He looks into my eyes. "There's other stuff we can do that isn't considered cheating."

Excuse me? "Are you...are you referring to oral sex?"

"Well...kind of."

Who does this guy think he is? Somehow I don't think Andrew Marvell was attempting to convince his coy mistress that she should take her ball of sweetness and give him a blow job.

If I knew more Tae Kwon Do I would snap-kick him in the groin and damage him permanently.

"Fuck off," I say and walk away. Not an original exit line, but effective nonetheless.

I call Wendy. "You're not going to believe this." I tell her the evening's events.

"What number did he give you?" I recite the number. "That sounds like a cell number. You should have known that a guy who gives you his cell doesn't want you calling at home." I don't know how a Connecticut girl who went to school in Philadelphia and lives in New York knows anything about Boston cell phone numbers, but in Wendy I trust.

"I feel cheap."

"Yeah well, think how much worse you'd feel if he'd given you his pager."

At three in the morning I think I hear muffled groaning through the walls. I imagine Sam and Marc having wild make-up sex. At 3:30 I hear groaning in the living room. Gross. Why are they having sex on the couch? What if I'm hungry? Steps echo back and forth through the apartment. I fall back asleep.

At five the phone rings. Sobs echo through the receiver. Who is it? I don't think I said that out loud. "Hello?"

Sob.

Where's my call display?

"It's me," a voice says. "Are you awake?"

"Yes." Why do I always say that? I am *not* awake; I am very much asleep. "What's wrong?"

"I've already eaten all the chocolate chip ice cream and now I'm working on the cookie dough." Sob.

"What happened?"

"He said he needs space. He doesn't want to live with me. He doesn't love me."

"Who *is* this?"

"What?"

Oh—Sam. I've never spoken to her on the phone before. Her voice sounds much younger than she does in person.

"*City Girls* says that when a guy says he wants space it means he can't decide if he wants to take off or get off the runway—"

"Where are you?"

"In the living room. I'm on my cell."

"I'll be right there."

But first, a pit stop in the kitchen. Did Sam say something about chocolate chip ice cream? Right. All gone. Maybe I'll grab some cheesies. To even out the sweet/salt ratio. Better make that the whole bag. It could be a long night.

Chapter Nine

But I Want to Be a Princess!

Sunlight gushes through the cracks in the living room blinds, illuminating the dust particles floating in the air. I'm lying on the couch in the pretzel position. Not the Fashion Magazine Fun Fact pretzel position, but the I-stayed-all-night-on-the-couch-because-I'm-a-really-nice-roommate position. Over myriad magazines and photos neatly piled on the counter that divides the living room from the kitchen, I can see Sam sitting at the table, staring up at the ceiling.

"Good morning," I say hoarsely.

"Shitty morning," she says, not blinking.

Oh, yeah. Space. Sam gave Marc the ultimatum, and she was not pleased with his response.

When I dragged myself into the living room last night, she was completely hysterical. Sobbing, she couldn't command her lips with enough control to form words. "He…sai-ai-aid…he-he-he…doesn't…kno-ow-ow…if…I'm the wo-wo—one."

She continued sobbing until I was about halfway through the cheesies. Then she started screaming. "That stupid bastard says I'm not the one! He thinks he's going to find someone better than me! Better than me? Let him try to find someone who gives more of a shit than I do! Let him find someone else who's willing to put up with his shit! Shit! Shit! Shit! Is it normal that he's so immature? Is it normal?"

After the cheesies, I finished the cereal, and then we just sat there at the kitchen table. We watched the sun eat the edge of the sky and turn it blue. I felt like a piece of gum chewed too long. Then I must have crawled back to the couch and fallen asleep.

"Have you been up long?" I ask.

"Since yesterday morning."

I try to sit up. Omigod, I can't move. Parts of my body I don't even know I have hurt. Is it from falling asleep on the couch? From staying up too late? "Owwwww," I whine. What's wrong with me? What if I have some kind of muscle disorder? Omigod, I heard about this: one minute you're fine and the next your muscles tense up and you have meningitis. I only have a few minutes left. My last breaths are being wasted in my living room instead of at a café in Paris or in bed with Jeremy. "I think I have meningitis."

"You don't have meningitis," she says flatly. "It's the karate."

Oh, yeah. "Not karate. Tae Kwon Do."

She doesn't answer. She's too busy looking at the kitchen table.

Something looks different. "Did you do something to the table?" I ask her.

"I Pledged it." Pause. "I Pledged it? Why on earth would I Pledge a glass table? No wonder Marc doesn't want to live with me."

I don't really know what she's talking about, but I do know that I should take a shower. My foot slides across the floor when I slide off the couch. Ow…hurts to stand… What's wrong with the floor? "Did you do something to the floor?"

"I polished it. It looked scruffy."

I look around the living room and kitchen in awe. The counters are sparkling. I peek down the hall. My bathroom smells like bleach. "You cleaned my bathroom?"

"Don't worry, I wore gloves."

"But didn't I just do it last week?"

"I know, but now it's clean."

This calls for further investigation. I slide to my room and find that my bed is made, my floor swept. I open my closet door and discover that my sweaters are now organized by color. The identifiable object that was hanging over the edge of my hamper has been identified and laid to rest.

This is not normal.

I take Sam shopping to the mall. I'm not sure what else to do with her. She has five hundred dollars put away for a rainy day. I tell her this is a rainy day. Thank God it's not really raining; the only parking spot left in the whole lot is so far from Macy's that we'd have to take a cab to the entrance. A couple holding hands push through the revolving door.

"I want to go home," Sam says.

"No, you don't. We're going shopping. Don't you remember the breakup rules?"

"I'm just not a high-black-boot type of girl."

"Shame on you! Search your soul. The black-boot girl buried inside will shine through."

She sighs. "Okay. Whatever. I just don't want to think anymore. My head hurts."

I steer us toward Macy's. Makeup and perfume counters make everyone feel better, don't they?

I paint silver nail polish on my left thumb. Pretty. Oooh. What's that? It smells nice. I spray a bit on the inside of my wrist. Janie once told me that women put perfume on the inside of their wrists because men used to kiss their hands. I actually believed it, too, until I read it was because of pulse points or something like that. This is a terrific red polish. Looks like blood. Pretty. I'll try it on my right hand. What's that perfume? Very nice.

Oooh. Brand-new winter colors! Funny, they look just like last year's winter colors. Three women in this year's brand-new winter colors smile at me from behind the *Jolie* counter. Suddenly I am struck with a brilliant idea: Sam will get a makeover, and it won't cost a thing. Everyone knows that makeovers are free—

foundation, blush, eyes, everything but cellulite and hair. The implicit understanding is that you're going to buy the makeup afterward, but you don't have to buy a lot. (It's a good thing, too, because the price of all the products they use totals close to one month's rent).

However, you should probably buy *something,* just to be polite; think of it as a tip. But don't buy lipstick; this would be a waste since you'll probably get a gift package with whatever else you buy, kind of like the loot bag you used to get after a birthday party when you were a kid. Except that this loot bag will contain lipstick, though never in the color of your choice, and certainly never in a brand-new color for winter.

The only problem with makeovers are the technicians who perform them. They're scary. They're either chic women who have Nighttime Barbie perfectly painted faces and bookend pearl earrings, flamboyant drag queens whose faces also look like Nighttime Barbie, or middle-aged women with pencil-drawn eyebrows and lip-extended smiles.

For Sam, I choose Nighttime Barbie number one.

"Hi," I say and smile. "My friend is looking to buy some makeup. Do you think you have time for a consultation?" Consultation is the euphemism for free makeover.

I push my lethargic roommate onto the stool. The crispy cosmetician tells her she has beautiful skin, although some coverage would definitely help.

"Okay," Sam says, a twinge of hope creeping into her voice. I can picture her mind processing the quasi compliment: if I have perfect skin, then surely Marc will want to spend the rest of his life running his fingers over it! But if I don't buy this coverage, then some other woman will, and he'll fall in love with her and I'll be all alone with my beautiful skin that's really not so beautiful because Nighttime Barbie says it needs some help.

Oooh. Pretty gold eye shadow. I dip some on to my finger and dab it on my eyelids.

"Would you prefer foundation or powder?" Nighttime Barbie asks.

Sam stares at her as if she has just spoken in Korean. Hanna twul zed ned?

Pretty blush. I put a bit on the apple of my cheeks. I love that phrase, *the apple*. Who thinks of this stuff? Why not *the orange?*

The woman seems oblivious to Sam's vacant stare and continues her onslaught. "A stick? A compact? A liquid?"

My reflection in the mirror looks like a four-year-old who's rubbed her mother's lipstick all over her face. Where's the makeup remover? Don't they usually keep it right near the mirror? Oooh. What a gorgeous bronze nail polish. I paint my left pinkie. Now I look as though I dipped my hand in caramel.

"Hydrating lotion? Would you prefer an oil-free formula? What about a time-release system?"

Sam bursts into tears.

Uh-oh. I've let N.T.B. number one scare my roommate. Time for a quick getaway. "I'm sorry," I say. "I don't think today's a good day for a consultation." I grab Sam's arm and pull her off the chair. She's in full-sob mode. "Let's go."

We walk slowly through the mall in silence. "What do you want to do?" I ask.

"Eat."

"Okay, let's eat."

Food: the dumpee's opiate.

Sam doesn't eat at food courts (germs, germs and more germs), so we find one of those fancy sandwich places in the corner of the mall. "I'm ordering a salad," she says, pulling a plastic knife and fork set out of her purse.

"Salad? As a meal? You mean with chicken?"

"Just salad. Not only do I have awful skin, I'm obviously fat, and that's why he doesn't want me."

"Obviously," I say, rolling my eyes. "It's not because you have an obsessive-compulsive disorder or anything."

"I worked in a restaurant one summer. Cutlery doesn't get cleaned."

"You were a waitress?" Somehow I can't imagine Sam handling food all day.

"A hostess."

That I can see.

I order a cheeseburger and she orders a green salad. "Can I get the dressing on the side, please?"

When the food comes, Sam takes one look at her plate and explodes. "What kind of lettuce is this? This isn't lettuce, these are frog flakes! This is sour. It doesn't taste good. Why do I want to eat something that doesn't taste good? Is it normal to charge a gazillion dollars for something inedible?" She calls over the waiter. "This is horrible. I want to exchange it." I'm not sure what she was expecting when she ordered the salad, exactly.

Obviously intimidated, the waiter nods vehemently. "Okay, miss, what would you like?"

"Unfortunately, this poor excuse for a meal has made me lose my appetite for something substantial. I would like a piece of strawberry cheesecake, please. Want a piece?" she asks me.

"No thanks."

"For me. Please. Have a piece. My treat. We'll be like *The Golden Girls*."

I sigh. The cheesecake lover in me is not buried that deep.

"Jack?"

"Yes?"

"Why do you look as if a child drew all over your face?"

Right.

After lunch, Sam insists on going straight home, which should be quite easy, a no-brainer actually, if we can only find my car.

"I know I parked in the D section," I insist. Unfortunately, we are standing in the D section and my car is not here. "Why don't we take one of these?" There is one BMW and two Mercedes, any of which I would like to be my car. My attempt at humor bombs; Sam doesn't laugh. A half hour later we find my car in the G section. "G rhymes with D," I say.

Sam's too depressed to even bother rolling her eyes.

Later that afternoon, Andrew comes over with two screwdrivers. Unfortunately, they're tools, not vodka and orange juice. After I order a large pepperoni pizza, we spread the instructions to my soon-to-be-bookshelf over my bedroom floor.

"Where's Sam?" he asks, while rolling back the sleeves of his J-Crewish black sweater. He doesn't smell like Jer today, thank God. He smells like Irish Spring.

"Sleeping." I say. Finally. She was tiring me out.

"I can't believe you've had this for four months and haven't put it together," he says, shaking his head.

True. It's been lying in pieces in a box under my bed. Maybe my procrastination has something to do with me knowing that as soon as I build the bookshelf, I'll have to unpack my books, and the last time I saw my books was when I packed them, and the day I packed them was the day the whole Jeremy fiasco began. Or maybe I'm just lazy. Whatever.

We start building the shelf, or more accurately, Andrew starts building the shelf while I sit on the bed and watch. It's really nice of him to come over and help ("help" being a euphemism for "doing the whole job"). "Who put up your pictures?" he asks, staring at the two prints on my wall. *The Kiss* is hanging over my bed, and the print Janie bought me about a year after she and my dad split up—the "I know you're an obsessive reader and I think maybe it's because the divorce has screwed you up and you're trying to escape reality but that's okay" present—is hanging above where my not-yet-built bookshelf will go. Janie's painting, *Woman Reading in a Landscape,* is by Jean-Baptiste Camille Corot. When I first hung up Jeremy's present at my Penn apartment, I was taking an introductory art history course. I learned that while *The Kiss* was straight out of the Italian Romantic period, Corot was a French Realist. How ironic is that?

"Sam and I did. I'm not completely useless you know."

"I never said you were."

He tries to pay for the pizza when it comes, but I insist on taking care of it.

"So tell me about Jess," I say after two slices have been consumed and two shelves nailed in place.

"She's all right."

What would Jess think if she knew she was being described as just all right? I think I'd throw myself in front of a train. "Not serious then?"

"No. She's fun to hang out with for now, but she's not the one." Translation: I like sleeping with her but I don't want to sleep with *only* her.

"Pig," I tell him.

"Me? Why?"

"Because you're using her for sex."

"I'm not using her. We're just enjoying each other's company. Sexually."

"And at the movies."

"Prelude to sexually."

"So what's wrong with her?"

He pauses. "I shouldn't say. It's inappropriate."

"Don't be a tease. Tell me. I'm not going to say anything."

He frowns. "She's a princess. She expects me to do everything. It's like we're living in the fifties. I have to call her all the time. I have to pick her up all the time. She never even offers to pay for anything. And it's not that I mind calling and paying, but she acts like she expects it. It's exhausting. And…I don't think we really click. You know?"

"So why do you keep seeing her?"

He smiles slyly. "Well she's really hot."

"See? You're a pig. And you're never going to meet 'the one' as long as you're still seeing 'the two.' You should be dating other people. I'd offer to fix you up with someone, but all my friends are presently slightly insane." I nod in Sam's direction.

"Sam's cute." Sam and Andrew? The initials S and A are just

not as amusing as S and M. Anyway, I can't imagine anyone with her other than Marc.

"Just promise not to try to fix me up with Natalie again."

"Why not?"

"Too flaky. She's even more of a princess than Jess."

Hmm. Why is all this anti-princess talk making me uncomfortable? Oh right. I slide off the couch onto the floor next to him and pick up a screwdriver. "So what can I do to help, kind sir?"

I am an awesome roommate and here's why:

1.   I put all the pictures of Sam and Marc and all the teddy bears he gave her (all eight of them, and not the crappy, carnival kind either—I'm talking Gund here) in a large green garbage bag, and stuff it in the front closet behind my long black pea jacket that I haven't worn in years but won't throw out because you never know, the style could come back.

2.   I convince Sam to hang up the phone the three times I have a sneaking suspicion she's going to call him. I can tell when she's going to do it. First she starts fidgeting. Then she gets really quiet. A minute or so later, she attempts a casual stroll into her room and closes the door behind her. It reminds me of when my baby sister Iris used to crawl into the corner of a room to go to the bathroom in her diaper. When my intuition tells me that Sam is about to call, I barge into her room just as she picks up the phone, and convince her to hang up, insisting she'll thank me later. Pretty good system—I've only had two misses. Both times she called him when I was asleep, and tearfully confessed the next morning. The both times she spoke to him made her feel worse.

3.   I bought five more boxes of tissue and watched at least thirty-five episodes of *Beautiful Bride* with my broken-hearted friend. "Better to get it out of your system," I tell

her. It's addictive, this cheesiness. I can't help but wonder, Who watches this show on a regular basis? Are women that obsessed with getting married? Every episode is about a bride worrying about her flowers and veil and frilly dress. My wedding dress is going to be far more sophisticated than the ones on that show. I think I want a scooped neck, princess sleeves, and a puffed skirt. None of that bow crap. Elegant is going to be the operative adjective. "Don't worry," I find myself telling Sam. "There's a lid for every pot." I can't believe I said that. God save me, I'm beginning to sound just like my father.

Week One A.M. (After Marc) seems to go on forever.

On Monday, Natalie comes over for some girl bonding. Her head-cheerleader smile and perky anecdotes are a little too much for us. Sam feigns a headache and goes to sleep. I'm stuck bonding.

On Tuesday, Sam cleans the house.

On Wednesday, I turn on *Law and Order* by accident. "...the criminal lawyers who prosecute the offenders. These are their stories...." Logan/Mr. Big finds a male body in the trunk of an abandoned car, and Sam gets a sad, wistful look in her eyes. I turn off the TV. Sam cleans the house again.

On Thursday, Andrew and I drag her to half-price night at Charlie's Wings. I'm not crazy about eating wings in front of a guy, even Andrew, because I have a habit of getting hot sauce all over my face. I stare at Andrew as he holds a wing by its tip and carefully chews off the meat, leaving the bone completely stripped. He then gently licks the sauce off his lips with his tongue. How can anyone eat wings with so much style and sex appeal? I'm perfectly content to sit next to Andrew and study his technique, when boom, Sam sees Marc's brother's best friend sitting two tables over. I spend the next half hour trying to coax her out of a locked bathroom stall.

On Friday morning I wake up to the sound of Gloria Gaynor's "I Will Survive" blasting through my walls.

"Hello?"

"Good morning!" Sam says, throwing open my door.

"Morning," I say.

"Good, good, good morning!" she sings brightly. "For the first time all week I actually wanted to get out of bed."

"Good."

"I'm a new me."

I'm unsure if that statement requires a positive or negative response.

She plops down on my bed. "I will be less anal, I will have female friends, and I will find a new man. And from now on I will be called Samantha."

"Good for you," I cheerlead sleepily. My three weeks of singleness allow me the insight that she is not quite ready for a personality overhaul, but I decide to humor her.

"I'm not wasting any more dating time. Marc is an infant. He wants space? I'll give him space. He'll have more space then he knows what to do with when I go fuck every other man on this planet."

The word "fuck" sounds funny coming from her mouth, almost as if she has a mouthful of peanut butter. "Good for you," I say uncertainly.

"It's time to find a *mature* man." She pushes up her breasts and stares at the responding cleavage in my mirror. "I'm ready."

"For what? For sex with mature men?"

"No. For Orgasm."

Talk about out of the frying pan and into the fire. I try to talk her into going to a more shall-we-say sedate bar, like Aqua, an after-work bar on the fifty-sixth floor of the Tyler Building, but she's insistent. Natalie, thankfully, manages to set her straight later that evening, pointing out that Orgasm is for the under-thirty crowd, while Aqua is *the* place to meet older, career-minded men. Mature men.

Natalie has consented to be the designated driver, which means she'll only have one glass of wine. I have a feeling Sam is going to want to wallow, and being the good friend I am, I can't possibly allow her to wallow alone. Natalie even insists on paying for parking, and because of our perpetual state of brokeness, Sam and I don't argue.

"These things are killing me," Sam says. She is referring to the Band-Aids strategically placed over her nipples, in case she gets cold. She's wearing one of Natalie's backless tank tops, and she gets too "nippy" when she goes completely coverage-free.

"Wait 'til you take them off," Nat says. "Now that's pain."

"So how do I look?" Sam asks.

"Stunning," I answer. She does look great. Almost slutty (this is good). Definitely hot, although I'm not sure after-work appropriate.

We're standing in front of the elevator to the bar, when a short woman standing behind a counter tells us that although there's no cover charge, we have to check our coats, which will cost us each ten dollars.

All three of us cross our arms in front of our chests. "Actually, I'd prefer to keep my coat, if you don't mind," Natalie says. It's not the money; she doesn't trust strangers with her possessions.

"So try it," the woman says. "But they're going to send you back down."

"No, they won't," Natalie mutters under her breath. "I always bring my coat up."

So up we go in one of those superspeed elevators that made me wish I was chewing gum to ease the pressure mounting in my ears.

The elevator drops us off directly in front of the hostess.

"Hi," Natalie says. "Table for three, please."

The hostess looks us over. "Sorry, we're full."

I notice an empty place by the window. This calls for drastic measures. The three of us form a huddle, and after an agonizing five minutes of deliberation, settle on the grand sum of ten dollars.

"The table is now free," says the hostess in a candy-coated voice. "But you need to check your coats downstairs."

"We'd rather keep our coats," Natalie says.

"Sorry. I can't seat you until you check your coats."

Silently I press the down button on the elevator and pass out sticks of gum.

When we arrive at the bottom floor, we all stare at the ground. "We'd like to check our coats." Natalie says. Sam and I giggle. I look up at the woman behind the counter and smile. She smiles back.

Five minutes later, the elevator drops us off in front of the hostess a second time. "Our table, please," Natalie says, pointing to the still-vacant spot by the window.

"Sorry, we're full."

We form another huddle, and fifty dollars poorer than when we first arrived, we're sitting at a corner table overlooking the city.

Natalie and Sam place their cell phones directly beside their napkins. In case. "So has he called?" Natalie asks. She is referring to Marc, of course.

"No."

The moment is punctuated with silence. What can be said after that? On one hand, you want to cheer her up and tell her he'll call, but on the other hand, you want to tell her he's not worth it, he's a jerk, and she's better off if he doesn't call—but what if he does call? If he calls, then they'll get back together and hate you for saying all those horrible things. Remember *How to Recover from a Breakup* rule number three? Only mediocre friends should say terrible things about ex-boyfriends.

We order three glasses of wine—red for Sam and Natalie and white for me.

"He likes being tied up," Sam announces.

"Excuse me?" I choke slightly on my wine.

"Tied up. And he especially likes handcuffs. He likes being spanked, too."

I am unable to swallow my wine. I guess Sam did understand the S & M significance of their names after all.

Natalie laughs. "Do you get off on that stuff?"

"Sometimes. Kind of weird, though."

I will never again be able to look at Marc in the same way.

"Do you think," Sam wonders aloud, "he'll use his handcuffs with another girl?"

"You don't buy a new box of condoms every time you sleep with a different guy," Natalie offers wisely.

At this point, I feel compelled to add my two cents. "I think you should buy a new set of handcuffs for each partner. It's like comparing apples to oranges. Handcuffs, I assume, are so personal, so individual, but it stands to reason you wouldn't buy new condoms if you still had some left over. It's only the used ones I'd object to."

"I don't know," Sam says. "I'm going to keep my vibrator."

Sam and I are on our second round of drinks when we notice the two *GQ*-ish men at the bar, both in their early thirties, both wearing suits, one talking on a cell phone, the other slightly in need of a shave, both very sexy.

"Let's call them over," Sam says, downing her wine.

I'm not sure how you're supposed to call men over. You can't wave and shout, Come and get it boys! Wouldn't they sense our desperation? "Maybe we should just stare them down."

"Definitely not," Natalie says with disgust, tapping the rim of her wineglass. "We don't call *or* stare."

Well excuse me. "So what do you think we should do?"

"We laugh a lot and look as though we're having the most wonderful time. And we ignore them completely."

"That's the plan?" I think it's time Nat started paying closer attention to Fashion Magazine Fun Facts.

"That's the plan," she says.

Sam sticks her finger in her glass in an attempt to suck up whatever alcohol might be left. "I'm going to need some more wine."

"Just finish mine," Natalie offers, handing over the glass.

I see the mental turmoil on Sam's face. Should she take the wine along with all of Nat's potential germs? Or should she give in to her anal ways and pass up the free beverage? I put my hand on her shoulder. "The new fun, fearless you, remember?"

Courageously, she nods. "Thanks." At first her facial expression reminds me of someone drinking toilet water, not that I've ever had the good fortune to witness such an event. But then she relaxes and I feel like a proud aunt.

Natalie throws her head back and laughs out loud, startling me. Apparently, the let's-pretend-we're-having-fun-so-we-can-attract-men show has begun.

Ten minutes later, the *GQ* men are sitting at our table. Natalie is flirting with Needs a Shave and Sam is flirting with Cell Phone. I would have thought that watching Sam flirt would be like spotting a girl on the street with her dress tucked into the back of her panty hose, but she is surprisingly talented. Once she introduces herself as Samantha, she morphs into a nymphet. She starts off with the pretending-to-be-interested-in-what-he-says technique and asks a dozen questions, and then subtly turns the spotlight on herself.

"I teach fifth grade," she says in response to the standard so-what-do-you-do. If he asks what sign she is, I swear I'm going to throw up.

"You don't punish your students, do you?"

"Not usually. The girls are pretty good. The boys sometimes misbehave. But that's okay. I know how to handle naughty boys."

Is that a cell phone he has in his pants or is he just happy to see her? Hmm. Maybe there's something to this spanking thing after all.

In the elevator, Needs-a-Shave asks when they can see us again.

"Unfortunately, that won't be possible," Sam says, surprising the rest of us. "It was nice to meet both of you." She kisses both of them on the cheek.

Huh? Did I miss something here? "Didn't you want to meet them?" I ask when they're out of earshot.

"Forget it. They didn't even offer to buy us drinks." Sam waves her hand in the air as if to shoo away an annoying fly.

"But we didn't say we wanted anything," I protest.

"Cheapskates," Sam adds, and Natalie nods her head.

"Besides," Sam says, "what kind of sleaze hits on a girl at a bar?"

Fifteen minutes later, Natalie lets us off at the apartment, and as I turn the key into our door, Sam says, "Guess what we're doing tomorrow."

"Sleeping in?"

"Yes. And after that, we're getting belly button rings."

This Samantha character is beginning to scare me.

Chapter Ten

Fifty Bucks to a Whole New You

Natalie tells us that her pierced friends got it done on Willington Street.

"Maybe we should find out the exact name of the store," I comment as we peer through the dirty windows of a used clothing store.

"If we wait, we'll never do it," Sam replies. "There's no time for extensive research."

"I'm not asking for extensive. Superficial will do."

"Let's try here," she says, and I follow her into a place called *Spider.* The tattoo machine's reverberating buzz makes me think of a sixteenth century torture chamber.

Sam asks the scary alternative man at the desk if he performs navel piercings.

"No inglés," he replies.

"I think the possibility of having the wrong body part pierced here is alarmingly high," I whisper, my voice coated with nausea.

Sam thanks the man, not that he understands, and we slip back out the door.

Further down the block a window advertises "expert exotic piercing" and a "reputation that is earned, not assumed." Hoping that their reputation goes beyond the local panhandlers, we enter.

The expert, I use that term loosely, looks a little wild—with various insect tattoos and nineteen pierces that I can see. I'm guessing ten is the minimum for employment. He convinces us that a navel ring is well worth his fifty-dollar quote.

Being the responsible millennium-girl that I am, I ask him about his hygiene practices.

"I always wear fresh plastic gloves, and all my needles are disposable," he answers.

This is good, I think. Disposable needles. Wait…needles? What needles? What happened to the good, old-fashioned piercing gun? When I got my ears pierced way back in the third grade, two women used a gun on each ear, and it was over in a momentary thunderous explosion.

"Would you kindly both sign these waiver forms?" he asks nonchalantly. Forms? What forms? Why do I need to sign a waiver form? I read: "…in the unlikely event of excessive bleeding, permanent scarring, loss of consciousness…" Loss of consciousness?

Somehow it is decided that I should go first, possibly because Samantha looks more like an about-to-be-sick Sam. Lucky me. I sit in a big black leather chair and without going into details here, I tell dear Samantha it only hurts for a second.

Her turn.

Screams from the leather chair.

I lied.

The Reaction—Scene One

Natalie: You really did it?

Me: Yeah. I don't think I'll ever be able to do up a pair of pants again.

Natalie: Maybe I'll get one, too.

Me: You should. Didn't hurt a bit, although it's a little sore now.

Natalie: Maybe I will. But it's kind of cheesy, don't you think? And everyone has one.

Me: (Muttering.) Thanks a lot, Nat. I guess I'm a conformist with bad taste.

*   *   *

The Reaction—Scene Two

Iris: That is so cool! I want one. Is it red? I bet it's red. The red will go away, won't it? My friend Mandy got one and she didn't tell her mother, and now whenever she takes a shower she has to wear a bathing suit just in case her mother barges in or something, and she doesn't know what she's going to do in the summer; she has a pool and won't her mother think it's weird she doesn't wear bikinis anymore? I asked Mom if I could have one but she said no, not a chance. I'm so getting one the second I turn eighteen. One year, five months and three days left of a belly-pierce-free me! It's not going to get infected, is it?

The Reaction—Scene Three

Janie: Couldn't you have just highlighted your hair or something?

The Reaction—Scene Four

Dad: So what's new?
Me: Nothing.

The Reaction—Scene Five

Wendy: (Voice on speakerphone while I paint toenails.) I'm wondering why our generation chooses to mutilate our bodies.
Me: It's not just our generation. Piercing has gone on for centuries all over the planet.
Wendy: But why is American culture piercing stomachs, tongues, nipples, and other parts I won't mention?
Me: Maybe it's a tendency of the politically correct to embrace cultural relativism?
Wendy: Perhaps to produce an aesthetic effect.
Me: (Blows on toes of right foot.) Or a spiritual one.
Wendy: Or a sexual one.

Me: (Feigning indignation.) I didn't pierce my clitoris.

Wendy: Maybe there's just nothing left to attack but our own flesh.

Sam (a.k.a. Samantha): (Barges into my room.) Isn't it cool? (Pulls up her shirt.) Can we take a picture?

Wendy: It'll definitely give your kids something to laugh about.

The Reaction—Scene Six

We're eating an early dinner at the Asian Grill, one of those places where you pick your own meat, vegetables, noodles, sauces, whatever, and watch how a small plate of food can cost you thirty dollars.

Andrew: (Sitting across from me in a two-seater booth.) I can't believe you did that.

Me: (Arms folded tightly across my T-shirt.) Why? I didn't realize body ornamentation was a character-altering ordeal. (The following words are unspoken.) Uh-oh. Will men find me sexually repulsive?

Andrew: I guess I always thought belly rings were for Alanis-type girls.

Me: Puh-lease. There's even a Miss America contestant who proudly sponsors one. Miss Springfield or whatever.

Andrew: Can I see?

Me: You want me to lift up my shirt in the middle of the Asian Grill?

Andrew: (Eyes growing large.) Yes!

Me: (Lifts up the bottom of my shirt.) Happy?

Andrew: Why is it so red?

Me: I just got needles stuck in my stomach, what do you expect?

Andrew: (Eyes growing to size of English muffins.) It's, uh, kind of, well, sexy.

Me: (The following word is unspoken.) Good.

Finis

* * *

After work on Monday, Sam and I go for a grocery run. Not that we can even walk properly. For the past thirty-six hours I've had to leave my jeans undone, and every time something comes in the remote vicinity of my stomach—an arm, clothing, air—I momentarily pass out.

We put the regular staples in our cart: juice, milk, and macaroni and cheese. Then Sam goes for the gourmet stuff and throws in a slab of salami, a six-pack of beer, a chunk of hard cheese, and a package of antihistamines.

I stare in bewilderment at the produce. "Are we visiting a frat house?"

"No. We're making our apartment guy-friendly."

"Is this the if-you-build-it-they-will-come philosophy? Let me guess, *Cosmo*? *Glamour*? *City Girls*?"

"*City Girls.*"

"What else does *City Girls* say?"

"That we should get a dog. Guys will come up to dogs on the street and start conversations with their owners. Us."

"You're allergic to dogs."

"That's why we're trying the food route instead. But maybe we can borrow someone's dog. That's what the antihistamines are for."

Who is this woman and what has she done with my roommate? Sam has a bunch of other suggestions, all of which I veto:

1.   Take a computer class. (We have no time for that. We're very, very busy.)
2.   Suck lollypops at bars. (Although lollypops turn your mouth to various tastes, which in itself is not a bad thing, they also turn your mouth to various inappropriate colors.)
3.   Hang out at Home Depot. (So *not* happening.)
4.   Take a salsa class. (Me: "No way—we can't dance." Sam: "That's why we should take classes." Me: "No way.")
5.   Turn socks into voodoo dolls. This, she says, is not to help us meet men but rather to cause Jeremy and Marc se-

vere physical pain, emotional embarrassment, and financial ruin. (Fun idea, but would put us in the "we're psychotic" category.)

I counter-suggest visiting a bookstore. I figure since I'm in publishing, my degree is in lit, and I read a lot, it would make sense for me to date someone who also appreciates the written word.

"I don't understand," Sam asks. "You want to meet a guy who reads romance novels?"

"No, that would be weird." I'd prefer him to read something manlier. Something Hemingway-esque.

We end up at Barnes and Noble. My watch says it's now six. Sam and I decide that we won't leave until we each hand out our phone number to at least one potential husband. She makes a mad dash for the business section. I'm still debating: Soul (fiction) or good job (computers)? It's a tough call, but I cave in favor of nice car over nice library; I'm just about to head up the escalator to fiction, when I cop out and veer toward the computer book area. Okay, so I'm weak.

La, la, la. The computer section consists of three walls of books. I figure I'll start at the right and work my way left.

"Can I help you with something?" a Barnes and Noble woman asks.

"No thanks. Just looking."

One cutie is glancing through a hardcover. I'll just bide my time, wait for a good opportunity...not that I know what I'm going to say to this man. Oh, I know! I'll ask him to recommend something. This is good. Brings out the hero quality.

"Excuse me?"

"Yes?"

What am I supposed to ask here? "Do you know a good book on...computers?"

He looks at me as though there is something horribly wrong with me, as if I'm wearing odd shoes, or I have no eyebrows. "You should probably ask someone who works here."

Damn. Time for a latté break.

Six coffees and four hours later, I'm over-caffeined and bored. I've encountered three men whose wives/girlfriends/women didn't appreciate me moving into the periphery of their territory, two men with kids (I don't think I'm at the stage in my life where I should be stepmom/mistress), and one Trekkie geek whose incessant staring forced me to temporarily abandon my post. The Barnes and Noble woman thinks I'm a complete freak. About every ten minutes she asks me if I'm sure I don't need any help.

"I'm beyond help," I respond.

Then I meet Josh. He's standing by the C++ shelf, scanning through a book called *The Joy of Programming*. He's tall and cute and has a nice smile (he has two adorable dimples), but I'm tired and want to go home. I stick out my hand and introduce myself, abandoning all pretense at preliminary mating rituals. I'm in a hurry here. He tells me his name, we chitchat for a few minutes, and in the middle of his telling me about his cat and dog and five microprocessors, I say, "Call me." I write out my phone number on a piece of carefully prepared paper from my purse (they're presprayed with perfume), throw it at him, and go look for Sam. Mission accomplished.

Sam is sitting on a couch deep in conversation with Jerry Seinfeld's look-alike. I wave. She doesn't respond. I wave again. I'm sure she's ignoring me. Time for another coffee.

"How do I look?" Sam asks and twirls. She's wearing a very low-cut black dress that ties behind her neck, and a brand-new pair of her version of high black boots—black sling-backs. She's going on a first date with Philip—the guy she met in the business book section. It turns out he owns his own business and he reads a lot of Grisham. Okay, fine, *The Firm* isn't exactly *For Whom the Bell Tolls,* but at least it's fiction. He can read. And he called. It's been five days and Josh has not. Serves me right for trying to date yet another jackass whose name starts with J. Serves me right for not stalking the business section. Computer section—

please. Guys who read computer books are about as trustworthy as the start-up Internet businesses they left their safe, monotonous jobs for.

Seven days. Why didn't I do the travel section? Even the cooking section would have been better. Once Natalie met a psychologist in the how-to section; with my luck, I would have probably run into a psycho.

I bring my frustration to Tae Kwon Do.

"Hanna. Twul. Zed. Ned. Dasso," Lorenzo says. "Spread your legs! Wider!"

Believe me, I've been trying.

After class, Lorenzo offers to help me with my first form. He puts his hands, those big Tae Kwon Do hands, on my shoulders and molds them into the proper form position. It's 7:30 p.m. and I'm daydreaming of a nice tall bowl of macaroni and cheese, but I say thank you and let him help me. I need to know this form before I can be tested for a yellow belt. And yellow belts are far more slimming than white belts. Presently I imagine I look like the giant Pillsbury marshmallow in *Ghostbusters*.

"Sir?" I ask. You have to call everyone here Sir. Yes, Sir. No, Sir. Thank you, Sir. Throw me up against the wall and kiss me, Sir.

"Yes?"

"When can I get my yellow belt, Sir?"

"You've only been to one class, Jackie."

"Oh. Right, Sir." Hmm. "So how many classes do I have to come to, Sir?"

"At least twenty." Lorenzo is looking at me with confusion.

Twenty? That's twenty hours of working out! That's also twenty hours of working out with Sir Sex-God-Lorenzo. Never mind. I think I'll remain a white belt forever. I think I'm in love.

"Do you know who you look like?" Sir Sex-God-Lorenzo asks. His hand is on the curve of my back and I'm having difficulty breathing. I'm still trying to figure out who *he* looks like. So familiar, yet I don't remember ever meeting him.

"Who?" An actress? Your first girlfriend?

"Chelsea Clinton."

Get away from me, Sex-God-Lorenzo. You smell, Sir.

"I don't see what the big deal is," Sam says. I'm sitting on the countertop in her bathroom, watching her expertly apply white stuff all over her eyelids. She's getting ready for her second date with Philip. She's been single for less than two weeks and she has a second date. A second date! Unbelievable.

"Chelsea Clinton is notorious for being ugly." I squirm, realizing that I am sitting on Sam's wet pouf.

"I don't think she's ugly."

"That's not the point, is it? The point is that she's *known* for being ugly. Letterman and SNL make fun of her constantly. How can someone think it's a compliment to tell me I look like someone who's notorious for being ugly?"

"Maybe he finds her attractive."

"Irrelevant subjective opinion." There's no use arguing anyway, because Sam's not even paying attention. Tonight Philip is taking her to a wine-tasting class. A wine-tasting class! How ridiculous is that? He obviously just wants to get her drunk and sleep with her.

Fine. I'm jealous. Horribly green-contact-eyed jealous.

"Do my eyes pop?" She bats them at me.

"Snap and crackle." What am I going to do tonight? It's Saturday night. Sam's on a date. Natalie's on a date. Even Andrew's on a date with Jessica the Sweet Valley Twin.

I sit down on my couch, wrap myself in Sam's afghan, and in desperation, call my sister Iris.

"Omigod. You're not going to believe what happened!"

"What?"

"Omigod. The guy who my best friend has obsessed about for seven years wants me, and I like him *so* much. What do I do?"

Teenage angst. Sigh. The good old days. "Mandy likes him?"

"No, Tamara."

"I thought Mandy was your best friend."

"Mandy used to be my best friend, but now she's more like my second best friend. So what do I do?"

"What do you want to do?"

"We were all at a party last night and every time Kyle came over to talk to me, Tamara kept shooting me looks so I couldn't talk to him except when she went to the bathroom, and it's really absurd because she's liked ten guys in the past year and she can't call dibs on every guy she's ever liked! Don't you agree?"

I think I lost her at the Mandy and Tamara confusion. Not that she waits for a response. She rarely comes up for air.

"He works part-time at Abercrombie, which proves he's hot, because every guy who works there is hot…"

After fifteen more minutes of listening to how hot Abercrombie-Kyle is, I am inexplicably tired. "Iris, I'm going to sleep."

"It's ten o'clock! On a Saturday night!"

Yeah, so? "Leave me alone. I'm tired."

"Don't you have any plans?"

Plans? What are plans? I decide to lie. "I did, but I decided to stay home instead. Are you going out tonight?" *Beep.* "Hold on, call waiting."

"Hello?"

"Jackie, you're my literary lifeline and you have sixty seconds to answer this question. The timer is starting now—" It's Bev, my stepmother. I haven't a clue what she's talking about.

"I'm your literary *what?*"

"I'm playing *Who Wants to be a Millionaire* with your father and some friends and I don't know the answer to this question. You're my literary lifeline."

I have a question of my own: why are my parents having more fun than I am on a Saturday night? Final answer?

"Hold on! Let me get off the other line." I press the flash button. "Iris?"

"Haven't you been listening to anything I said? I'm going to a party at Angie's, and both Tamara and Kyle are going to be there."

"Can we discuss this tomorrow?"

"But the party is tonight!"

"I have to go."

"Why?"

"Bev needs something on the other line."

"Fine. Pick your other family over me." She slams down the phone.

I switch back to Bev. "Okay."

"Ready? Timer on."

"Am I on speakerphone? I hate speakerphones. Hi, Dad! Can you take me off?" There's no way anyone else is going to hear me make an ass of myself.

This whole lifeline thing is making me nervous. What if I get it wrong? What is Bev losing exactly? How much does she already have? I need to know what I'm up against here. Suddenly it grows very quiet. I'm off the speakerphone.

"Who did T.S. Eliot dedicate *The Wasteland* to? Was it Andrew Marvell, Ezra Pound, his wife Jennifer Eliot, William Carlos Williams, or none of the above?"

None of the above? Wait just a moment here; there's never a "none of the above." "Five choices?" I ask.

"We try to make the home version slightly more challenging."

Okay, okay. Calm. Stay calm. I read this in my survey course, my modernism course, and my twentieth-century poetry course. I never really understand anything in it beyond the title. Okay. I know it's not Marvell. *The Wasteland* was written at the beginning of the twentieth century. Wait a minute. I know this. "Marvell," I say.

"Are you sure?"

No! No! Why did I say that? I knew it was wrong! Can I change it? Is it too late? Have I lost? "Not Marvell! I meant Ezra Pound." I should have finished my master's! Why didn't I finish my master's?

"Okay. Ezra Pound. Are you sure?"

"No. It could be William Carlos Williams. I'm not sure. I think it was Pound."

"What's the percentage possibility of it being Pound?"

''Fifty-one percent Pound, forty-five percent William Carlos Williams. Four percent his wife. Wait. I'm not sure if he *was* married.''

''Then it could have been his wife if he was married?''

Maybe. ''I don't know. I think it was Pound.''

''Okay. Thanks. Good night.'' And she hangs up.

Good night? Good night! How can I possibly sleep when she didn't tell me if I was right? Thankfully, my bookshelf is now in full working order. The top shelf is filled with school anthologies, the second shelf with classics, the third shelf with commercial trade books, the fourth shelf with my nineteenth- and twentieth-century books, and the fifth shelf way at the bottom with all the romances. I organized each section by publisher—an extremely entertaining time-wasting activity that caused me to miss some pretty heavy-duty prime time TV, an extremely entertaining time-wasting activity that I should have saved for a night like tonight.

I find a copy of *The Wasteland* in one of my Norton Anthologies. It is in fact dedicated to Ezra Pound.

Thank you, God. And thank you, T.S. Maybe I should start calling myself F.J. in tribute.

Never mind.

My phone rings at exactly 1:07 a.m.

''Hello?''

''Good. I didn't wake you.'' It's Iris.

''You did wake me. I told you I was going to sleep three hours ago.''

''I know, but this is an emergency.''

''Why?''

''Because Kyle left the party early and Michael gave me his number and said I should call him.''

''Call Michael?''

''No, call Kyle.''

''Who's Michael?''

''Kyle's friend.''

"Did you call?"

"Not yet. Should I?"

"Won't Tamara be mad?"

"She won't find out. I'll just call and we'll talk and hopefully, he'll ask me out or something. All my makeup is still on."

"You're going to go out now? It's 1:08! Don't you have a curfew?"

"Yes, but if necessary, I can climb out the window. Desperate times call for desperate measures."

"So call."

"Okay. But I want you to stay on the phone. I'm going to call three-way."

"But what if I laugh?"

"Don't."

"What if I can't help it? Is this a good idea?"

"Please? Please? Please? Please?"

"Okay, fine."

She does some speed dialing (she's obviously programmed a button for him), and then I hear a deep male voice answer, "Yeah?"

"Is Kyle there?"

"It's me."

"Hey, what up? It's Iris."

"Hey, Iris! What up?"

What is "what up"? Why are they forgetting the S?

"Nothing, I'm just sitting at home. What are you doing?"

"You know. Chilling at my pad."

This boy has a pad? Why does he have a pad? How old is he? Why is he chilling? Is he on drugs?

"Oh." This from Iris.

Silence. More silence. Should I interject something here? *Breeeeeeep.* Oops. That was an accident, I swear.

"Well, have fun," she says. "I'll see you later."

"Okay." I hear a twinge of confusion in Kyle's one-octave-lower-than-I-expected voice.

"Okay, 'bye." Iris disconnects Kyle. Again, silence.

I howl.

"Stop!" Iris says, unable to suppress her own laughter.

"Nice work! I'm very impressed."

"Omigod. Omigod. Omigod."

"Why does he have a pad?"

"Omigod. Omigod. Omigod. At some point in my life I'll be able to treat boys like normal people, right?"

"I'll keep you posted."

All this laughing is killing my navel.

Chapter Eleven

Oh, Brother

I'm about to start editing *The Sheik Falls in Love*, when the words *New Mail* flash across on my screen.

More comma meetings I cannot take.

But wait, what's this?

Jackie,
This is a picture of my brother, Tim. If you're interested, let me know and I'll give him your number.
Julie

Humph. What kind of horribly superficial person does she think I am? Does she really think I'll only go out with her brother if he's physically attractive? What about personality? Intelligence? Sense of humor? Money?

I open the attached file.

He's *cute*.

And tall, standing at least a foot taller than Julie beside him. It looks like a professional picture, with that pale blue screen in the background. A present for their parents' twentieth wedding anniversary? As far as I can remember, I always wanted to have my picture taken professionally. But my dad had this fantasy about being a photographer, and when I was little he always had a camera and a huge lens slung around his neck, ready to snap at anything. He looked like a tourist at Disneyland. "Oh, look, Janie!" he'd shout. "She's smiling!" or "Oh, look, Janie! She has a new tooth!'' I'm just grateful my parents split up long before I got my first bra.

It's not that he was so embarrassing, which he was, it was because in all his pictures people came out with no feet, or no heads. Weird. In all my early years on this planet, I didn't have a decent picture of me. But when I was thirteen, I thought of a plan. I convinced Janie to have Glitzy Image done for her birthday. These are funky professional pictures where they do your makeup and hair, and dress you up in fur scarves or glittery bustiers. I told her I'd pay for the shoot, and all she'd have to pay for were the prints. Of course, once we arrived at the studio I wanted to get my pictures taken, too, and the bill came to twenty-five dollars. That is, twenty-five dollars for the shoot and four hundred fifty dollars for the actual pictures. But they were good pictures, I swear it. Especially the ones of me.

It was *so* worth it. For me, anyway.

This guy isn't just cute, he's hot. He has broad shoulders, and soft brown hair that looks like it wants to fall into his big, brown puppy eyes. Come here, doggy. Over here.

Why didn't she just tell me she has a hot brother? What's his name again? Right—Dad. I mean Timothy. Timmy. Tim.

What a conundrum. If I say I'm interested in meeting her brother, she'll know it's just because of his looks, otherwise I would have said yes earlier. Do I e-mail her back, thereby admitting I'm superficial? Or do I respond that I haven't had time to look at the picture? No, that would sound fishy. Maybe I'll tell her that my computer can't open attachments but that I'd love it if she could fix me up with her brother anyway, sight unseen. Come to think of it, why is she doing this in the first place? Did she see through my lie that I have a boyfriend? Or does she think I'm a slut who will see two boys at the same time? Or, God forbid, does she think I did have a boyfriend but that I am totally incapable of maintaining a relationship?

I hit reply. No reason to think too hard about this.

Dear Julie,
Hook it up!
Jackie

Send.

He calls at exactly eight that evening. Amazing. Completely implausible. He got my number today *and* he called today. See? Not all guys play games. There are some men out there who don't sing at plays, don't run off to Thailand, and don't cheat on their girlfriends. I hope so, anyway. It would suck *big* time if Tim has a girlfriend, is planning a trip to Thailand, and sings at plays.

What if he wants to take me to a play? What if he buys tickets to *The Apartment?* Do I have to go again?

"Jackie!" Sam yells from her room while I'm watching the end of *Ally McBeal.* "It's for you!"

"Tell them I'll call back later!" I scream back. Damn, just when the sappy music is about to come on. Why would someone call during *Ally?* How annoying is that?

Two minutes later I yell, "Who was it?"

"Some guy...Jim? No, Tim."

"Tim? Why didn't you give me the phone?"

"You said you'd call back."

"Yeah, but I thought it was Iris or someone. I didn't think Tim would call so soon."

"Just call him back. I took down his number."

"What did his voice sound like? Smart? Cute? Funny?" I don't need Sam to tell me if he sounded hot. I already know he's hot. At least I *hope* he's hot; he was hot in the picture. But wait. What if it was airbrushed? "Did he sound hot?"

"How does someone sound hot?"

"Never mind. Did he sound funny?"

"No. He just asked to speak to you."

"You can't tell me anything?"

"He was polite."

Polite's better than rude. "Okay, I'll call him back." Uh-oh. "I *can't* call him back. What if Julie answers?"

"He lives with his sister?"

Good point. I hope not. But they might. "What if they do? Do I say hello? This is way too stressful."

"If you don't call him back, he's not going to call you again."

True. A definite bind. Aha! "I'll leave an internal message!" The miraculous capabilities of the virtual answering machine. I can call through the message service. This way it looks as if I tried to call but didn't get through.

"Are we going to have dry-run messages again?"

Hmm. "No, I'm not even nervous because I don't like him yet. Watch. I can do it cold." She hands me the phone number and watches me dial.

"Hello. You've reached the Mittmans. We can't come to the phone right now. To leave a message for Tim, please press one. For Norman or Sandra, press two." Beep.

I press one. "Hi, Tim, it's Jackie. Julie's friend. Call me back when you get a chance. Call me back when you get a chance. 'Bye." I hang up. Hee, hee. I'm not sure why I pulled a Jon Gradinger, but I couldn't resist.

"So? What does his voice sound like?"

"Old. I think it was his dad."

"His dad? He lives at home?"

"I guess." Uh-oh.

"How old is he?"

"I don't know."

"How old is Julie?"

"I don't know!" What if Tim is really Timmy? Eighteen-year-old Timmy. Eighteen-year-old Timmy still in school.

"What does he do for a living? Does he have a job?"

"I don't know." I probably should have done a touch more research than simply ogle his picture. If he doesn't have a job, do I have to pay for the date?

The phone rings. "I'll get it," I scowl. "Hello?"

"Hi, can I speak with Jackie, please?" His voice didn't crack. Good sign. He's not twelve.

"It's Jackie."

"Hi, this is Tim, Julie's brother."

"Hi, Tim." Nice voice. This is good.

"Hi, Jackie. I'm glad I reached you."

"I'm glad you reached me, too."

"Good." Pause. "So apparently you're my type," he says.

Cute opening line. Three cheers for Timmy! "I've never been told I'm anyone's type before."

"From what my sister says, you're everyone's type—cute, smart, and sweet."

Two points for Tim. Four points for Julie. Wait a minute. There's something a little off-color about being everyone's type. However, for the moment, I will give him—and Julie—the benefit of the doubt. "Thank you."

"You're welcome." Pause. "Would you like to meet me for coffee this week?" Cutting right to the core, aren't we?

"I'd like that." I hope you're not a creep.

"Are you free on Friday night?"

Friday night? Friday night is Orgasm night—and since you're not a sure bet yet, Timmy dear, I can't quite give that up. Who goes for coffee on a Friday night, anyway? Friday night is bar night.

"Um…Thursday night is better."

"Oh? During the week? Okay. It's just that I get up at 5:30 and I'm pretty zonked at night. And I have to get up early the next day…"

Is that half past five in the morning? What could one possibly have to do at 5:30? I decide to save the questions until the date to ensure we have potential discussion material. "What about Saturday?" I ask, taking what I know to be a huge risk. A Saturday night first date? That's like playing the two-dollar slots instead of the quarter ones.

"Perfect," he says.

Yay! Now I can still go to Orgasm *and* have Saturday night plans, too.

"I'll call you Saturday afternoon to get your address."

And he's even going to pick me up at my apartment, not on a street corner! He must have been deposited here from the nineteenth century! "Okay, speak to you then."

"Good night."

"Good night." I hang up the phone.

"So? How does he sound?"

"He sounds…nice."

"Nice is good…isn't it?"

"I don't know. You'd think, wouldn't you?"

We go to Orgasm on Friday night, we meaning Sam, Natalie, and myself. I am wearing a jean skirt, a white blouse tied at my waist, a cowboy hat (all purchased at a nearby drugstore), and Sam's cowboy boots. She still hasn't given me a good reason as to why she owns these boots. Unfortunately, they are slightly too small and are presently doing damage to my feet. My hair is in pigtails and I drew little freckles on my cheeks. No, I have not decided to commit fashion suicide—it's a Halloween party.

Natalie is not in costume; she's far too cool. Sam is wearing skintight black leather pants, a navel-exposing black crop-top, *Playboy* bunny ears, and a bushy tail. She is determined to act out her costume, and has begun flirting with everyone in sight, including Andrew, who has appeared by my side in a black turtleneck, black pants, black shoes and a sign around his neck that says, "I'm a nihilist, I care about nothing." I forgive him for the turtleneck; after all, it's just a costume.

"Did you get that idea from *The Big Lebowski*?" I ask, laughing at his creativity.

"Yup. But I think you're the only one who gets it."

Ben is dressed up as the town drunk—oh, yeah, that's his normal attire. When he sees Sam's costume, she becomes the receiver of his sleazy hello. When he buys the five of us shots, she's the one he drinks a toast to.

"What happened to toasting my soft skin?" I whine.

"You've been replaced." At least he's honest. His hand drops to Sam's waist, below her waist, and then rests on her butt. Does she smack him? Gently move his hand? No. She giggles and leans into him.

"How come *you're* not wearing a crop-top?" Andrew asks, eyeing my clothed stomach.

Um...no. "Only special people get to see my belly ring."

"I saw it." He smiles.

"You must be special." I lean over and kiss him on his freshly shaven cheek. I guess it's a good thing that I never went for Andrew. Knowing me, I probably would have just screwed up our friendship.

"What's happening with Philip?" I ask Sam later in the ladies' room. After the wine-tasting, he took her out two more times, bringing the grand total to four dates.

"What about him?"

"Aren't you kind of dating him? How come you're all over Ben?"

"First of all, we're not dating-dating, we're just dating. I am not getting back into another relationship. I like being single. I need some 'me' time. I can flirt, date, and sleep with whomever I want. Second of all, Ben is cute. But just because I'm flirting doesn't mean I'm going home with him. Okay, Mom?"

How is it possible that Sam sounds so adjusted? It's only been two weeks and already she's a swinging single.

Tim calls at 3:00, we reconfirm, and I give him my address.

Big Tim (a.k.a. Dad) calls at seven to confirm that I'll be spending Christmas with him and Feed-Your-Spirit (a.k.a. Bev). "Yes, I'm coming home."

Like I have anything else to do. I can't believe it's almost Christmas. Have I been in Boston for half a year?

Iris calls just before eight to ask why I can't come visit her.

"Because Janie doesn't celebrate Christmas, and my father does."

"Fine. You love that side of the family more than me."

"Iris, don't be a baby. I spent two weeks with you this summer before I moved here."

"Oh, now I'm a baby. Thanks. Thanks a lot." She slams down the phone.

Tim (my date, not my dad) buzzes me at eight. I intercom him not to bother coming upstairs. I'm not in the mood to introduce him to Sam, and I'm not in the mood to make my bed, pick up my socks from all around the living room, et cetera, et cetera.

It's strange, Single-Swinging-Sam hasn't harassed me to clean up anything these days. Maybe the breakup has caused her to profoundly reevaluate the world and her place in it, forcing her to realize that she cannot control everyone around her like puppets. Or maybe she's just so busy being slutty that she hasn't thought about it.

I'm wearing my first-date outfit, of course. But I've left my hair curly. No use in making myself too gorgeous, in case I don't like him. It's hard to shake a guy who's crazy about you once he's hooked. I'm assuming.

He's standing beside a long, pale blue car—you know the type, the kind Kevin Arnold inherited from his grandfather in *The Wonder Years*. Fortunately, he's far better-looking than his car. And Kevin. Good for Julie, for having such a cute brother. I wonder if it's hard for her, being the uglier sibling. Is she at least the smart one? I hope not. Not that I know what that feels like. My sister looks like I did at sixteen, only she's shorter, skinnier, and wears a D-cup. We both look like Janie—we both have her face, Iris has her boobs, and I have her thighs. And to top it all, we're both exceptionally intelligent. No sibling rivalry there. Just conceitedness. I wonder if Julie and her brother are close. I wonder if girls befriend her just to get to know her brother. They would if he's older than she is. I wonder if he's older, or if he's my age.

Tim smiles at me, or the guy I assume is Tim smiles at me, since he's the only one standing there, and he looks a lot like the Tim in the picture. So unless Tim has a secret twin and they're playing one of those stupid jokes on me like in *The Parent Trap,* it's probably him. He doesn't look exactly like his picture. Then again, no one ever looks exactly the way they do in pictures—he's a little less broad-shouldered than I had thought (was he wearing shoulder pads in the picture?), but his smile is nicer, so it kind of evens out.

Instead of going for coffee, he invites me to see an exhibit at the Museum of Fine Arts. He scores three points for this: one for creativity, one for having a place to go and not saying, "I don't know, what do you want to do?" and one for being cultured and knowing about stuff like exhibits.

We make small talk in the car about Julie. I still don't know a whole lot about him. Like, for example, where he works. I really, really want to ask but it's such a sensitive question. I don't want him to think I'm the type who only goes for guys who make a lot of money, but I do want to know if he's a waste of life. What if he makes black-market porn? Don't I have the right to know this immediately?

I ask him where he's from.

"Boston."

"Oh."

He doesn't bother circling when we get to the museum; he just pulls into a pay-by-the-hour lot. Another point. Wants to impress me. Although this could signify laziness.

Apparently, the museum hops on Saturday nights. Who would have thought? I guess culture is in. He pays for the tickets. (My fake reach-into-my-purse maneuver leads to his "Don't be silly, I asked you out and it's my pleasure" line.) Yay! Another point for Timmy!

As soon as we step under the high, white, slightly intimidating ceiling, a Helen-the-editor look-alike asks us if we would like headsets. There is no cost, but the Helen clone makes it very clear that a donation to the museum would be much appreciated.

"I'll get them," I say, and offer her four dollars. That would be my financial reciprocation. Or, as I see it at this point, an investment in my future. But as I put on the earphones, I become acutely aware of my grievous error. How am I supposed to get to know Tim if we can't talk to each other?

Too late. A nasal recorded voice is already ordering me to look at the painting on my right. Tim is concentrating next to me. I wave. He waves back. I am officially an idiot. Plus, I must look like Princess Leia.

I should have asked for one set so that we could share—the modern day version of one milkshake and two straws.

Here goes. We see some abstract paintings, some sort of ancient art, a Renoir…more Impressionist paintings. And then I see it. A painting by the French painter Paul Gauguin, called *Where Do We Come From? What Are We? Where Are We Going?* Now these are excellent questions. Where do I come from? That I know: Danbury. But what am I? Where am I going? These are more baffling. The oil painting features groups of what I'm assuming are Tahiti natives (the recorded voice tells me he went to Tahiti to search for unspoiled society and I infer the rest). I must own this painting. Or at least the print. I must be able to look at it constantly. For some unknown reason it makes me feel less baffled knowing that Tahiti natives are baffled, too.

An hour later, we reach the end of the tour and remove our headsets. "Do you mind stopping at the gift shop?" I ask. "I must have a print of that Gauguin."

Just my luck, the gift shop is closed.

"Do you want to grab a drink?" I motion in the direction of the museum café.

"Actually," he says. "I have to call it a night, if you don't mind. I have to take my grandmother to the airport tomorrow morning. Maybe we can do something again next week."

Omigod. That is the worst brush-off I've ever had. Why does he have to contaminate his grandmother with his dirty lies? What guy says no to a drink? So he'll be a little tired in the car tomorrow. I spend half my life as if in a coma. Big deal. "Sure," I answer. "Whatever." Why isn't he interested? I'm not…what?

Good-looking enough? Witty enough? He doesn't like Star Wars? Listen, mister, you're cute but not exactly exploding with personality, either.

Back in Grandpop's mobile (he probably stole the car from Grandma, and then left her stranded on a street corner), I reason that since he's obviously not interested, I might as well look crass and ask him what he does for a living.

"I'm a high school social worker," he says.

Hmm. That's pretty cute.

"So why do you have to get up so early? Your school starts at six?"

"No, I jog in the morning and then volunteer as staff advisor for the yearbook before classes start."

"I was one of the yearbook editors for my high school," I offer. Wendy and I decided to do it together. But we never met before class. In fact, I tried to schedule as many meetings as possible during class. And we definitely didn't have a staff advisor who looked like Tim. "Do you want to run your own practice someday?"

"Maybe. Right now I like being able to be hands-on with so many kids."

If anyone else would have said that I *might* have taken it the wrong way.

Okay, so he'll never be rich, but he does have integrity. Isn't that just my luck. I finally meet a guy who's cute, a planner, cultured, loves kids, and likes to use his hands, and he doesn't want to have anything more to do with me.

Why why why? What's wrong with me?

He drops me off at my door.

"I'll call you," he says.

"Good night," I say, holding back tears. Why doesn't he like me? What am I going to say to Julie? She'll be terribly uncomfortable around me, like when you see someone with food stuck in her teeth. You don't want to look, but you can't help it. She'll ignore me when I walk into the coffee room. Maybe she'll feel so guilty for setting me up for heartbreak, she'll bring me some chocolate. Or sour berries. They're sweet and sour simultaneously. Like the way you feel when you pluck your eyebrows. Mmm. I think I have a package at home.

Goodbye, my sweet and sour Timmy.

Maybe I should have straightened my hair.

Chapter Twelve

Abstinence Makes the Heart Grow Fonder

Week 1, Monday

9:15 a.m.
From: "Jacquelyn Norris" <JacquelynNorris@cupid.com>
To: WendyBerger@petersonmarcus.com
Subject: I don't get it

Hi!
Okay, get this. He called last night. Does that make sense? We went out on Saturday, he made up a lame excuse, and then he called. He said something about his grandmother insisting on taking an early flight. And then I asked, "Is she the type of grandmother who eats dinner at five o'clock?" And then he said, "Don't all grandmothers?" And then I asked, "Do you think it's a sudden thing that happens when you reach a certain age, or is it a gradual sliding into, this condition that makes you eat dinner at five?" And then he said, "I always eat at six on the dot because that's when I get home from soccer practice." He played in college and now he coaches JV after school. Can you imagine? Yearbook *and* soccer? If he were doing his college applications now, he'd be a shoe-in.

So then he asked me what sports I played. From his loud sigh I could tell that my "Me?" was the wrong answer. Luckily, I remembered the Tae Kwon Do and I told him how much I love it. Then he asked me what belt I was. When I answered white, he said, "That's cool." So it's possible he thinks white belts are advanced, like right before black or something. And then he asked me if I wanted to do something again next Saturday.

I am in love. I think. But what's his deal? Why blow me off one night only to ask me out again the next? And why ask me out almost a whole week in advance?

11:00 a.m.
From: "Wendy Berger"
<WendyBerger@petersonmarcus.com>
To: JacquelynNorris@cupid.com
Subject: Re: I don't get it

You do not love Tae Kwon Do. You never even go.

11:04 a.m.
From: "Jacquelyn Norris" <JacquelynNorris@cupid.com>
To: WendyBerger@petersonmarcus.com
Subject: Re:Re: I don't get it

Yes, I do. What do you know? Do you have a hidden camera in your computer or something? I don't think so. I just love it most when there's only five minutes left in the class. Fine, I love it the most when I'm sitting in my pajamas, freshly showered after the class.

Why is he so weird?

2:00 p.m.
From: "Wendy Berger"
<WendyBerger@petersonmarcus.com>
To: JacquelynNorris@cupid.com
Subject: Re:Re:Re: I don't get it

Is it possible he's a gentleman? Maybe he didn't want to risk the possibility of falling asleep at the wheel and driving poor Granny off the side of the highway. Maybe he called to reserve you for next Saturday night because he believes you are so incredibly popular, and if he doesn't bid for a prime night like Saturday way in advance, you will undoubtedly have made plans with an alternative party.

2:05 p.m.
From: "Jacquelyn Norris" <JacquelynNorris@cupid.com>
To: S.Emerson@speedymail.com
Subject: Fw: Re:Re:Re: I don't get it

What do you think? Could Wendy have a point? (See below.)

From: "Wendy Berger"
<WendyBerger@petersonmarcus.com>
To: JacquelynNorris@cupid.com
Subject: Re:Re:Re: I don't get it

Is it possible he's a gentleman? Maybe he didn't want to risk the possibility of falling asleep at the wheel and driving poor Granny off the side of the highway. Maybe he called to reserve you for next Saturday night because he believes you are so incredibly popular, and if he doesn't bid for a prime night like Saturday way in advance, you will undoubtedly have made plans with an alternative party.

3:00 p.m.
From: "Sam Emerson" <S.Emerson@speedymail.com>
To: JacquelynNorris@cupid.com
Subject: Re:Fw:Re:Re:Re: I don't get it

I think he's a freak!

3:02 p.m.
From: "Jacquelyn Norris" <JacquelynNorris@cupid.com>
To: S.Emerson@speedymail.com
Subject: Re:Re:Fw:Re:Re:Re: I don't get it

But so far he's been nice.

3:05 p.m.
From: "Sam Emerson" <S.Emerson@speedymail.com>
To: JacquelynNorris@cupid.com
Subject: Get It!

"So far" is the operative phrase! There's no statute of limitations on when a nice guy can become an asshole!

3:07 p.m.
From: "Jacquelyn Norris" <JacquelynNorris@cupid.com>
To: S.Emerson@speedymail.com
Subject: Re: Get It!

I like Wendy's opinion much better. Please stop drowning your e-mails in exclamation marks. You're giving me a headache.

3:20 p.m.
From: "Sam Emerson" <S.Emerson@speedymail.com>
To: JacquelynNorris@cupid.com
Subject: Re:Re: Get It!

Didn't you say Wendy hasn't dated in over a year? What does she know? I must go teach.

3:30 p.m.
From: "Jacquelyn Norris" <JacquelynNorris@cupid.com>
To: WendyBerger@petersonmarcus.com
Subject: Strange behavior

Every single morning since I've been working at Cupid, I've run into Tim's sister Julie in the kitchen. *Every single morning.* I've never been sick. She's never been sick. We both have slight coffee addictions, and therefore repeatedly visit the coffee machine. And the bathroom. So tell me, why is it that today, the Monday morning after my date with her brother, she suddenly pulls a disappearing act? I haven't seen her *all* day. Maybe he told her he doesn't like me. Maybe she realized *she* doesn't like me and no longer wants me fraternizing with her family members.

4:00 p.m.
From: "Wendy Berger"
<WendyBerger@petersonmarcus.com>
To: JacquelynNorris@cupid.com
Subject: Re: Strange behavior

Maybe she bought a thermos and stopped by Starbucks this

morning. It would have to have been decaf (not a diuretic), otherwise you would have met her in the bathroom.

4:30 p.m.
From: "Jacquelyn Norris" <JacquelynNorris@cupid.com>
To: WendyBerger@petersonmarcus.com
Subject: Re:Re: Strange behavior

Because of Julie's AWOL behavior, I have not been able to hear the lines I've been dying to hear, like "I hear you guys hit it off," or "I hear you two love birds are going out again," and "I'm sorry I ruined your date by not offering to take Granny to the airport." Speaking of which, once Tim and I get more serious, we'll need to have words. I'm planning on reorganizing the unbalanced proportions of his family responsibilities.

Friday

1:00 p.m.
From: "Send-a-Smile" <Send-a-smile@e-cards.net>
To: JacquelynNorris@cupid.com
Subject: A smile for you!

You have a greeting from *Send-a-smile*! Please open the attachment!
(Binary attachment):
   I think we'd make a great pear!
(Picture of pear inserted here.)
Can't wait for tomorrow!
Tim

1:05 p.m.
From: "Jacquelyn Norris" <JacquelynNorris@cupid.com>
To: S.Emerson@speedymail.com;
WendyBerger@petersonmarcus.com
Subject: Fw: A smile for you!

Isn't this sweet? *Really* sweet. (See below.)

From: "Send-a-Smile" <Send-a-smile@e-cards.net>
To: JacquelynNorris@cupid.com
Subject: A smile for you!

You have a greeting from *Send-a-smile*! Please open the attachment!
(Binary attachment):
  I think we'd make a great pear!
(Picture of pear inserted here.)
Can't wait for tomorrow!
Tim

3:30 p.m.
From: "Sam Emerson" <S.Emerson@speedymail.com>
To: JacquelynNorris@cupid.com;
WendyBerger@petersonmarcus.com
Subject: Re:Fw: A smile for you!

What about the exclamation marks!!! And you don't even like pears.

3:36 p.m.
From: "Jacquelyn Norris" <JacquelynNorris@cupid.com>
To: S.Emerson@speedymail.com;
WendyBerger@petersonmarcus.com
Subject: Re:Re:Fw: A smile for you!

It's not that I don't like them, they make my teeth itch. I like them; I just can't eat them.

4:00 p.m.
From: "Wendy Berger"
<WendyBerger@petersonmarcus.com>
To: JacquelynNorris@cupid.com; S.Emerson@speedymail.com
Subject: Re:Re:Re:Fw: A smile for you!

I hate when you say that! Your gums itch, not your teeth! I think the card is cute. Let me know how the date goes.

*   *   *
Week 2, Monday

9:08 a.m.
From: "Jacquelyn Norris" <JacquelynNorris@cupid.com>
To: WendyBerger@petersonmarcus.com
Subject: Where are you?

I have to tell you about my date! (Note the exclamation mark.) Why didn't you call me all weekend? I've left at least four hundred messages on your cell phone, work phone, home phone, and beeper.

Tim brought me red tulips. Wasn't that sweet? They were *so* pretty. Three points. Two, actually. When he showed up at my door with his hands behind his back, I could see green stems peeking out from behind him, and I thought he had brought me roses. It's not that I'm disappointed he brought tulips—that would be ridiculous since I wasn't expecting anything at all—but what girl doesn't prefer roses?

This time he came up to my apartment, I assume so that I could put the bouquet of nonroses in a vase. Not that I have a vase. An empty bottle of Zinfandel served me nicely.

Actually, he gets only one point for the tulips. Why didn't he bring a vase?

Sam said he was cute. Not to his face, naturally, but knowing Sam these days, I wouldn't have been surprised if she had.

He took me to the Starlight Bowling Alley. Bowling! Can you imagine? It's essentially a regular bowling alley with glow-in-the dark lanes and the same glow-in-the-dark stars my sister has on her ceiling. I've never actually been bowling on a date. Don't get me wrong, I like bowling—kind of. It's just that I've never been crazy about the shoe situation. Sam would have freaked. I can see her thoughts on the subject as clearly as call-outs in an Archie comic: "Wear shoes that have been worn by hundreds of others?" "Don't you understand the germ potential?" "Don't they watch *20/20*?" I have to be fair, she's been a lot less neurotic since the breakup. The other night, I made chicken soup for dinner, and she asked if she could try some right from my bowl. She fearlessly swallowed all the contaminated liquid. Except that she used her own spoon, of course.

Anyway, Tim and I put on our imperfectly fitting bowling shoes—mine were too big, his too small—and took our places at an assigned lane. In the lighting, his teeth glowed like little halogen light bulbs. I'm glad I wore my charcoal pants and black sweater, but I prayed I didn't have dandruff, because the girl in the lane next to me did and the whole bowling alley could see it.

Anyway, I knocked down two pins with my first ball. My second got me one more. So I'm thinking, three's pretty good, right?

Wrong. It was a good thing I'd already told him I wasn't an athlete.

Tim got a strike. What does good bowling aim say about a man's sexual performance?

A couple of turns later, I unexpectedly got a strike. Yay! So I did the strike dance—you know, the little jig I do to imitate the dancing motions of the stick figure on the screen above the lane. In a way, my spontaneous dance was a test. If I'm as weird as I want to be, will Tim still like me?

Apparently so, since he actually *laughed* (with me, not at me—note the distinction) when I explained what I was doing. And when he got a spare, he ridiculously attempted a dance of his own. Arguably, his dance was a lot more difficult than the one I did, since the spare stick figure on the screen prances around on only one foot.

Then he offered to teach me to bowl with one hand, but said, ''Not that you don't look extremely cute doing your two-handed throw.''

I said, ''Advise me, advisor.'' Wasn't that a good line?

He held my arm and helped me with my swing, just like in a cheesy TV show! Wasn't that sweet? Jeremy would never have done a thing like that. In fact, we hardly ever went anywhere. For dinner sure, but not bowling. Never to a museum.

After bowling, he took me to a small bar I'd never heard of. Not that I'm an expert on Boston bars. He took my hand and led me to a booth beside the back windows.

And then...

He told me I looked just like Sarah Jessica Parker.

Much better than Chelsea Clinton.

Later, when we were sitting in front of my apartment in his grandfather-mobile, he asked me out again for next weekend. *A full week in advance!* Not six days in advance, but I repeat, a full week. And of course, I said yes, not that you can actually say no to someone's face. You'd have to go home, wait a day, and then leave a message on his voice mail with an excuse like you've come down with Ebola, or you have to pick up your grandmother at the airport—no, scratch that second reason. Luckily, I want to see him again so this isn't a problem.

Anyway, I just sat there, waiting. I figured after two dates, a kiss would definitely be in order. Except I wasn't exactly sure how it should take place. A normal guy would have been all over me by this time—if of course, my other A.B. (After Breakup) dates could be considered normal. So there I was, wondering if maybe I should lean over and kiss him good-night on the cheek. But what if I he thought I was making a move? What if I leaned in too much and missed his cheek, pecking him on his forehead, or his chin, or God forbid, his nose? How ridiculous would that have been? I placed my hand on his arm. "Good night," I said in my most demure voice. "I had I great time."

"Good night," he replied.

I held my breath. Was it going to happen? Would he be the one to make the lean?

"I'll call you this week," he said.

Weird. So what do you think?

11:30 a.m.
From: "Wendy Berger"
<WendyBerger@petersonmarcus.com>

To: JacquelynNorris@cupid.com
Subject: I'm here!

Sorry I didn't get back to you this weekend. My workload is out of control. I don't have a second to eat, never mind talk on the phone. Judging from your thesis, you're not quite as busy as I am at the office.

I hate my life.

What am I saying? I don't have a life.

He sounds like a sweetheart. Don't screw it up.

Wednesday

10:30 a.m.
From: "Jacquelyn Norris" <JacquelynNorris@cupid.com>
To: WendyBerger@petersonmarcus.com
Subject: List

A.

Good things about Tim:

1.   He's sweet.
2.   He's cute.
3.   He cares about his grandmother.
4.   He plans fun activities. (Maybe he'll take me skiing, or even apple picking. Or karaoke. I've always wanted to try karaoke, but you always refused to come with me.)
5.   He's sweet.
6.   He's cute.
7.   He likes kids (not an immediate bonus, but definitely good in the long run).
8.   He's cute.
9.   He thinks I'm cute.

B.   Bad things about Tim:

1.   He lives at home. (Will he be allowed to sleep over?)
2.   He goes to sleep really early. (What's the point of having a boyfriend if Sam is the last person I usually speak to before I go to asleep?)

C.   Conclusion:

Good presently outweighs bad. Yay!

* * *
Week 3, Monday

9:30 a.m.
From: "Jacquelyn Norris" *<JacquelynNorris@cupid.com>*
To: WendyBerger@petersonmarcus.com
Subject: Third date

He brought chocolates. Wasn't that sweet? And they're the kind that are filled with pastel crème. Except he said, "Hope you like them, babe." Now I have to make a revision to "Bad things about Tim." New entry (B3): He called me "babe."

We went for Italian in the north end. We had to wait a half hour outside in the freezing cold for a table, but Tim swore they made the best Caesar salad in the city. He insisted on treating, even though I did the fake reach. The Caesar salad was pretty amazing, but I was so looking forward to dessert (if you get my drift), that I hardly tasted a thing.

When he pulled up in front of my house I told him I had a great time. "Me, too," he replied.

It was *so* time for the kiss. I was freaking out at this point, wondering if I should just kiss him and get the ball rolling. Should I just grab him? But wouldn't he do the grabbing if he were really interested? What would the Fashion Magazine Fun Fact be to speed up this painstakingly slow process? To draw attention to my lips? Oh, why didn't I bring a lollipop?

I started licking my lips.

"Are your lips dry?" he asked. "I have some Chap Stick, if you'd like."

"Uh...no thanks." And then I decided that if he didn't kiss me in the next twenty-five seconds, our relationship was over.

He put his hand on my cheek and then—get this—asked, "Would it be okay if I kissed you?"

How sweet was that?

And he did.

5:00 p.m.
From: "Wendy Berger"
<WendyBerger@petersonmarcus.com>

To: JacquelynNorris@cupid.com
Subject: Re: Third date

   So? I want kiss details!!!!!!!

                        Tuesday

9:15 a.m.
From: "Jacquelyn Norris" <JacquelynNorris@cupid.com>
To: WendyBerger@petersonmarcus.com
Subject: Re:Re: Third date

   It was pretty good. Except that he tasted like Caesar salad dressing.
   By the way, I called him last night to ask him if he wants to see a cheapie movie tonight.

11:30 a.m.
From: "Wendy Berger"
<WendyBerger@petersonmarcus.com>
To: JacquelynNorris@cupid.com
Subject: Re:Re:Re: Third date

   You called him? You're joining the women's movement after all!
   P.S.
   What happened to the once-a-week plan?

11:35 a.m.
From: "Jacquelyn Norris" <JacquelynNorris@cupid.com>
To: WendyBerger@petersonmarcus.com
Subject: Re:Re:Re:Re: Third date

   I've evolved.

2:37 p.m.
From: "Wendy Berger"
<WendyBerger@petersonmarcus.com>
To: JacquelynNorris@cupid.com
Subject: Re:Re:Re:Re:Re: Third date

   So how long are you going to wait…?

2:40 p.m.
From: "Jacquelyn Norris" <JacquelynNorris@cupid.com>
To: WendyBerger@petersonmarcus.com
Subject: Re:Re:Re:Re:Re:Re: Third date

Not much longer!

4:42 p.m.
From: "Wendy Berger"
<WendyBerger@petersonmarcus.com>
To: JacquelynNorris@cupid.com
Subject: Re:Re:Re:Re:Re:Re:Re: Third date

How long is not much longer?

4:50 p.m.
From: "Jacquelyn Norris" <JacquelynNorris@cupid.com>
To: WendyBerger@petersonmarcus.com
Subject: Re:Re:Re:Re:Re:Re:Re:Re: Third date

What time is it now? Ten to five? The movie will be over by twelve, right? In a little over seven hours the six-month dry spell will be over!

4:59 p.m.
From: "Wendy Berger"
<WendyBerger@petersonmarcus.com>
To: JacquelynNorris@cupid.com
Subject: Re:Re:Re:Re:Re:Re:Re:Re:Re: Third date

SLUT!!!!!!!!!!!!!!!!!! :-)

Wednesday

9:30 a.m.
From: "Jacquelyn Norris" <JacquelynNorris@cupid.com>
To: WendyBerger@petersonmarcus.com
Subject: Fourth date

Unfortunately I'm not a slut. But I am trying very hard.

There wasn't even any hand-brushing in the popcorn (but that's because I had sours instead), or a secret shoulder squeeze in the dark.

Even the movie was good.

I invited him up later. I kissed him in the elevator. He kissed me back. He sat down next to me on the couch. I turned on *Law and Order*, which was just starting (the movie was shorter than anticipated).

Technically, it was his turn to kiss me.

But no.

Ten minutes passed. He still hadn't puckered up.

Twenty more minutes passed. We were already at the Order part…

I didn't understand what he was waiting for, considering that he supposedly gets up early and it was already almost midnight. He was too fixated on the TV to notice my impatience—or my existence altogether. At the commercial, I attempted a snuggle.

Finally, he remembered he wasn't alone, and the kissing began. But ten minutes later, he yawned and asked me out for Saturday night (all in one breath). And then he left.

Why would he have asked me out *again* if he doesn't want to fool around? Do I have B.O.? Please tell me the truth.

Did I tell you he volunteers for Just-a-Meal? In the winter he drives around Boston, handing out sandwiches to homeless people. And he organizes the Boston blood drive. He has lots of causes. I think he may be a saint. Do saints wait longer than normal people to have sex? Do saints even have sex?

How can I make my practically regrown hymen one of his causes?

Thursday

3:00 p.m.
From: "Wendy Berger"
<WendyBerger@petersonmarcus.com>
To: JacquelynNorris@cupid.com
Subject: Re: Fourth date

You have to be dead before you can be canonized.
You do not have B.O.

Week 4, Monday

9:30 a.m.
From: "Jacquelyn Norris" <JacquelynNorris@cupid.com>
To: WendyBerger@petersonmarcus.com
Subject: Fifth date

There was physical contact, sort of. His hand lightly grazed the outside of my shirt. The whole scene played itself out on the couch.
I'm seeing him again tomorrow. I'm trying to convince Sam to sleep at Philip's (the guy from the bookstore). I don't want anything around to distract him.
Why do you have to be dead before getting canonized? They do it to pets all the time. Kidding.

3:00 p.m.
From: "Wendy Berger"
<WendyBerger@petersonmarcus.com>
To: JacquelynNorris@cupid.com
Subject: Re: Fifth date

Better keep Sam around. Sounds as if Tim can use all the help he can get! Also kidding.

Wednesday

11:26 a.m.
From: "Jacquelyn Norris" <JacquelynNorris@cupid.com>
To: WendyBerger@petersonmarcus.com
Subject: Sixth date

I think I have a boyfriend. We escaped the couch last night and made it to my room. My bra finally came off. But that's all that got off last night.
This is all taking a lot longer than anticipated. Do you think my boyfriend is a sexual?

3:00 p.m.
From: "Wendy Berger"
<WendyBerger@petersonmarcus.com>
To: JacquelynNorris@cupid.com
Subject: Re: Sixth date

Do I think he's a sexual what? Or do you mean "asexual"?
Don't you get paid to proofread?

Friday

11:00 a.m.
From: "Jacquelyn Norris" <JacquelynNorris@cupid.com>
To: S.Emerson@speedymail.com
Subject: Help!

Have I ever given you permission to go to sleep before I
come home? I needed to talk to you!! I saw Tim again last
night and he still hasn't made the big move. It's been a month!
Is there something wrong with him, or am I fat and ugly? Be
honest.
    P.S.
    The kids at his school have gone farther than we have.
What's wrong with this picture?

2:00 p.m.
From: "Sam Emerson" <S.Emerson@speedymail.com>
To: JacquelynNorris@cupid.com
Subject: Re: Help!

I think he's gay.

2:06 p.m.
From: "Jacquelyn Norris" <JacquelynNorris@cupid.com>
To: S.Emerson@speedymail.com
Subject: Re:Re: Help!

Why would he keep asking me out if he doesn't like
women?

2:10 p.m.
From: "Sam Emerson" <S.Emerson@speedymail.com>
To: JacquelynNorris@cupid.com
Subject: Re:Re:Re: Help!

Gay.

2:18 p.m.
From: "Jacquelyn Norris" <JacquelynNorris@cupid.com>
To: S.Emerson@speedymail.com
Subject: Re:Re:Re:Re: Help!

He doesn't seem gay. It would be far too wasteful for
womankind if he was gay. And he has all these causes. And he
wears great clothes. *Manly* clothes. Do you think he's just
taking his time? Maybe he doesn't want to rush things.

2:20 p.m.
From: "Sam Emerson" <S.Emerson@speedymail.com>
To: JacquelynNorris@cupid.com
Subject: Re:Re:Re:Re:Re: Help!

Nope. Gay.

Week 5, Wednesday

1:30 p.m.
From: "Jacquelyn Norris" <JacquelynNorris@cupid.com>
To: WendyBerger@petersonmarcus.com
Subject: I give up.

It's been five weeks and he still hasn't tried to sleep with
me. I'm starting to think he's a virgin. A twenty-six-year-old
male virgin. And here I thought he was a real hands-on kind of
guy!

I know some (a few) female virgins, but male virgins? Do
you think he's all moral and waiting for marriage, or just
hasn't found anyone to do it with? I've heard about this
"abstinence" trend.

A lot of the heroines in Cupid books are virgins. I don't

think any of the heroes are, though. Wouldn't that be
something a guy would mention? Virgin men should wear a
painted sign around their necks. A big, scarlet V. It should be a
law.

Does this mean we're never going to do it?

Thursday

11:10 p.m.
From: "Wendy Berger"
<WendyBerger@petersonmarcus.com>
To: JacquelynNorris@cupid.com
Subject: Re: I give up

Maybe abstinence will make him propose faster. Have you
met his parents yet?

Friday

9:22 a.m.
From: "Jacquelyn Norris" <JacquelynNorris@cupid.com>
To: WendyBerger@petersonmarcus.com
Subject: Re:Re: I give up

No, I keep telling him that it makes more sense for him to
come to my place than for me to go to his. Besides, we've
only been dating for five weeks! We're not really at the meet-
the-parents stage yet.

11:03 p.m.
From: "Wendy Berger"
<WendyBerger@petersonmarcus.com>
To: JacquelynNorris@cupid.com
Subject: Re:Re:Re: I give up

Let me get this straight. You haven't known him long
enough to meet the people he lives with, yet you've known
him long enough to share the most intimate experience two
people can share—exchanging bodily fluids…and I don't mean
kissing.

* * *
Week 6, Monday

11:00 a.m.
From: "Jacquelyn Norris" <JacquelynNorris@cupid.com>
To: WendyBerger@petersonmarcus.com
Subject: Re:Re:Re:Re: I give up

So what are you suggesting, that I shouldn't have sex, or that I should meet his parents?

Helen just plopped a huge manuscript on my desk. I don't even know why she's giving this to me. Shauna's the one who usually circulates this stuff. This one doesn't have any of the proper forms—getting sloppy, are we, Helen? I'm not even finished with *The Virgin Sighed with Pleasure,* but she wants me to get started on this right away. It's called *The Millionaire Takes a Bride.*   Now that's original.

Not that I'd mind meeting a millionaire. Or being a bride. But why aren't these books ever about normal, everyday guys? Like social workers?

11:10 a.m.
From: "Wendy Berger"
<WendyBerger@petersonmarcus.com>
To: JacquelynNorris@cupid.com
Subject: Re:Re:Re:Re:Re: I give up

On second thought, forget the parents. Go for the gusto. Your challenge will be an inspiration to all womankind! Go forth and conquer!

Friday

1:05 p.m.
From: "Jacquelyn Norris" <JacquelynNorris@cupid.com>
To: S.Emerson@speedymail.com;
WendyBerger@petersonmarcus.com;
Nat.Moore@speedynet
Subject: HELP!!!

Calling all girls! It's been six weeks! It's going to be this weekend or never! Any suggestions?

2:00 p.m.
From: "Natalie Moore" <Nat.Moore@speedynet>
To: JacquelynNorris@cupid.com
Subject: Re: HELP!!!

Six weeks! Six weeks and you haven't slept with him? Why don't you just make the first move already? Just *tell* him you want to have sex. Or say, "I want you." Even better, tell him, "I want you *inside* me." That one's a killer. You always tell me never to underestimate the power of prepositions. So use one!

Orgasm tonight?

3:15 p.m.
From: "Jacquelyn Norris" <JacquelynNorris@cupid.com>
To: Nat.Moore@speedynet
Subject: Re:Re: HELP!!!

I doubt if I could say that without laughing. But you've given me an idea. First I'll read him an excerpt from *The Millionaire Takes a Bride,* the book I'm editing. Here's a good line: "His fingers slipped between her silky thighs to toy with the tiny pink plug that lay there waiting, the trigger to her passion, and a searing heat raced through her veins." Then I'll manage to allude to the sentence (indirectly) while we're watching *Law and Order.* Logan will pull out his gun, and I'll wink and say, "Do you think he's toying with his gun?" Or maybe, "Do you think there'll be a bang?"

I can't come to Orgasm tonight. Tim and I have plans. Actually, I have plans for *him.* Tonight's the night. It's the weekend. It's Friday. Sam's staying at Philip's. I'm going to straighten my hair. I'm even making dinner.

Do you think macaroni and cheese is an aphrodisiac?

Chapter Thirteen

The Quasi Girlfriend Sighed

My night starts off just like page ninety-four of *The Millionaire Takes a Bride*. Except that the hero's not a millionaire and I'm not his bride.

After dinner they move into her bedroom. He devours her with kisses, his mouth pulled toward hers by an indefinable magnetic attraction. He unbuttons her pale azure blouse with agonizingly deliberate motions, never once abandoning her lips. Finally, he removes her blouse, exposing the creamy smoothness of her flesh (and her wonderful cleavage, thanks to Victoria's Secret). His hands caress her soft shoulders, her upper arms, the curvaceous swell of her belly (my euphemism for she hasn't been doing her morning sit-ups), and he dips beneath her bra. He unclasps it (it's a front enclosure; she's surprised he's worked that out so quickly), and her pale breasts spill onto his eager hands. He caresses her right breast first, and then the left (our hero is very methodical), and then flicks his tongue across her silky, erect nipples (again, right first, left next). Slowly, ever so slowly, he lowers his hands down to the small of her back, and with an urgency he can't deny, crushes her against his taut chest.

She sinks into him, resting her luscious mouth against his earlobe. Her hips involuntarily writhe against him, as she hungrily pulls him on top of her. Intense heat burns through her thighs, threatening to consume her body and soul. Her fingers clench his hair, his back, his shoulders.

With a groan (he's a noise-maker! Yay!), he rips her skirt and panties away. (What girl actually uses the term "panties"? Oh, and his jeans have already been removed—did I forget to mention this?) She reciprocates by pushing off his boxers. (Boxers? What kind of a hero wears boxers?) The moment has arrived.

An alarm rings in her head. "Do you have any…"

"No, I didn't think…"

"I did and I have." She reaches into her side drawer and pulls out a condom. She opens the wrapper and slips it onto his ready, eager manhood.

Wrapping her legs around his waist, she slides him into her wetness, her heart a hammer in her chest. He lets out another groan, and then bingo—here's where any semblance to *The Millionaire Takes a Bride* comes to an abrupt end.

Comes being the operative word here.

He explodes in orgasm.

Explodes in orgasm?

That's it? That's what I've been pining for? That's why I cooked him dinner? What business does a hero have coming after only one thrust? What happened to hours of passion? What happened to my multiple climaxes?

Do guys realize when they're bad in bed, or is it the phenomenon similar to ugly people not realizing they're ugly?

But wait, hold on a minute. (I wish *he* had held on a minute. Better yet, an hour.) What if he *was* a virgin? That would account for his, well, let's just call it overzealousness.

Should I be flattered?

But what if he knows he came too fast and was expecting me to say, "It's okay, dear. Don't worry about it, dear. It doesn't matter, dear."

Yeah, right.

"I don't want to go home, babe," he says in a muffled voice. He's still on top of me, his head resting above my shoulder.

"So stay." I'd actually prefer to have the bed to spread out in, but whatever. At least we get to try it again. However, at the present moment I'm having difficulty breathing under his weight. I close my eyes. He should really get off me before the condom rolls into me and we have to rush to Emergency to get it surgically removed.

I nudge him gently. Good God, has he fallen asleep? "Tim?" No answer. "Tim?" I nudge him again. "Tim!" I shove him off my body. "I have to use the washroom." The Fashion Magazine Fun Fact # 6 is to pee right after sex to avoid getting a bladder infection. Or maybe it's a yeast infection. Not that what Tim and I did can really count as sex.

I use the washroom, running the water so he doesn't hear. Is this ridiculous? As if guys don't know that girls pee. I make a pit stop in the kitchen to pour two glasses of water. We're not at the sharing-one-glass stage just yet.

Am I being too hard on him?

When I climb back into bed, I notice the time. It's 11:55. He's sitting up in bed, waiting. I notice there's a tent under the sheets.

Now that's more like it.

Then it hits me. I suddenly remember reading about the let's-get-the-first-time-over-with theory. The guy deliberately comes quickly, knowing that afterward, little Timmy will be able to stand at attention for hours.

At 11:59 he's asleep again.

So much for that theory.

Four minutes? What is four minutes? Four minutes is a commercial break. Four minutes is a music video. Four minutes should not be sex.

We're spooning now, his arm wrapped snuggly around my waist. It's too hot in here. I'm never going to fall asleep. Oh, God, he's sleeping on my side of the bed.

Why is he sleeping here, anyway? Won't his mother be worried about him?

And what kind of guy doesn't carry condoms with him, just in case?

When we wake up the next morning, we have the standard how-many-people talk. It's probably the type of conversation you should have before doing the nasty, but whatever.

"Four," I say, "including you." If I can even count you, that is, which I still haven't decided.

"Who were they?"

Aren't we nosy? "My first time guy in college, one minor indiscretion my sophomore year, and Jer, my ex. What about you?" He'd better not tell me something lame like he's been waiting his whole life for someone as special as me.

"Um…more than four." More than four? It must be five.

"Five?"

"More than five."

This game is getting old fast. "I give up. How many?"

"Thirteen. Including you."

Thirteen? Is it possible that he's slept with twelve other women and no one, not one single one of them, has ever told him that one thrust is not sufficient?

Maybe I'm just unlucky thirteen. Maybe he's had fantastic sex with the previous twelve. Or, maybe I'm so attractive that he couldn't control himself.

Yeah, I like that last explanation best.

"So what do I do?"

"Train him," Natalie says.

"Leave a *Cosmo* opened on a sex page or something," Sam says.

"But he doesn't realize he needs training! He wasn't even embarrassed! It's as if he's oblivious to every film, literary, musical and television reference to sex ever made. What does he think 'All Night Long' is alluding to? Talking?"

"There are tricks to solving this kind of problem," Sam says knowingly.

Can you trick someone into having good sex? "Like what, for instance?"

"Like the stop-start technique. Have sex for a few minutes, then stop and do other stuff. Then start again," Sam explains.

"Do what other stuff?" I ask. "Order a pizza? Besides, it's

not easy to stop when there's a condom involved. I mean, what happens to it during the shrinkage interim?''

''Maybe condoms are your problem,'' Natalie offers.

''That makes no sense. Condoms should technically slow down the process, not speed it up,'' I reason. ''If we hadn't used a condom, the whole show would have been over in half a thrust.''

''Try two condoms,'' Sam pitches in.

''No.'' Natalie shakes her head. ''Two condoms might make him come faster. He'll be so worried he won't feel a thing through all that plastic, that he'll overcompensate.''

''Try it again,'' Sam advises. ''It was probably first-time jitters.''

Nope.

You've got mail.

A message from *Send-a-smile* flashes across the screen. ''Hi, babe!'' the text says. Next to it is a large graphic of a pistachio, and more text that says, ''I'm nuts about you!''

Twenty minutes later. *You've got mail* pops up on my screen again.

Another message from *Send-a-smile.* ''A whole day without you is the pits.'' A cherry pops up on the screen.

How symbolic. I'm starting to feel like a virgin again where Tim is concerned.

This problem requires in-depth analysis. I'm about to e-mail Sam, when I realize that immediate feedback is called for. Why doesn't someone develop a vocal e-mail system in which the sounds are transmitted instantaneously? It would work something like a chat room, only with voices, and fast. There would be a dial tone to indicate that the server is up and ready, and a system to record your voice if the recipient is not at the computer or is busy chatting to someone else.

I pick up the phone.

Sam is probably home by now, so I try her there. ''Help! I

tried every trick in the book. For example, in the middle of his first thrust I said, 'Wait, don't come yet. It feels *so* good.' He said okay, he'd try, but then two shoves later it was all over, and he rolled over and went to sleep. How can I have a relationship with this guy? Let's say we end up having sex three times a week, and each time takes five minutes. I'll be spending only fifteen minutes a week having sex, while I spend 174 $1/4$ hours doing other stuff! This is a ridiculous proportion. How can I spend only 1/700 of the week having sex? What will I do the rest of the time?''

"Oh, hi, Jackie," Sam says. "What's up?"

"Is it possible I don't like him anymore because he likes me? Is the challenge over? Am I that screwed up?'' I'm nearly hysterical. "Maybe Bev is right. Maybe I need therapy. Do I only like men who don't want me? Am I going to spend the rest of my life chasing men who don't care about me, while ignoring the men who worship me? He wants me to meet his parents. I do not want to meet his parents. Why would I want to meet his parents? I can't marry a 1/700 guy.''

"No," Sam replies, "you don't need therapy. You don't like him because he's terrible in bed. Life's too short for bad sex. Dump him. I have to go now.''

So much for in-depth examination.

"Jacquelyn?" Yuck. Helen.

"Yes?"

"Thanks for copyediting *The Millionaire Takes a Bride*."

Thanks? Thanks? Since when does Helen thank me? "Oh. You're welcome. It *is* my job.''

"Right. It is.''

For some reason Helen seems flustered. Does she know I'm sleeping (kind of) with her other copy editor's brother? "So, um…what did you think?'' she asks.

Think? When is thinking involved? "Think of the book?''

"Yes. Did you like it?''

"Yeah. Good plot.''

"Really? What else?''

Well, once she's asking… "Okay. I have a few editorial suggestions. First of all, you know when he first sees her? I think
the author needs to add a few more sensory details. The scene is
a little bland. I can't smell him. What does he smell like? Is he
wearing cologne? Right now there's too much telling, not enough
showing. And the wedding scene needs a bit of a point of view
tune-up. It's a little jarring. The narrative jumps all over the place
without finding a home. I know the author wants the reader to
identify with both characters, but it's annoying. Just as I get into
the hero's head, I'm yanked back to the heroine. I need to be
able to get a bit more comfortable. And I especially don't care
about the mother's point of view during the wedding. Letting her
thoughts come through is a mistake. And the aunt? She has no
purpose. All her lines can be said by the mother. Tell the author
to exercise her finger with the delete button and get rid of her."

She looks stunned. Well, she *did* ask. Apparently she didn't know
I could talk. "I'll be sure to incorporate your opinions into my edit."

"Oh, one more thing. Great sex scenes. This should not be in
True Love. It's so *Love and Lust*."

She smiles. "Thank you."

"You're welcome." That was fun.

You've got mail.

If this is another cheesy card from Tim I'm going to kill myself. No, I'm going to kill *him*. If he tells me how special I am
one more time, I'm breaking up with him.

Hi, Jackie,
I'm home! I'm at my parents in New York. How's every-
thing? I had a fantastic trip. Can't wait to show you pictures.
Give me a call or write back.
Jer

Omigod. Omigod. Omigod.

Should I call him? I can't call him. But he wants to see me.
He wants to show me pictures. He's home. Will the Dutch bimbo

be in the pictures? Will he try to avoid hurting my feelings by removing all bimbo-related pictures from his album? Will he have two separate albums, one specifically bimbo-free for me, and one for his psychologically stable viewers? Would he put in that kind of effort for me? Does he love me that much? Is he still planning on moving to Boston to do his masters program? If so, he'll hang out at Orgasm. Will he live in Back Bay, also? Does he have an apartment already?

I'm going to lose five pounds for when I run into him at Orgasm. I'm going to have a gazillion men surrounding me, and he's going to spot me from across the bar, amazed at how fantastic I look. I'm going to be wearing my hooker boots and a slutty skirt and top, and he'll forget why he ever left me in the first place.

If he wants to talk to me so badly he could call. Or e-mail again. If he e-mails again, I'll write him back.

You know something? I haven't seen Wendy in a while. Maybe I should visit her in New York over Christmas. I'm sure she'd love to see me. We can have girl talks. I want to go to New York. To see Wendy. I want to go to New York because I haven't seen Wendy in months. I am going to New York because I miss Wendy.

"I'm thinking of coming to visit you," I tell her that night.

"Now's really not a good time," she tells me.

Don't say that. I'm coming. I have to come. "Why not?"

"I don't leave work until one in the morning. I won't be able to spend any time with you."

"But it's Christmas!" Maybe she can just leave me the keys to her apartment?

"Which, being Jewish, I don't celebrate."

"But your company does. They can't expect you to work when everyone else is off."

"This is true. I suppose I can take one day off. A half day at least. Maybe."

There is a God. "That's good."

"You're going to come all the way to New York to see me for one day?" Uh-oh. I think she's suspicious.

"I miss you."

"And your visit has nothing to do with Jer being in New York?"

Nailed. "How do you know he's back?"

"Our department was having its Christmas dinner at Katsura, the new trendy Japanese restaurant, and I ran into him at the bar."

"You saw him and didn't tell me?"

"I didn't want to upset you. I know you're in dangerous Tim territory, and I thought that this tidbit of information would throw you off-balance."

She saw him and didn't tell me? How could she do that? She should have phoned me immediately from the bar. "What do you mean, upset me? Who was he with? Was he with his Dutch bimbo? Tell me he wasn't with his Dutch bimbo. Is she pretty? Is she prettier than me?"

"I'm sure his Thailand fling didn't come home with him. He came to the bar with some Penners—Rob, Jon, and Crystal."

Crystal, huh? He always liked Crystal. "Was he *with* Crystal or just with Crystal?"

"He was with a whole group. I didn't even see him talking to Crystal."

He once told me that he thought Crystal Werner, who was on the student council with him, was cute. Like I wanted to hear that. He'd better not have been with Crystal.

"I don't care that he's back," I say for no reason. No reason because I know I'm lying and Wendy knows I'm lying, too. The only reason you should lie is because you think someone is going to believe you, and if that someone is not the person you're lying to, it should at least be yourself.

"You can stay with me if you want," Wendy says, reluctantly.

Well, yeah. Where else would I stay? Does she really think I'd even consider staying with Jer? I mean, I can always hope, but I wouldn't go to New York without a backup place. Can you

imagine the scene? Jer and I would be looking at a picture of a
Thai temple, and then he'd say, "This reminds me, where are
you staying?" As soon as he'd ask I'd know he wasn't expecting
me to stay with him, so I'd have to lie and say at Wendy's
because if I said a hotel he'd know I came just to see him, and
then he'd say, "That's nice. I'll call you a taxi." I'd have get
out of the taxi on the next block because I can't afford to ride
around in a cab all night, and I'd end up walking the streets of
New York, late at night, searching for a cheap hotel, and probably
get mugged.

"Thank you thank you thank you!"

"Are you going to call him?"

"No. *We're* going to run into him."

"*We* don't know his schedule."

"You ran into him once. I'm sure you can manage it again."

Yay! Christmas in New York!

It's a good thing I'm going away. Everyone is deserting Boston. Sam and her two brothers are visiting her grandparents in
Florida; Natalie and her parents are going on a Caribbean cruise;
and Andrew, like me, will be in New York, though visiting his
family, unlike me.

"Bev will be very disappointed." My dad is not pleased with
my change of plans.

"I know, but I just saw you Labor Day, and I haven't seen
Iris and Janie since July." Am I going to go to hell for lying
about where I'm going for Christmas? I could be the worst
daughter ever. My mother thinks I'm going to my dad's in Connecticut, and my dad thinks I'm going to my mother's in Virginia. Ah. I'm reaping the one benefit of having your parents
treat each other like strangers—they don't check up on each
other.

Tim, also, is not happy about me going away. "Why don't
you spend Christmas with me?" he suggests. "I dress up as Santa
at the orphanage."

Hmm. For some reason, the thought of Tim in a costume turns

me on. Maybe it has something to do with that man-in-a-uniform thing. Maybe it has something to do with me reading too many holiday romance novels. Should I give him one more chance? After all, a bird in the hand (Tim) is better than a bird in the bush (Jer). I refuse to take these bird/hand/bush puns any further.

Nah.

I think Santa could use a few more helpers. He just doesn't seem capable of ringing my sleigh bells.

Example 1: The other night he brought me a stuffed animal and a card that said, "I love you Bear-y much." How many bad puns can one person make?

Example 2: After Jer e-mailed me, I lied and told Tim I had my period. I was amazed he wasn't disappointed that we couldn't have sex that night. Amazed he didn't remember that I had just finished my period last week. Shouldn't guys remember these things? If a guy is such a good boyfriend, shouldn't he keep track?

I must end the insanity.

I hate breaking up with people.

Can't I just not return his phone calls? Is that wrong?

Now that I think about it, we've never discussed our relationship as being a relationship. Since I've never referred to him as my boyfriend (to his face anyway—and that's what's relevant here) and he's never called me his girlfriend, technically we're not even a couple. So technically I don't have to dump him.

All right, then. We're broken up.

Chapter Fourteen

Why is there a Worm in My Big Apple?

The first thing I see when I get off the train is Wendy frantically waving.

"Hi, stranger." I throw my arms around her, then step back. "You look fabulous!" I say and mean it. Her brown hair is tied back in a bun, and she's wearing a sophisticated pinstripe pantsuit with fancy black leather loafers. Very chic. And very skinny. Why is she so skinny? "Have you raided Ally McBeal's closet?"

"Hi!" she squeals. "Since I have no life, the only thing I have to spend my money on is ridiculously expensive clothes. Just one bag?"

"I'm here for only five days. How many bags do you want?" Maybe more than five days. Cupid closes down for the whole holiday, so I'm off work until the third. If Jer and I are getting along, maybe I can be convinced to stay over New Year's...

"Okay, here's the plan. It's three o'clock now. I'll take your bag with me to work, and you'll wander around the city for a few hours. Then you'll meet me back at my office at around nine. After that, it's up to you. Do you want to go out tonight? What about tomorrow? Tomorrow is Christmas Eve. Do you want to do something special? I may have to work in the morning, even though I'm pretty sure the office will close down later."

"Not really."

Hmm. I wonder where Jeremy is? How am I going to find him? Why didn't I call him before I came? What if he's not even in the city for the holidays? If he just got back, he wouldn't leave again so soon. But what if he did?

I'm a complete idiot. Who comes all the way to New York City to see a guy she doesn't even know will be in town? Should I call him now to ask what his plans are for tonight? But then he'll know I'm here specifically to see him. I have to accidentally-on-purpose run into him. How difficult can that be? The characters from *Friends* run into each other all the time.

I won't call him. I'm not going to call him. I think I'll do some window-shopping this afternoon. I love New York. I should move to New York. It's a little scary, though. I don't want to have to worry about getting mugged or murdered every time I step outside. They'd probably leave my body in Central Park, with no identification and no clothes—I can't even think about moving here until I lose a few pounds—and it would take the N.Y.P.D. weeks to figure out who I was.

I definitely watch too much *Law and Order.*

Speaking of losing weight, why is Wendy so thin? Is it all the walking? The hectic lifestyle? No time to eat? The city would go well with my new low-carb diet. I read about it in *City Girls.* No bread, no noodles, no fruit. The problem is that as soon as you start eating the stuff again, the diet is all over and back comes the weight. But that's fine, because it's only an I-haven't-seen-Jer-in-many-months-so-I-have-to-look-really-hot temporary diet. And it's working so far. I think. It's hard to tell. It's only been one day. Since breakfast, actually. After breakfast. And I had a salad for lunch. But no croutons.

My hands are cold. Why don't I have gloves? What happened to the pair I had last year? I think I lost them. The next time I buy gloves I should sew them to the sleeves of my jacket. But then I'd probably just lose the jacket.

By the time I meet Wendy at her office, my feet hurt, I'm starving, and my fingers are bloated and red. I change into a more appropriate going-out outfit—my high black boots and a little black dress—and we go to a trendy new Japanese restaurant for dinner. I order teriyaki salmon (low in carbs). Afterward, we go to a bar in West Chelsea for a drink. Wendy sees some investment banker people she knows, but no Jeremy. "I told you we weren't going to run into him," she says in her annoying I-told-you-so voice.

After an hour of me almost falling asleep at our table, we're on our way home. The good thing is that since I don't know anyone here, I can wear the same outfit tomorrow night.

We take a cab to Wendy's place in the Bronx. We're quiet when we open the door because her grandmother is already sleeping. I've pretty much known Bubbe Hannah as long as I've known Wendy, since she used to come to Danbury from New York to visit at least one weekend a month. She doesn't like me to call her Mrs. Teitelbaum. "It's Bubbe," she says in her thick Yiddish accent. So I call her Bubbe Hannah. Normally she'd be in Florida this time of year, but Wendy's cousin is having his bar mitzvah in the middle of January, so Bubbe Hannah had to postpone her trip. Supposedly the timing of the bar mitzvah caused quite an uproar among the geriatric crowd, regarding the necessary changes in their yearly migration schedules.

I'm sleeping with Wendy in her room, since the couch in the living room is covered in protective plastic, kind of like the sticky plastic stuff we had to cover all our textbooks with in grade school. It's not comfortable to sit on, never mind sleep on.

"You're not going to hog the entire blanket?" Wendy asks, throwing an extra pillow on her double bed.

"I don't hog blankets." Uh-oh. "I forgot to pack pajamas. Can I borrow?"

"Why am I not surprised?" She throws me longjohns and a T-shirt. "And you *do* hog blankets. You roll yourself around in them like a rolly-polly. Speaking of which, I'm going to get us some."

She goes to the kitchen and returns with slices of a dough roll rolled filled with jam, raisins, and nuts. Oh, well. I guess my diet officially starts tomorrow. We finish our snack, get washed and changed, close the blinds and the light, and crawl into bed.

"How many times do you think I stayed over at your house

in Danbury?'' I ask, rolling myself in the flower-patterned duvet. Just a little.

''At least once a week. How come you slept over at my place more than I stayed at yours?''

''You had brothers who would play with us. And better food.''

''True.'' Wendy sighs. ''I wish we still lived in the same city.''

''Maybe one day we will.''

''Maybe I'll quit my job and move to Boston.''

''Don't you like your job?''

''Not really. I mean, I guess the job's okay, sometimes, but I hate the hours. I really hate the hours. I'm usually there 'til eleven every night, sometimes past one. Is this a life?''

''But think of the money you're making! And you live rent-free! You're going to be filthy rich by the time you're thirty.''

''By the time I'm thirty! Are you crazy? I can't do this for another six years! I'll go insane! I'll lose so much weight I'll disappear!''

''So what do you want to do? Go to business school?''

''Maybe. But I don't have time to write all the essays. Maybe I'll do something fun like copyedit.''

''Yeah, real fun—I'm bored to tears. Inserting commas is not my ideal job. And you couldn't afford your fancy suits on my salary.''

''Maybe I'll just quit and take off some time to figure out what I want to do.''

''But you've always wanted to be in business.''

''Have I? Maybe I should have been a doctor. At least then I'd feel as if I'm contributing something to society.''

''So go to medical school.''

''Maybe I will.''

''You know what you're problem is, Wen? You've been focused for so long, you don't know how to be unfocused. You don't know how to just ease off and have a little fun. You know what I would do if I were you? I'd bum around the world for a while. Go to Italy, France, Greece. Just take off. No one to answer to. Just you and the unknown.''

''That's your style, Jack. Not mine. You're the one who just packed up and went to Boston. But you never know, maybe one day I'll do just that. Maybe one day I'll wake up and say, 'Enough! Goodbye nine to five, or nine to eleven, or nine to one, I'm off to join the circus!' ''

We have a moment of silence while Wendy, I assume, is contemplating how she would fit in with acrobats and clowns, what kind of wardrobe she would need, et cetera, et cetera...while my mind drifts to more immediate concerns.

''Should I call him?'' I ask.

''Now?''

''Not now. Tomorrow.''

''Why bother discussing it? You know you're going to call him.''

''No I don't.'' We both know this is not true, and laugh.

''Why do you miss him?'' she asks.

''Why?'' What kind of question is that? ''I don't know. I just do.''

''So then call him.''

''I shouldn't.''

''So don't.''

I'll worry about this tomorrow. Right now I'm too tired to exert the kind of energy this decision requires. ''Can we go to sleep now?''

''Yup. Good night.''

When the alarm goes off the next morning, I am quite pleased it's not for me. I fall back asleep and wake up at eleven to Bubbe Hannah knocking on the door.

''Vake up! Vake up, sleepyhead!''

''Hi, Bubbe Hannah,'' I mumble, sitting up. She kisses me on the cheek.

''Are you hungry? I made lunch.'' All her Us sound like Os, all her Ws like Vs.

''You really didn't have to,'' I tell her.

"Vat you talking about? I made chicken soup and lokshin, broiled chicken, raisin kugel, and my rolly-polly, of course."

What are the chances these are all carb-free?

I sit down at the table as five dishes are brought to me at once. Hmm. The chicken looks fine. The soup smells great, but it has lokshin noodles in it. I guess I can eat around them. The raisin kugel and rolly-polly are definite no-nos.

"Thank you so much for lunch," I say.

"It's my pleasure. My Vendy doesn't eat. No time, she says. No time to eat? Vat kind of life is that? Maybe you vant something else? Bread? Let me get you some bread."

"No thank you."

"No bread?"

"I'm on a special no-bread diet."

"Vy are you on a diet? You're too skinny. You girls today are all too skinny. Eat, bubelah, eat."

Too skinny? Me? I love this woman. Maybe I'll move in. Why can't I have a bubbe? "It's just a short-term diet. It's the new trend in diets these days. No bread or pasta."

"I've heard of it," Bubbe Hannah says, nodding. "It's called Passover."

I eat in silence for a few minutes.

"So tell me about Boston," she says.

"I like it."

"Vat do you like?"

"I like my job."

"Good. That's good. And your boyfriend? He's good, too? I'm happy you have a boyfriend. Vendy has no boyfriend. It's not good. It's not good for a girl so old to not have a boyfriend."

"Ah, come on, Bubbe Hannah. Wendy's still young. There's plenty of time for her to meet someone and get married."

"Time for her, maybe. But I'm not getting any younger. She vorks too hard. She comes home very late. She's not going to get married. Not like you. You I don't have to vorry about. So ven's the vedding?"

"Uh, we haven't decided, Bubbe Hannah. But soon. Real soon."

"Good. Just leave the plates on the table ven you finish. Don't you like the lokshin? Vy did you leave the lokshin? Eat the lokshin, bubelah." She leaves the kitchen to watch *Veel of Fortune*.

I eat the lokshin. I don't want to be rude. The diet starts right after lunch.

After lunch I take the subway to Thirty-fourth Street to look at the Macy's window display and to do some last-minute holiday shopping. I stop in front of the store window and look at my reflection. Why do I go on letting Bubbe Hannah think I'm with someone? What if I never meet anyone I want to marry?

Every Cupid book is based on the premise that the heroine and hero were meant for each other right from the start. My dad always says, "There's a lid for every pot." But this doesn't make sense. What if two people are perfectly matched but live in different countries? This would imply that luck plays a greater role in life than fate. I mean, what if the stars schedule you to meet your one true love at exactly three o'clock, but at one minute to three you sneeze and have to search through your handbag for a tissue? By the time you find one and are done with blowing your nose, the love of your life has rounded a corner and is out of your life forever. Is this what it all comes down to? A sneeze? No wonder we end up marrying whomever we happen to be dating in our mid-to-late twenties. We get desperate because we haven't met our soul mates. No wonder there are so many divorces.

My hands are cold. I need a new winter jacket, too. If I had gone to Danbury to visit my dad, I would have raided his company's coat inventory.

Should I call Jer? No, I'm not going to call him.

I could always call and hang up, just to see if he's home. He might not even be in town. He's probably not in town. I should check. Just to see if I'm wasting my time.

Where's a pay phone? I need to find a pay phone. I find a pay phone and dial his number before I change my mind.

Why am I doing this? It's ringing. What if his parents answer? I can't talk to his parents. What if he's not there?

"Hello?" It's his voice. He's home. He's on the phone. I'm on the phone with him.

"Hi," I say. "It's me."

"Hey!" His voice feels both strange and familiar. "How are you?"

"Good. How are you? Happy to be back?"

"A little. Happy to be clean. Miss the life. You know."

"Of course." Not really. What does *a little* happy mean?

"How's Boston?"

"Good," I lie. My job sucks, I have no friends except for Nat and Sam, and I miss you. "How are your mom and dad?"

"Good. They're away. Hawaii."

"You didn't want to go with them?"

"I just got back. I'm trying to settle in."

Pause. I can't hold in my whereabouts any longer. "I'm here."

"Here? In New York?"

"In New York."

"Where in New York?"

"Outside Macy's."

"Come over," he says without hesitation.

Do I want to go over there? Of course I want to go over there. "Okay." I need to find a place to change. Good thing I brought along Wendy's knapsack with my knee-high boots, black tights, a cute skirt, and my first-date shirt. Just in case.

I step out of the cab in front of his parents' apartment building on the Upper East Side. I smile at the doorman, and he calls up to the eighteenth floor to tell Jeremy he has a visitor. Two, three, four...you'd think such a fancy building would have a faster elevator. What am I doing what am I doing what am I doing? Don't think don't think don't think. About twelve hours later, the elevator opens. Why am I here? Why do I always react based on primal instincts rather than on rational thought?

He's leaning against his door, his arms crossed in front. Our eyes lock and I'm moderately concerned my knees may do the same.

The first time you see an ex after a substantial time, you kind of hope he looks a little worse. Not ugly—you don't want to wonder what you were doing with him in the first place. You want him to be just slightly less attractive to prove to yourself that he's not doing quite as well without you around.

He looks at home in dark jeans, a navy sweatshirt that make his eyes look even bluer, and an incredibly sexy twelve o'clock shadow.

And he's tanned. So much for him looking a little less attractive.

"Hi, there," he says.

"Hi."

Why does he have to be wearing that cologne? The one he knows I love?

I lean over to kiss him on the cheek, kind of, and he pulls me into him. Before I realize it, his lips are on my lips, my neck, and then back on my lips. We're still in the hallway and I'm touching his shirt, his arms, his face, and his hands are in my hair, on my back, on my skirt…

And so it goes.

"Do you want to see pictures?" he asks, wrapping the covers over my shoulders with one hand, fingering my belly ring with the other.

"Sure," I reply sleepily. "Only if it involves us not getting out of bed."

"No problem, they're right here." He kisses my forehead and pulls out two packages of photos from the drawer in his nightstand. "I haven't had a chance to put them in an album yet."

Only two rolls? I'm surprised. On one of our weekend ski trips he took four rolls. I guess he was too busy this time to be camera happy.

I wade through a stack of photos of him standing next to native Thai people. When he pulls out the second batch, I'm sure I'll have a heart attack. "This is the group I traveled with for about a month," he explains. "We moved through the country together." The first picture is of him, some French guy named François, and four girls. Two of the girls are tall blondes, one is a skinny redhead, and one is a short brunette. How do I know which one is the bimbo? I can't ask. Why is he showing me this picture? He shows me about five more pictures of the same group. Is he trying to kill me? I'm going into cardiac arrest.

Wonderful. A bikini shot. Which one is she? *Which one?* Could he have slept with all of them? Maybe he was sleeping with all of them. For some sick reason that makes me happier. If he was sleeping with them all, he couldn't be in love with only one, right? Maybe when he wrote me that he'd met someone, he actually meant he'd met more than one someone.

There are no pictures of him and some girl posing in front of a sunset on the beach. No cover shots. Hmm. He usually buys rolls of thirty-six. Have I seen seventy-two pictures? I don't think I have. I think I've only seen sixty-six, maybe sixty-seven. Gasp. He must have taken some out! He's hiding them! Or maybe some of the pictures were overexposed. It happens.

He places the photos back in their envelopes. "I'm going to take a shower. Wanna join me?"

"No, thanks. I'm too comfy." I want to have a better look at these photos, without him surveying over my shoulder.

I wait to hear him turn on the water. I remove the pictures from the envelopes and look through them again. I'm guessing one of the blondes. But that would be the obvious choice, wouldn't it? He expects me to think that, but it's really the brunette.

I'm unclear as to what happens now. Are we back together? Do I just forget the last few months? Can I do that? Can I trust him again? Earlier when he reached into the drawer of the nightstand to get a condom, I noticed the box was open. Did he take home an opened box from Thailand? It couldn't have been here before he went over there, because for the last two years I was with him, I was on the pill.

It would be really wrong if I searched through his drawer to investigate the matter further. Really wrong. Morally wrong. Legally wrong.

Hmm. I can still hear the pounding of the water against the tiles.

I open the drawer and take out the box. Let's see. It says on the package there should be twelve condoms inside. And the box is in perfect shape—meaning that there's no way it was anywhere near a backpack. So he didn't take it back with him from Thailand. It could have been a new box, mind you, and he could have opened it just after I called. In expectation. In eagerness. I'll buy that. But there had better be eleven in there, since we used one. Let's see. Four. There are four condoms left. Four? Only four? Is there a secret compartment? Like the spare tank in your car when your gauge says empty? Why are there only four? Where are the missing seven?

More importantly, where *were* they?

The water stops and I frantically return the box and the pictures to their original homes.

Seven. He's had sex seven times in the last two weeks. His vacation sex I'm prepared to forget about. But New York sex?

I am having difficulty processing this information.

When he walks back into the room, I'm sitting cross-legged on his bed. The lower half of his body is wrapped in a black towel. The wet tips of his hair fall in front of his eyes. He is so *cute* wet. Very distracting.

"I'm starving," he says.

I pull him back to bed. "What do you want to do for dinner?" I decide to give him the benefit of the doubt—for now. He could have bought the box months ago, intending to bring it to Thailand, but at the last moment decided to take only seven condoms.

"Actually…"

Yes? Order in? Dine out? He rests the back of his head against my knee. "I have this Christmas Eve dinner thing tonight," he says.

"Oh." That sucks. I guess I'm going to make Wendy take the whole day off from work, after all. "You can't get out of it?"

"Unfortunately, no. You didn't tell me you were coming in." I watch as his eyes change from blue to gray. They do that sometimes, depending on the light. "If you had given me some sort of notice, I would have been able to take you."

Excuse me? A look of death must be clouding across my face because I sense him tensing up. Or maybe he's tensing up because he realizes what he's just said and knows he's busted.

"You're taking someone else." This is not a question.

"I…"

I just slept with him and now he has a date. I just *slept* with him and now he has a *date*. Tonight. After I slept with him. I shove his head off my knee. "Who? Who's your date?"

He pauses. Again. "Jackie, I don't think you want to know."

Omigod. I know. I know who it is. "Are you dating Crystal Werner?"

Another pause. This man sure takes a lot of pauses when he's being busted.

"You're dating Crystal." I'm going to kill myself. Did he always like her? Did he like her while he was dating me? Was he just waiting for her to break up with her boyfriend? Was I just the bed warmer? "Good for you, guys. I hope you two have a long and happy life together."

He laughs. I can't believe he laughs. I'm contemplating suicide and he's laughing. "It's not serious. It's really casual. We don't want to get too attached to each other. I'm moving to Boston in a week, remember?"

No, I do not remember. He never did give me a date as to when he was coming. And what does he mean by "we"? Is he saying that he would have considered getting serious with her if he *weren't* moving to Boston? Which makes me now wonder about our whole relationship. Did he sleep with other girls when we were together and tell them that we weren't serious, that we were only casual, because he was going to Thailand?

If he cared about me, even a little, he would not have done

this. He would not have started up with Crystal. He would not have started up with anyone, in Thailand or elsewhere. He would not have made me an afterthought, an if-nothing-else-works-out-there's-always-Jackie kind of girl.

I have to get out of this apartment immediately. If I stay here a moment longer, I might explode—and I mean into actual physical pieces, not verbally. Where are my clothes? Where are my damn clothes? I hate him. I really hate him. I hope he dies. I hope he dies an excruciatingly painful death. Like getting eaten by a shark. While still conscious. Or being burned to death, but not passing out from the smoke. I wish I had one of those sock puppet voodoo dolls. I know exactly where I'd prick him.

As I step back into my skirt and boots (I would put on the comfy clothes that are in the knapsack, but I don't want him to know I dressed up for him), I feel him watching me. I ignore his gaze. "Have a merry Christmas with Crystal," I say and slam the apartment door behind me. I am not going to cry. I will not let him matter that much to me. I will not cry. He is not worth it. Raindrops on roses? Snowflakes that stay on my nose and eyelashes?

I walk into the closest grocery store and ask the woman behind the counter where the nearest phone is. She points me to a phone booth near the fridge at the back of her store. I need to speak to Wendy.

"Hi," she says. "So are you staying at Jeremy's?"

"No. I want to go back to Bubbe Hannah's."

"Now?"

"Yes."

"What happened?"

"Nothing," I answer, my voice shaking. I won't cry. I can't cry. I cannot start sobbing while the grocery woman is watching me while she stocks the fridge with milk cartons.

"What happened?"

"He's dating Crystal Werner." I am not going to cry in a

grocery store. I am crying in a grocery store. The grocery woman passes me a tissue.

"It's okay," she says soothingly (Wendy, not the grocery woman). "He's an ass. Nothing new."

"I know." The tears are now running freely down the sides of my face. "So why am I surprised? It's not as if he's inconsistent."

She tells me to stay where I am. She's coming to pick me up in a cab in half an hour.

I wander around the store for five minutes, buy a chocolate bar, and then decide to try Sam's cell.

"Jack! How's New York?"

"Horrible. I hate this place. When will you be home?"

"Day after tomorrow. The twenty-sixth. What happened with Jer?"

I don't feel like revisiting the experience just yet. "Me, too. I'm coming home."

"Aren't you supposed to be coming back on the twenty-eighth?"

"I'm coming home early. I don't want to talk about it. Tell me about Florida."

"I met the cutest lifeguard at the pool!" she exclaims excitedly, and goes on to describe all the men she's met.

Twenty minutes later (good thing I memorized my dad's calling card number way back when), I see a yellow cab pull up outside the store. I hang up in the middle of some story about mouth-to-mouth resuscitation and, sobbing, join Wendy in the backseat.

We order kosher Chinese food for dinner (Bubbe Hannah wants to join us) and rent *Love Story, Titanic, The Other Side of the Mountain* and *Madame X.* I'm in the mood for a good cry.

"Jim called," Bubbe Hannah says.

"Jim?" I ask.

"Who's Jim?" Wendy asks.

"Not for you. It was a boy for Jackie. A boy didn't call for *you*. Unfortunately."

Wendy rolls her eyes. "Do you mean Tim?"

"Yes, Tim. I thought your boyfriend had another name. But I'm old. I forget."

"You're not old, Bubbe. You're chronologically challenged." Wendy pecks her grandmother on the cheek. "What did he say?"

"To call him."

So not happening.

"I have a Hanukkah present for you," I tell Wendy the next day. It's Christmas morning. I pull the present I purchased for her yesterday out of my bag. It's not wrapped or anything, and there's no card, but still, it's a present.

"You didn't have to buy me a Hanukkah present. Friends don't exchange presents on Hanukkah. Anyway, I've known you for over fifteen years, and you never bought me a Hanukkah present before."

"I know, but I wanted to." I hand her a copy of *Let's Go Guide to Europe*. "To inspire you."

"This is fantastic," she says flipping through it. "Oooh… Italy. One day for sure, I'm going to Italy."

"I wouldn't care where I went," I tell her, "as long as I don't ever have to come to New York again." I hate New York. Maybe I'll create a new line of hats and T-shirts with that logo.

"I have a present for you, too," Wendy says.

"You do?" Yay! A present! She hands me a box wrapped in shiny, green paper, tied with a swirled pink ribbon. She's included a card, one of those text-free ones with a pretty scenic picture of a couple holding hands next to a large Christmas tree—obviously purchased before the calamity. Inside, she wrote, "Happy holidays to a wonderful best friend. You are strong, brilliant, and beautiful. Anyone who doesn't realize this immediately does not deserve to be in your presence." I assume this was written after. I sniffle.

Under the wrapping paper is a Bloomingdale's box with two pairs of identical fuzzy gray gloves.

"They're gorgeous!" I tell her. They really are. "But why two pairs?"

"You are to immediately place the second pair in a safe-keeping drawer. They are for when you lose the first pair."

So clever, that Wendy. How could I ask for a better friend? Someone who gives me a backup plan.

Instead of someone who makes me the backup plan.

Chapter Fifteen

The Milkrun—Literally

I'm reading in *City Girls* about how to lose those extra five Christmas pounds when the lights in the train go out and sparks start flying by my window. They kind of look like the tail of firecrackers before they explode. Then the window turns black and the train comes to a stop. Someone turns on a flashlight, and in the dim light I make out the silhouette of the woman sitting next to me. She's eating a ham and cheese sandwich. Instead of putting the sandwich down, which is what most people would do under the circumstances, she continues eating. What kind of person continues eating when the train might be exploding? Say you have one more minute of life—do you finish your sandwich? I, on the other hand, choose to reflect. Not on my own life, mind you, but on the eating habits of the woman sitting next to me.

We'd better not be stopped for long. I've already spent far too much time on this train, which for some reason, has taken the most convoluted route from New York to Boston. Hmm. What's the fastest way to get from A to B? I know, take a side trip to C, stop a little at F, and then pop over to U. Ridiculous.

My head hurts. I shouldn't have been reading without my contacts. I took them out as soon as I sat down on the train because I figured I'd take a nap to try avoid thinking about the misery of Christmas, and I hate napping with my contacts in because then I wake up with dry and sticky lenses. I should get that eye laser surgery, but it probably costs more than I make in a year. An image of a peeled mandarin springs into my mind every time I think of it. I don't like mandarins, especially when they remind me of eyes.

Suddenly everyone around me begins whispering and laughing nervously. More flashlights are turned on, and I squint and look around. An old woman donning a round hair-sprayed nest is standing up on her seat. She appears to be wearing a long red raincoat, and in my contact-less vision looks like the devil getting ready to flash. In the row behind her, a man wearing a gray and black checkered suit stands up, too. "I'm a lifeguard," he says. "Does anyone needs assistance?"

Why, is someone drowning? Weirdo. Two kids across the aisle from him apparently also find this declaration amusing, because they start to flap their arms up and down in their seats as if performing some kind of ritual dance, something that reminds me of what Dad nostalgically refers to as "the swim."

Do I smell smoke? I smell smoke. Isn't this wonderful? I'm going to burn to death on a train the day after Christmas. At age twenty-four. Alone. I'm going to die a nobody. No one will care because no one but Wendy even knows I'm on this train, and she won't find out about me for weeks because she never leaves the office. My parents each think I'm in different cities, and Sam will assume I decided to stay longer.

If I go to sleep, will I wake up in Boston?

Where are my glasses? I can't find my glasses. It's too dark to put in my contacts. My glasses are in my bag. I need to get my bag.

A woman at the back stands up. "Can everyone please sit down?" she yells.

A man in a stripped uniform opens the sliding doors to our car and tells us to get off the train, adding that we should take whatever belongings we have at hand and not to worry about our bags stacked at the front. I only have my purse and a magazine with me. All my stuff is packed in my bag. I must save my black boots! Who am I without my black boots?

I wait in line to disembark. A woman who smells like anti-septic talks to the lifeguard, and I eavesdrop. I wonder if they know each other from before or if this quasi tragedy has brought them together. I am never traveling alone again. I am never going to pack my boots again. Traveling rule number one: always carry or wear anything you consider important, which in my case, is everything. If it isn't important, why bring it at all? Traveling rule number two: always carry a pair of running shoes; you never know when you'll have to run from a burning train.

I'm sitting on a layer of snow, my legs pulled into my arms. The first car of the train is on fire, and the second one is in immediate danger of being chewed by the flames.

"Jackie?" a voice says. Is someone talking to me? Was there another Jackie on the train?

"Yes?" I call out into the darkness.

"I can't believe you were on this train, too."

Andrew! It's Andrew! Andrew was on my train! Thank God. Thank God thank God thank God. I jump up from the snow and throw my arms around him. "I am so glad to see you, you have no idea."

He hugs me, and sits down beside me. "Didn't you see me waving at you? Were you sleeping with your eyes open?"

Great. He thinks I'm a freak. "I took my contacts out in case I fell asleep, and I haven't had a chance to put them back in. Aren't you supposed to be off for another week? Why are you coming home now?"

"Too much to do in Boston."

Hmm. Running back to a warm woman's embrace, maybe? "Can't wait to get back to Jess?"

"No. I took your advice and ended it. There was no point. Well, there was a *point,* but you'd just call me a pig again."

He doesn't elaborate and I don't ask.

People are clustered in twos and threes, clutching whatever belongings they had at their seats, watching the train burn. If only we had marshmallows. The woman who smells like antiseptic is still talking to the lifeguard, and the she-devil in the raincoat is talking to herself. The firemen are on their way, I hear the lifeguard say, but apparently they'll be a while. It's not like it's an emergency or anything.

Don't worry about us. It's only a twenty-car-train-burning catastrophe. No rush here. It's not as though we're stuck in a void somewhere between nowhere and nowhere, thank you very much.

I give Andrew half the muffin I bought at Union Station. He thinks it's blueberry until he looks closely and realizes it's chocolate. I'm lactose intolerant, he says and gives it back. Why is everyone these days lactose intolerant? Maybe I should be lactose intolerant, too. That seems like a better diet than the no-carb one. No chocolate, no ice cream…but no cheese? Never mind. I don't want to be lactose intolerant. I reach into my purse and hand him my only package of sour berries. "Save me a couple, they're my favorite."

The sky is layered with stars. We lie our heads down on his knapsack and stare up. "My head hurts," I say, and I think he thinks I mean against the ground when I really mean I wish I had an aspirin. He removes a sweatshirt from his knapsack and rolls it into a pillow for me. It smells like Bounce dryer sheets— a dead giveaway he went home for the weekend.

"The sky looks like art class," he says.

"You take art class?" He takes art class? What guy takes art class? Business and art? Is this permissible? Doesn't the registration office block this kind of combination to protect the Alpha A-type man from becoming Alpha B?

"Yeah. I'm kind of artistic. When I was a kid, I used to dip toothbrushes into white paint, and tap them with Popsicle sticks to make stars." He sits up suddenly. "Hey, doesn't the sky kind of look like an Impressionist painting?"

A thick gray cloud of smoke spreads across the sky, threatening to obliterate the so-called painting. In my blurry vision, the flames look more like smeared red and orange finger paints.

Can I like Andrew?

His eyes seem lighter, as though bleached by the fire. He lies down again, this time on his side, and leans on his elbow. What do I do if he leans over and kisses me? Do I want him to? Will it be good? Why do I want him to kiss me? How can I get him to kiss me? Will he taste the chocolate on my lips? Will he need to take a lactose pill?

"I'm assuming you went to see Jeremy."

Oh, right. New York. I don't answer at first. "Kind of," I say reluctantly.

Can I like Andrew? I think I like Andrew. Does Andrew like me? I can't tell. Why do I always have to like someone? How can I tell if I really like Andrew or if I just like him this second because of the stars, the fire, the bleached eyes, the clean sweatshirt?

A man who seems to be in charge—he's wearing florescent—directs the waiting crowd to a farmhouse where buses are waiting to take us back to Boston. I remove my jacket and make a show of putting on Andrew's sweatshirt. I put my coat back on, but leave the zipper undone. In my contact-less, surrealistic condition, I imagine this is supposed to be suggestive. We trudge through a path in the forest, tripping over broken tree roots and scraping our shoes against the jagged edges. Maybe it's a good thing I'm not wearing the black boots. I heard the she-devil say that a path was cleared to enable us to reach the road, but my feet are arguing otherwise. And I don't remember seeing any bulldozers.

Andrew's ungloved hands are freezing; they look as if they're about to turn blue. I squish one of his artistic hands next to mine inside my glove. (I'd have given him the other pair if they weren't in my bag.) I tell him the reason I'm taking his hand is to reduce the chances of my walking off into a tree. Which, given my eyesight and the darkness in the woods, is not exactly a lie. Also, at least one of his hands will be kept warm. Of course, he can always shove his hands into his pockets, but this I don't suggest. Our feet move at the same time as we try to walk in rhythm. Left right, left right, one foot, the other foot.

"I feel like I'm a character in *The X-Files*," he says.

The lifeguard, who happens to be walking in front of us, turns around. "They say some kids put rods on the tracks, and that's what caused the fire." Why are people always blaming kids? My dad does that, too. Anytime he hears about some act of vandalism, he says, "Those damn kids!" I hate that. When I'm an adult I'm never going to blame kids. I'll say, "Those damn adults!" instead. Oh, right. I *am* an adult.

The woman walking with the lifeguard turns to us and says, "We also heard that the first car filled up with smoke so fast, the passengers had to break the windows and climb through the broken glass to safety."

"Was anyone hurt?" Andrew asks.

"No, thank God. A few people have been taken to the hospital as a precaution, though."

That certainly makes the story less exciting. Wow, that's a really awful thing to think. Am I an awful person? I am an awful person. I deserve to lose my boots; it's instant karma all over again.

Wait just a minute. I could be on TV! Am I going to be on TV? I've only been on TV once, and it was during a school assembly for a Christmas/Hanukkah show. Except I was dressed as a tree and was totally unrecognizable.

"There's the bus," Andrew tells me. Does he think I'm blind? Oh, yeah, I am blind, sort of. Ah, we are finally out of the woods—literally speaking. He helps me climb aboard. (I might as well milk this blind thing for all it's worth). We take two seats in the back. He sits near the window, and puts his arm around my neck. Aha! He *does* like me. Maybe. The bus driver puts on the movie *Speed*, which we think is a very strange thing to do, considering the movie is about an exploding mode of transportation. The red glow of the screen provides the only light in the pitch-black bus.

He smells yummy. And not like Jer anymore. "You smell good."

"Thanks. My parents bought me a new cologne for Christmas."

"I like it. What time is it?" I ask.

"Almost midnight."

"We were supposed to arrive in Boston at nine." I feel his breath on my cheek. Should I turn to face him, or should I continue staring ahead at the mesh seat pouch directly in front? Why am I staring at the mesh seat pouch directly in front?

If I turn around we are going to kiss. It's going to happen, I just know it. Is it going to happen? I think maybe. I'm not sure.

He's not moving. His arm is still on my neck. Still. On. My. Neck.

Is he going to make a move? Should I make a move? Should I do the lean? Do I want this to happen?

It's happening. Why is it two hundred degrees inside a freezing bus?

I turn toward him.

His face is less than two inches away from mine. Omigod omigod omigod.

"I don't mind," he says without moving.

What? What? He doesn't mind being late or the fact that we're about to kiss? "I guess I don't mind, either."

Lips. So. Close. This is ridiculous. Why doesn't he just do it already?

"It's not like I'm in a rush or anything," he says.

"Yeah, I'm not in a rush, either," I answer.

Lips. Right. There.

This is stupid.

I do the lean and kiss him.

I can't believe I did that.

Not that he seemed to mind.

A few strobe lights of screen color later, I pull away.

A perfect kiss.

I fall asleep against his shoulder.

The phone rings at eight in the morning, jarring me out of my REM sleep. I presume it was REM sleep anyway, since a person can't actually know she's in one—see what near tragedy does? It makes you question everything.

"Hello," I mumble. Somehow I know it's Tim.

"Babe! You…worried…" I have difficulty following what he's trying to say, since I keep falling back to sleep. "…thank God…heard on the radio…your train…worried… Why didn't you call me?"

Okay, I'm awake now. Kind of. It's Tim. When I checked my messages five hours ago, I saw that all ten messages were from him. Apparently, he called me in New York again, and Bubbe Hannah told him I had left early.

How did he get that number in the first place? It's not even listed.

"I'm fine." I'm fine except I don't like you anymore. And I slept with Jeremy even though I think I like Andrew.

"I was so worried. I couldn't sleep all night. I'm coming over."

"No, Tim. Please don't."

"Why not?"

Is it wrong to break up with someone over the phone? Here goes nothing: "I don't think this relationship is working out."

Silence. And then, "Can't we talk about this?"

I thought we just did. "I'm really tired, Tim."

"What about New Year's? Does this mean we're not going out?"

"Uh, no."

There's another silence at the other end, and I'm not sure whether or not I've fallen back to sleep.

"Okay. Take care, Jackie."

"'Bye."

I know I'm being a bit heartless here. But isn't it less cruel to break it off swiftly and cleanly, for example, over the phone or via e-mail, than to prolong the agony? Remember Fashion Magazine Fun Fact # 5? It's better to be cruel at the beginning than to string him along. Okay, okay, so we're not exactly at the beginning of our relationship, considering the fact that we've had already had sex (sort of), but isn't the concept basically the same?

*   *   *

The phone rings again a few hours later, once again waking me up.

"Get over it, Tim," I mumble into the receiver. We're history. Kaput. Dead.

"I called you at your father's, but you weren't there." It's Iris's accusing voice.

Uh-oh. Busted.

"Don't worry," she says, "I can keep a secret. I kind of found out by accident. When I called, your father seemed a bit confused as to why I was calling. And then he asked, 'So how are you and Jackie enjoying your holiday?' I put two and two together and then I had to come up with some reason as to why I'd be calling your father when you're not even there, so I remembered that he sold coats or something and I told him I loved your coat and could he order me one. He said he couldn't remember which one you had so I basically described my dream coat, and he said he remembers it and now he's going to send it to me! He's such a sweetheart. I saved your ass, didn't I? So where were you, Jackie? Hmm? Hmm?"

"I went to visit Wendy, and if you ever tell—"

"Guess what?" she cuts in excitedly. "I got on Kyle!"

I try to understand what this means. I'm not sure if it makes no sense due to the fact I'm exhausted, or because it just makes no sense. She physically climbed on top of him? At the risk of sounding geriatric I ask, "What does that mean? You actually got on top of him?"

"It's an expression, Jack. An expression. Never mind. We fooled around."

"You didn't sleep with him, did you?"

"No. Relax, I'm still a virgin."

"You'd tell me if you weren't, right?"

"Yeah, sure."

I'm going to kill her if she's lying. Not that I'd know if she's lying. "Want to come spend New Year's with me? We can party all night." I'm feeling a bit guilty for neglecting her over Christmas. And I'm dateless on New Year's, anyway. How did I manage that? Oh yeah, I broke up with Tim. Andrew's face suddenly flashes through my head. If he liked me, wouldn't he have called by now? Wouldn't he have asked me out for New Year's? Shouldn't he at least want to know how I am after our near fiasco? Our fiasco meaning the fire, not the kiss.

"No."

No?

"The fossils are going to Arizona. They're leaving me alone for New Year's."

"Don't have a party."

"Of course I'm having a party! It's New Year's and I have the house all to myself. Anyway, Janie said I could."

"She did?" I find this hard to believe.

"She said that I'd probably be safer at home than out wandering the streets."

Makes sense, I guess. "But I bet they don't know about Kyle."

"I'll kill you if you tell them. But I guess we're even now. I won't tell about New York if you don't tell about Kyle."

What happened to "Don't worry, I can keep a secret?"

When I wake up for the third time, it's because I sense I am not alone. And that's another thing. Since the fire, I have developed ESP. Some people who have near-death experiences see a bright white light and then they develop the ability to talk to the dead. But I wasn't wearing my contacts at the time, and because I wouldn't have been able to see the white light, my experience resulted in a completely different phenomenon. Bruce Willis, move aside! I now have the ability to sense a person's presence before it reaches my consciousness. How else could I have known that Tim was on the phone the first time? His leaving ten messages has nothing to do with it. And the fact that I can hear someone breathing has nothing to do with it.

"What?" I ask, opening one eye. Sam is sitting on my bed, staring at me.

"Oh, good, you're awake. Were you on that exploding train?"

"What time is it?"

"Late. I just saw you on the news."

I jump out of bed. "Really? I was on TV? Did you tape it? Was it a good shot? Did you see me with Andrew?" How many times do they show the same news before the news becomes old? Two? Three? At least four, for sure. Yay! Jeremy is going to see me with Andrew!

"How could I tape it when I didn't even know it was going to be on? When did you get in? I didn't even hear you. Are you okay?"

"I'm fine. I split a cab with someone who lives nearby." The lifeguard.

I shove a tape in the machine, and set the dials to record the news at a later time. A few hours later, the clip of me is on TV again. The shot lasts for about a half a second—I'm alone, sitting in the snow, staring into nothing. I look like an idiot.

"You look so sad," Sam says and pats my head.

There *has* to be more of me. This is my one moment of fame! The burning train appears on the screen. I try another station. The reporter gives a brief account. The image shifts to the woods being bulldozed. Switch. We're walking through the woods. Switch. We're getting on the buses. Switch. Getting off the buses. Switch. The fire again. Switch. Left, right, left right. Switch. An interview with the woman with the hair-sprayed nest and the long red raincoat. How come she gets an interview? She gets a two-minute interview and I get to look sad for half a second.

The woman who was talking to the lifeguard fills the screen. Even she gets to talk on TV! "I was terrified," she says. "Absolutely terrified. The flames were consuming everything in sight."

"She's full of shit—she wasn't terrified. She found a boyfriend on the train! She probably made out with him on the bus!" Slut.

"You know her? You know the woman on television?"

I hush Sam with my hand and watch the fire blazing on the screen. Switch. The reporter is cross-examining a mechanic on how this could have happened. Switch. I hate the news.

Cupid is closed for the holidays. Actually, it's kind of disappointing, since this would have been an excellent excuse to call in and tell them I need a mental health day. I wonder if I can claim a delayed reaction next week. It's not every day a person has a close encounter with death.

That night, Andrew comes over to watch the video I made of the news. At my suggestion, I regretfully have to add.

"You looked so sad," he says, referring to my half-second cameo appearance. Then we watch *Speed 2*. He's on one end of the couch, and I'm on the other.

There has been no physical contact so far. When he buzzed, I unlocked the door and pretended to be cooking something in the kitchen. Well, opening something anyway. So I could avoid the potentially awkward kiss on the cheek hello. There has been no mention of the obvious, either. Isn't it strange that we're both too wimpy to mention the one thing we're both thinking about?

"Jess called me last night." He's staring at the TV and not looking at me. Why isn't he looking at me? Uh-oh. Why is he bringing up Jess? I hate that he's bringing up Jess. For the past few months I was on one side of camp—the platonic side. The train ride yanked me onto the other side. And now he wants me to mosey on back to the platonic side while he discusses his previous relationship in-depth? I don't think so.

"And? Does she love you even more now that you've proven you're commitment phobic?"

He throws a pillow at me, while still looking at the TV. "I'm not commitment phobic. I just don't see the point in wasting my time with the wrong woman. That's why I've never had a lasting relationship."

No kidding. A lasting relationship kind of implies you're in one now, right? Otherwise, by definition, it's unlasting. Is he trying to warn me off? Is this his way of telling me he doesn't want a relationship? Who says I want a relationship?

"You've never had a real relationship?" Note the switch from "lasting" to "real."

"Once, when I was in tenth grade."

"What happened?"

"I fooled around with her best friend."

"Very classy."

"She dumped me."

"Good."

"My longest relationship was in college. It went on for two months." He sighs dramatically. "Women don't want me for a boyfriend. All I am is a boy-toy."

I can't help myself from laughing. "Yeah, most women are only interested in a one-night stand. Relationships and estrogen? Like oil and water."

"It's true. Maybe I need to read a *Dating for Morons* guide."

"I could write that." But maybe I'll call it *Dating Morons*.

"What would your first chapter be about?"

"The first date, of course. Picture it. Boston. Saturday night."

"Saturday night? Waste a Saturday night on a first date? What happened to Tuesday?"

"Quiet! Pay attention, now. You're pulling up in front of my house. What do you do?"

"Um…honk?" He scrunches his forehead as if I've asked him a trick question. "Twice?"

"There you go!" He's kidding. I hope. I quiz him further. "And what do you say once I'm in the car?"

"Hi?"

"I'm looking for compliment, here. I got all dressed up, you know."

"Ah. I'd tell you that I prefer natural woman. I'd ask you to leave the makeup at home next time."

"Very good! And where do you take me?"

"I'd insist on meat. Ribs, probably."

"You're a regular Don Juan! And what happens when I do the reach?"

"The reach?"

"The bill comes and I reach for my purse."

"Well, if you're offering to pay, then you must want to, right?"

"Of course I do! I'd be embarrassed if you insisted."

"And then we'd walk back to the car, holding hands." He grabs my hand and swings it back and forth. "And then I'd tell you I had a great time...babe."

"That's it. I draw the line at babe."

"But everyone likes being called babe. Or doll. Or hon."

"I'm not everybody."

He looks up at me and his face grows serious. "No, you're not."

He's still holding my hand. He's still holding my hand. Why is he still holding my hand?

I hear Sam's key in the door. "I love not having to go to work!" she sings out brightly a moment later.

He drops my hand.

Thanks, Sam. Thanks for ruining everything. "Where were you?" I ask, noting her disheveled outfit.

"With Philip."

"And who's on for tomorrow?"

"Ben."

"You are certainly one busy girl," Andrew remarks.

Her face clouds over. "I have to decide which one I'm going to kiss at New Year's. This could be a problem."

"You can't kiss both?" he asks.

She thinks about this for a second. "Maybe I could."

"Please don't," I say. "Where are we going, anyway?"

"Orgasm." She flashes me a huge smile. "Huge party. The place to be. But we have to buy tickets."

"How much?" I ask.

"A hundred."

"A hundred?" A hundred dollars? I guess I'll have to dig into my therapy money. "And I bet that doesn't even include drinks. Maybe we should pre-drink here before going out. A party before the party."

"Who should we invite?" She looks at me inquiringly.

"Let's just go the four of us." Is this too presumptuous? Will Andrew think I'm assuming I'm his date? I figure I have nothing to lose by my suggestion. If he thinks it's just platonic between us, I've nothing to be embarrassed about. If he's hoping it's not…then for sure I made the right move.

"Did you open your package?" Sam asks.

"What package?"

"The huge present FedEx brought earlier today while you were still sleeping. You didn't see it?"

"No! Where is it?" What package?

"In my room."

"How was I supposed to know I had a package in your room? Why is it in your room?"

"Because I didn't want to wake you."

"And the living room was a problem because…"

"Whatever. Can you open it? I'm dying to know what it is."

Sam and I go into her room. A Christmas-paper-wrapped huge object is leaning against her bed. The note scribbled in marker across the paper says, "It's nonrefundable. Merry Christmas. Tim."

I tear open the wrapping paper. The *Where Do We Come From? What Are We? Where Are We Going?* print stares up at me.

Omigod.

I can't believe he bought it for me.

I can't believe I was such a bitch.

Tomorrow, I have to call and thank him.

We return to the living room.

"So what was in the package?" Andrew asks.

"A gift from an admirer," I reply. He thinks I'm joking.

"What are we watching?" Sam cuts in, plopping down on the couch between me and my potential New Year's Eve date.

I shoot her one of my best get-lost looks, but she's already absorbed in the movie.

Can I get away with sending Tim an e-mail?

Chapter Sixteen

Why Can't I Just Turn into a Pumpkin?

My favorite romance covers are the glamorous ones. The hero is dressed in a tuxedo, and the heroine, draped in some sort of velvety, silky, sparkling, emerald strapless gown, looks a little like Cinderella or at least the prettier of the two evil stepsisters. He gazes into her eyes. She gazes into his. There's lots of gazing going on. Tonight I get to be Cinderella—minus the glass slippers and the silver carriage drawn by horses that is actually a pumpkin pulled by singing mice. And I get to put my hair up, wear a three-quarter-length satiny black dress with spaghetti straps, and lots of eye makeup. Sam is wearing a floor-length maroon skirt and a matching tank top. We look fabulous, if I do say so myself.

Andrew is nothing to balk at, either. He and Ben are wearing dark suits. Yup, Sam chose Ben over Philip to be her date for New Year's.

I ask Sam to ask Andrew if he'd mind posing for a picture with me so that he doesn't suspect that I want a picture of us together.

"Smile! Say cheese!" She snaps us in front of the blind-covered window. "Okay, now you can resume your natural dispositions."

He keeps his arm around my shoulder. I stay smiling.

Janie calls to wish me a happy New Year.

"Where are you?" I ask.

"Pheonix. We love it out here. It's sunny. Why do people choose to live in cold climates when they can live out here?"

"I don't know. Why don't you move?"

"We're thinking about it."

Uh-oh. Poor Iris. She'll lose it if they even suggest it. "I thought you liked Virginia."

"I'm not crazy about it. I prefer a dry heat."

I hear the tinkle of glasses. I hear my friends laughing in the kitchen.

"I gotta go."

"Why? What are you doing tonight?"

"Just going for drinks with some friends."

"So who do I hear in the background?"

"Some friends. We're having some drinks."

"I thought you were going out for some drinks. Are you having a party?"

"No, we're going to a party."

"So who's there now?"

"Just friends."

"Why are you having drinks if you're going out for drinks?"

"Why not?"

Pause. "Jackie, do you have a drinking problem?"

Oh, God. "No, I do not have a drinking problem. What are you talking about? I have to go."

"Okay. Ration yourself. Happy New Year."

"You, too."

I enter the kitchen just as Ben is topping off our drinks. He lifts up his glass. "To a wonderful new year. May it be filled with lots of sex."

"Here, here," Sam says. Then they kiss. Right in front of us. Especially weird because Andrew and I just stand there, watching. There's been no kissing action between us since the train.

"We should go soon," Andrew says. What's his problem? Is he uncomfortable with all the coupling in here? He'd better get used to it…fast. Because tonight's New Year's Eve. Is there a better time to launch a relationship than at midnight, New Year's Eve, the magic moment when all potential couples kiss?

Orgasm looks the way it always does, just slightly more dressed up. Black and silver streamers cover the walls, and waitresses are wandering around carrying platters of hors d'oeuvres. Mmm. Are there any mini egg rolls? I love mini egg rolls.

"Oh, God," Sam whispers when we walk in. "Philip is here."

"You're so getting nailed."

"What do I do?"

"You didn't promise either of them anything."

"You're right! I haven't even slept with either of them!"

What? "You haven't?" Oh. There goes my even-Sam's-doing-it theory. "Then what do you do when you sleep over at Ben's all the time?"

"We cuddle a lot."

Cuddle a lot? "Are you telling me you spend the entire night in the same bed and don't have—"

A very bad sight interrupts my train of thought. "Sam, Marc is here." I nod to where he's standing with his work buddies at the other side of the bar. Sam's eyes are popping and it's not because of her white eye shadow. I thinks she's hyperventilating.

"Calm down, calm down," I tell her. "It'll be okay."

"Is this normal? Is this normal?"

I think she's about to faint. I really hope she doesn't. Then I'll have to go home with her to make she's all right. I can't go home with her. I have to go home with Andrew.

"I need a drink," she says instead of fainting. This is good.

I motion to Andrew that we're going to the bar.

"I'll get us a table," he mouths back.

"Two Lemon Drops, please," I tell the bartender, who isn't my friend Ms. Cleavage but appears to have the same DNA.

We do our shots and stand by the bar. Sam sighs. "What am I going to do? I haven't spoken to him in over a month."

"What do you want to do?"

"I want him to leave. I despise him. I'm happy without him. Why does he have to ruin my New Year's? He's already ruined my life. Has he seen me? Look if he's looking."

I look. "He's not looking. I don't think he's seen you yet."

"I can't stand up anymore. I'm going to sit down."

Don't faint, Sam. Please don't faint. "Okay, let's go find Andrew. He said he was getting us a table."

"Wait," she says. "Fix your hair."

"What's wrong with my hair?"

"It's frizzy."

"So don't just stand there, fix it!" I hiss at her.

"I can't," she says, trying to run her hands over it. "You need to run water through it."

I can't run water through it. People with naturally straight hair do not understand the delicate procedure involved in blow-drying curly hair straight. You can't add water. That's like eating a chocolate bar while you're working out. What's the point? Luckily I have a bottle of silicone-coated hair gel in my purse. I always wonder if putting silicone in my hair is a good idea. I mean, if it's used in breast implants, won't it make my hair puffy?

"Okay. Sit down. I'll be back in a second." I elbow-squeeze my way through the holiday-crowded bar. In the bathroom, I bump smack into Amber in front of the mirror. Remember Amber? Too-skinny-no-my-father's-not-a-fireman-I'm-a-sadistic-dentist Amber.

"Hello." She gives me the once-over.

"Hello." Someone needs to force-feed this girl. "How are you?"

"Fine, thanks, how are you?" She reapplies her lipstick. I notice she has a dark lip-liner/lighter lipstick thing going on.

I open my bag and retrieve the gel, preparing to perform major surgery on my hair. There's no place to put my purse, since the counters are littered with various colognes and perfume sprays—and an honor basket in which to leave money should you choose to spritz. So in the sink goes my bag, after I verify that the ceramic is dry. Down comes my hair, in goes the silicone. (Look Amber, we're twins! The silicone in my hair matches the silicone in your breasts!) And *whoosh* goes the water into my purse. Why don't these places warn you that these things run on automatic sensors?

I stick my purse under the hand dryer for a full ten minutes, and then leave the bathroom. Amber's still fixing herself. She obviously needs a lot of maintenance.

As I make my way toward the table, Marc spots me. He's sitting at the bar with a group of cute boys. How come Marc never offered to fix me up with his any of his friends?

"Hey, Jackie!"

I pretend I don't see him. He starts to wave frantically, then approaches me before I can escape to my table.

Me: "Oh, hi, Marc."

Marc: "Hi, Jack. Where's Sam?"

Me: "Good to see you, too. How are you?" At least pretend to want to talk to me.

Marc: "I'm okay. And you?"

Me: "Fine."

Marc: "How's work?"

Me: "Fine. Your work?"

Marc: "Fine. What's up?"

Me: "Not much." Marc and I never did have much to talk about.

Marc: "Is she here?"

Me: "Is who here?"

Marc: "Sam. Is Sam here?"

Me: "Yes, she's here." That's all you're getting, Marc dear.

Marc: "Where?" He looks around the bar.

I point to the table that now has Sam, Ben, Andrew and…Jess? Is that Jess? Why is Jess at the table? Why is Jess at Orgasm? I thought it was over. What do I do? Do I go over? Do I let them talk? What if she seduces him?

"Who is that?" Marc asks, trying to sound casual.

"It's Jess!"

"I mean the guy. Who's the guy with Sam? Does Sam have a new boyfriend? Why is some guy's arm around Sam?"

"A guy she's dating. What did you expect?" Uh-oh. Jess is smiling up at Andrew. Why is Jess smiling up at Andrew? "You dumped her. She's trying to meet other guys."

"But she wanted to move in with me! How could she be over me so quickly?"

"She's not the type of girl to sit at home and pine." And now he's smiling down at her! What should I do?

Marc stares openmouthed at the table. "I—"

"Gotta run," I tell him. Not that there's anywhere to run to. Not that I could run anywhere in these heels if there *was* somewhere to run to. Yes, it's time for me to leave Marc so that he can be alone to ponder the error of his ways. Should I go back to the table? No. I think I'll just wander around the bar. Maybe some cute guy will offer me a drink and Andrew will see how popular I am. Who am I kidding? It's New Year's Eve and most people are part of a couple. Or at least part of a group. I can't even sit down with the group I came with. I don't want to go interrupt Andrew and his girlfriend.

I might as well drink.

I order myself a glass of champagne.

That's a nice solution. Maybe Janie's right about me.

Raisin-Eyes has spotted me. Remember Raisin-Eyes, the rating guy? My first Orgasm. And now he's ogling my spaghetti straps. Ew… Is this what my life has come to? Will my year-end destiny lie with Raisin-Eyes?

Fine. Andrew can talk to Jess. For now. It's only eleven. He has one hour before he has to reappear by my side and kiss me magically.

"Who's that with Sam?" Marc comes up behind me and points. Philip has Sam boxed between him and the bar. He kisses her lightly on the lips.

Ha! That was fantastic! "Another one of her suitors."

"I made a mistake, didn't I?" Marc asks, his voice rising a full octave. He sounds pubescent. Then again, his behavior was always pubescent.

Now that was perceptive of him. I mock sigh. "Yes, you did."

Are those tears glistening in the grown man's eyes? Where's my camera? Why don't I carry a camera?

"Do you think she'd get back together if I asked?"

"Actually, Sam's quite together as it is." With Ben, with Philip, with just about anyone... "She's witty and beautiful and caring, and you threw all that away. You screwed up because you were afraid of commitment. Now she's happy and single and you're alone. Deal with it." I don't care if I sound harsh. Who does he think he is? Why should he be allowed to break someone's heart and then expect it to be able to magically glue itself together again?

Sam, unknowingly (and brilliantly) chooses this exact moment to stretch her pale arms above the table, thereby exposing her newly decorated stomach to the world.

Marc turns white. "What is that? Is that a navel ring? Since when does Sam have a navel ring?"

I shrug. "She's a new person."

He continues staring at Sam while swigging the rest of his drink. "I'm leaving."

Good riddance. Go home. Thanks for stopping by.

Moments later, Sam pops up behind me. "What happened? I saw you talking to him. What did he say?"

I reiterate the conversation.

She looks at me incredulously. "You said *what?*"

"I told him you were happier without him."

"Why would you say that?"

"Because you are." Aren't you? I think you are. You said you were. Uh-oh. Did I miss something here? "What about Ben? What about Philip?"

"Who cares about them?"

This is not good. "You do. Don't you?"

"Where is he?"

"Philip or Ben?"

"Marc! Where is Marc?"

"He..." It's unfortunate this will not meet with a positive response "...left."

"*When?*"

"A few minutes ago."

"I have to go find him."

Find him? You mean leave? "You can't leave!"

"Yes, I can." And with that, she takes off, leaving me on New Year's Eve, at a bar, by myself. Oh, that's right. I'm not by myself. I'm with the happy-Andrew-and-Jess-couple. Isn't this perfect?

I hate this place. It's packed. Drunken fools are packed in here like hordes of sweaty commuters in a subway car at rush hour. Hundreds of people are in this bar, yet here I sit by myself.

Time for another shot. Never mind. Time for two more shots. Jess is still there. Why is Jess still there?

About four—five?—shots later—how much later?—Raisin-Eyes feels it's the appropriate time to start talking to me. Apparently, I'm sending out I-am-desperate-please-come-annoy-me signs. Am I desperate? Maybe I am. Jess is still there. Why is Jess still there? Oh, look, there's Amber! Maybe I should go talk to Amber. That's not Amber. And here's Raisin-Eyes! Maybe I should talk to Raisin-Eyes. Raisin-Eyes, Raisin-Eyes, weren't you once a nice, plump grape? Why are you looking at me with those raisin eyes, Raisin-Eyes?

What time is it? Is the new year here yet? Did I miss it? "What time is it?" I ask my dear friend Raisin-Eyes.

"Ten to twelve."

Now look what I've done. I've gone and broken the seal, and now we're having a conversation. Kind of like the first time you visit the bathroom after you've been drinking. After that, it seems you have to go every five minutes.

"What day is it?" I say. Get it? What day is it? It's New Year's! I start laughing so hard that I temporarily fall off my stool. Whoa!

"What's your name?"

"Amber," I answer, and I'm not sure why. I suddenly miss her. Where is Amber? We're like sisters, me and Amber, with our silicone.

"Why are you sitting by yourself, Amber?"

Can't you do better than that, Raisin-Eyes? Tell me I'm beautiful or something. C'mon, you can do it! Tell me. I'm serious.

He'd better tell me. "Because my friend left and Andrew's with Jess and I'm drinking."

"Oh."

"Oh. Oh. Oh. Oh, say can you see? So why are *you* by yourself?"

"I'm not. I'm talking to you."

Rate me, already, Grape-Face/Raisin-Eyes. Rate me, date me, but please don't hate me. "Why?"

"Why? What do you mean why?"

"Why are you talking to me?" I'd like a compliment, please.

"Because you seem nice and friendly. And you're beautiful."

That's better. 'Cept you forgot to mention easy prey.

"And because I don't meet a lot of women at work."

Hmm. He wants me to ask him what he does. Could he be any more obvious? I'm not asking. If he wants to tell me so badly, let him tell me. "You don't want to meet women?"

"I'd like to meet more women, of course, but I don't know any female investment bankers."

Puh-lease. That's the most pathetic excuse to sneak in what a guy does for a living I've ever heard. "You don't know any? In your whole company there's not one woman?"

"Well...I guess there are a few."

Gee, nice of you to pull your head out of the nineteenth-century's ass. "My best friend is an investment banker. My female best friend."

"I didn't say there weren't any."

"Yes, you did."

"I..." Yadayadayada. He keeps blabbing about investment banking. I watch his mouth open and close to the thumping music. He tells me about mergers and acquisitions, acquisitions and mergers, and...is he still talking? Why hasn't he asked me what I do? Why does it take guys hours to consider the possibility that I may also have a career?

"Excuse me," I say to the bartender. "Excuse me? Ms. Bartender? Uh, can I get some more shots please?"

"How many is some?" she asks. Rather obnoxiously, I might add.

"Some is three." Obviously. Or maybe a few is three. I don't know. Who cares? I take out my wallet and hand her *some* bills. Get it? *Some* bills. That's three dollars. However, Ms. Obnoxious says it's not enough. Thanks for offering to pay, Raisin-Eyes. He's too busy blabbing. Still. About his stupid job.

"Guess what?" I ask. "I work, too!" Shot one. Shot two. Shot three.

"You do? What do you do?"

"I work for Cup-id." I emphasize the P. I'm not sure why. "I'm an editor."

"Cupid?"

"Romance books."

"Do you know…" Don't say it don't say it don't say it. "…Fabio? Have you met him?"

What is it with everyone and Fabio? It's enough with Fabio. "Yes. Actually, we're sleeping together. And frankly," I look down at his crotch, "I don't think you'd measure up."

He stares at me in disbelief.

"Ten minutes 'til New Year's!" a loud DJ-esque voice announces from a hidden speaker. Where's Andrew? I must find Andrew. Andrew? Andrew! Where are you? There you are! There! You! Are! At the table. There you are at the table. Yoohoo, Andrew! I'm trying to get to you but there are all these people between us. Move over, people. Here I come! I wave to him. Wave wave wave. Arm up. Arm move. Dancing arm. Arm dancing. Back and forth. Hello. Hello, Andrew.

He sees me. He's looking at me funny. Why is he standing sideways? Why is everyone standing sideways? Why wait for midnight? Maybe I'll kiss Andrew *now*. I don't feel well. I don't feel well at all.

"Heyyyyy." Andrew is right here. And his voice sounds as though it's in slow motion and turned to a ridiculously loud volume. "Wheeeere havvvve yoooou beeeeeen alllll nighhhht?"

Where have I been? I don't know where I've been. "I've been

sitting at the bar watching you talk to Jess, that's where." So there.

Hi, Jeremy! Is that Jeremy? It can't be Jeremy. Why would Jeremy be here? "Jeremy?"

Now he looks really unhappy. I think I can see him clenching his teeth through his jaw. "I'm Andrew."

"I *know* that." Silly, silly boy. Giggle, giggle. "Are you in love with Jess?"

He looks at me kind of strangely. "We were just talking."

"Sure. Just talking. Whatever." What's wrong with this picture? If you knew tonight was the night, would you be rubbing up against your ex? "You guys can get back together for all I care. And I don't care. Don't care. Don't care even a smidgen of a bit."

"We should get some air."

"I don't need air. I need another drink."

"No, you don't. Come outside." He's holding on to my arm and pulling me outside.

"But it's almost midnight!" Where's my watch? How come I'm not wearing a watch? Do I have a watch? I don't have a watch.

"We still have five minutes. You look green."

"It's not easy being green. Kermit said that. In a song. I always liked Kermit. Do you know Kermit? I know Fabio." Cold air. Cold air on exposed skin. "I'm going to freeze to death, then will you be happy?" Spinning. Watch out! Orgasmic neon woman now spinning!

"Are you okay?"

Andrew kind of looks like Kermit. Have I mentioned that I always liked Kermit? If I kiss the frog, will it turn into a prince? "Fine," I say.

"Do you need some water?"

"Water? I need more than water. I need a boyfriend. *Boyfriend*. Do you understand? Not a friend who's a boy, but a real, live, honest-to-God, flesh-and-blood *boyfriend*. Not someone who wants to hang out with a Sweet Valley Twin on New Year's Eve.

Don't you know we're supposed to end up together at midnight?''

"Jackie—"

"Didn't you see *When Harry Met Sally*? Why don't men ever pay attention? It all comes down to New Year's!"

"You have to calm down."

"I don't want to calm down! You calm down!" Why has the sidewalk turned into a treadmill? "Can I sit down?"

He nods. I sit. The ground is hard and cold.

"Are you going to throw up?"

"No." I shake my head. Maybe. "I'm not sure."

"Come with me to the side of the building so you won't be embarrassed about this tomorrow."

Embarrassed? Why would I be embarrassed?

He takes me to a deserted brick wall that seems to belong to the bar. Only I can't be sure because it doesn't want to stay in one place.

This whole thing would not make my dad happy, especially me leaving a bar with a strange guy. He doesn't know Andrew, so in his eyes, that makes him strange. *Is* this Andrew? I look at his hair. Yup. It's red. It's Andrew. Unless someone else is trying to trick me and is wearing a wig.

Someone is counting over a microphone. "Ten...nine... eight..."

It's almost twelve! It's almost twelve! "Are you going to kiss me?" I ask. "I really need to know *now*."

If he doesn't kiss me, my carriage will turn into a pumpkin, and my prince will remain a frog. If he doesn't kiss me, I may as well forget him.

"Four...three...two..."

"I don't feel well."

"One! Happy New Year everyone!"

Should auld acquaintance be forgot and never brought to mind...

I throw up into a snow-covered bush.

Chapter Seventeen

Happy New Year!

Head. Hurts.

What day is it? I vaguely remember making a bad joke with that punch line last night. Where am I? I'm in my bed. That's good. What time is it? My clock says three. Why do I have perfect vision? My contacts must still be in. Why are my contacts still in? What is that smell? Oh, God, it's me. Why do I smell like crap?

Uh-oh. Memories are trickling into my consciousness like a bad aftertaste. Orgasm...Marc...Raisin-Eyes...Andrew. Uh-oh. I have a bad feeling about this. A *very* bad feeling.

Knock, knock, knock.

Is someone at my door or is that the pounding in my head?

"Who is it?" I call out. I doubt the person outside my apartment can hear me. I'm not sure if I even spoke out loud.

What did I say to Andrew? What did I do? I remember a bush...uh-oh. I remember him walking me home...giving me a glass of water...putting me into bed. I remember me getting out of bed and throwing up again in the garbage pail.

"It's me!" a shrill voice yells. "Open the door! I've been standing here for centuries!"

"Hold on," I mumble and get out of bed. At least I managed to get my dress off last night. Was it me who took my dress off? But why are my legs black? Oh. I slept in my nylons.

"Hurry!" the voice demands, still shrill, a siren in my ears.

Is that... "Iris?" I throw open the door.

"It's about time!" My sister is standing in the hallway, her little arms folded across her massive chest.

"Why are you here?"

"What do you mean why am I here? Can't a girl visit her sister? Why do you always have to be so suspicious?"

Let's see. It's New Year's Day, the day after her big bash in the house in Connecticut, the day after she supposedly got on what's-his-name. Ken? Karl? Kyle? She and Ken/Karl/Kyle have the whole house to themselves and she wants to visit her sister. I don't think so.

"I buzzed downstairs for an hour," she says, "but you didn't answer and finally, someone let me in. I need some money to pay the cabdriver. He's waiting downstairs and he's not very happy."

"You came all the way from Virginia to Boston with no money?"

"Yes and will you please hurry? I promised I'd only be five minutes!"

"Okay, hold on." Where's my purse? There it is. Hmm. Why is it so light? I open it. Why isn't my wallet inside? Shit, shit, shit.

I run through my room. Nowhere.

The kitchen. Nowhere.

"Will he take a check?" I call from the bathroom.

"I hope so."

"How much?"

"Thirty. And don't forget the tip."

I go back to my room to get my checkbook, write out the amount, and return to the door. Iris runs back to the elevator.

You're welcome, Iris.

Where's my wallet? I must find my wallet.

I search through the drawers in my room.

Nope.

In my closet.

Nope.

In the sheets.

Nope.

"Can't you at least help me?" Iris screams from the hallway. She's pulling a green duffel bag through the front door. "He insisted on keeping my bag as hostage until I paid him. Ridiculous. My Diesels are worth three times the price of the fare."

"Did he take the check?"

"Unhappily."

I help her drag the bag into the living room. "Why does this thing weigh a ton? Did you pack everything you own? How long are you planning to stay?" A warning alarm goes off in my head. "Enlighten me, Iris. What are you doing here? For real."

"What does it look like I'm doing?" She pulls her scrunchie from her hair and remakes her ponytail. "I'm moving in."

Hold on there a second. "You can't just move in. I have a roommate. How did you get here? Does Janie know you're here? Why are you here?"

"First of all, you won't have your roomie much longer. Sam is moving in with Marc."

What? How does she know this? "What? How do you know this?"

"I spoke to her this morning."

"Sam called you?"

"Don't be an idiot. Why would Sam call me? I called here this morning. Five times. You didn't answer." She makes a drinking motion with her hand. "Our mother thinks you're an alcoholic, you know."

Nice to know Janie's been sharing her theories with the rest of the family. "I didn't hear the phone."

"You were probably unconscious. You look like shit."

"Don't swear."

"I'm not six! You're not my mother!" she yells.

"Shh." Yelling does not mesh well with the present headache. "Why do you think you're moving in with me?"

"Because Mom called this morning to wish me a Happy New Year and said we're moving to Arizona. Just like that. Just like that she thinks she can rearrange my whole life. Well, I have news for her and my father. I am *not* going. Do you realize the psychological damage they're causing me? I called here hysterical this morning and Sam answered. She said she didn't want to wake you. So I told her how horrible my parents are and she told me she was moving in with Marc. Ew… What's the awful smell? You puked, huh?''

"Sam! Sam!" Where is she? Is she even home? She can't be serious, moving in with Marc! Doesn't she hate him? No, I forgot. She ran out of Orgasm last night, looking for him. But he doesn't want to move in with her. He broke up with her! I have to call Ben. Or Philip.

"She's not here. She's out with Marc. She told me she wanted to talk to you, but you were still asleep."

"I can't believe she would tell you before telling me."

"She *was* going to tell you, Sleeping Beauty. Actually, Sleeping Ugly right now."

This is not good.

"Can I have her room? You probably want to switch, right? I guess that's only fair. All right, you've been here longer. I'll take your room, but then you owe me. Do you have a TV?''

When did my life become hell? "You can't move in."

"But I have nowhere else to go!" She starts to cry. I can't tell if her tears are real, but she gets to me anyway. "Our mother is crazy! I tell you, there is something wrong with that woman. She's never happy. I don't want to move to Phoenix—I just moved to Virginia! And it's way too hot in Phoenix."

"But it's a—"

"I don't care if it's a dry heat! I don't want to move again. And I don't want to live with her anymore. I hate her. She only cares about herself. And I hate my father. He goes along with everything she wants. She's like, *so* selfish. I can transfer back to JFK High and live with you. At least I'll know people at school."

"You can't transfer in the middle of the year."

"Of course I can! I'd have to if I moved to Phoenix, anyway. You should really brush your teeth. You *did* puke, didn't you?''

I must think fast. "They're not going to want to move in the middle of the year. You have a half a year to work this out."

"According to Janie, January is not the middle of the year. It's the beginning."

"But it'll take Bernie some time to transfer!"

"There's an immediate opening in Phoenix, so they have to leave within the next month."

"Oh." That does suck.

"Oh? That's all you can say? My whole life is about to go down the drain again and that's all you can say?"

"I'm sorry, Iris."

"Not as sorry as I am. So can I live here?"

"They will never let you live here." I will never let you live here.

"Can't you adopt me?"

"I don't think you can adopt a sixteen-year-old. Besides, I have to find someone who can cover Sam's rent. I can't afford to pay for the whole apartment by myself."

"I don't have any money! You expect me to support myself *and* go to school? What a nice sister you turned out to be."

"It's not a matter of being nice. I just can't—"

Iris drags her bag into my room and slams the door behind her.

What a way to start the year.

I search the living room. No wallet. Did I leave it somewhere? Did I leave it at Orgasm? I think I did. Yes, I did! I must have forgotten to put it back in my purse after paying for the drinks.

I search for Orgasm's number in the phone book and dial. Easy. No problem, except for the fact that even my fingers have a headache—I must have really tied one on last night. What if I'm still drunk and Iris is a hallucination and I can't see my wallet even though it's probably right under my nose?—one can always hope. Nah, Iris's duffel bag is too big to fit into anyone's hallucination, and I probably left my wallet at the bar. Maybe one of the busty bartenders found it and is keeping it safe for me.

Ring. Ring. Ring. They'd better be open. Why wouldn't they be? It's 2:00 p.m. New Year's Day, that's why. It's a holiday. It's the middle of the day. They're probably out maxing my Visa.

"Orgasm." They're open! Yay!

"Hi. I think I left my wallet at your bar last night."

"I didn't find any wallets."

"Are you sure?"

"Yes. No wallets. Sorry."

"Can you at least check? Please?" My voice is wavering on hysteria. I don't think this guy realizes what a crucial element he is in this investigation.

"Hold on."

I hear him shuffling in the background. Five minutes later he returns. I thought he forgot about me.

"No wallet. Sorry. Are you sure you've looked everywhere?"

Why do people always ask this when you lose something? What answer do they expect? Oh, yeah, thanks to your incredible insight I realize I forgot to check behind the couch? "Yes, I'm sure."

"Do you remember where you left it?"

"Yes, at your bar."

"Sorry. Someone must have taken off with it."

Gee, thanks.

Damn that Raisin-Eyes.

I call Sam at Marc's.

Marc answers the phone. "Hello?"

"Hi, Marc, how you doing?"

"Fine. How you doing?"

"Fine. Can I speak to Sam please?" I have no time for one of Marc's nonexistent conversations. Personally, I think Sam should have stayed with Ben. He, at least, has a personality, albeit he's a drunk.

"Sure. One sec."

I hear giggling. "Hi!" she squeals. "How are you?"

"How am I? How do you think I am? Please tell me what the hell is going on."

"I was just going to call you. Good morning! Happy New Year!"

Why must everyone scream? "Shh. Happy New Year to you, too."

"I'm not mad at you anymore, if that's why you're calling. Everything's good. We're back together." She giggles again.

"So I hear. Apparently, you're moving out." Why is she so happy when I'm so miserable? Shouldn't friends commiserate?

"Uh...you spoke to your sister, huh? Sorry about not telling you myself. I didn't want to wake you when I left. You weren't exactly in top form last night. Did you get sick?"

Why are we still talking about me here? "Why did you tell my sister she could move in?"

"Tell your sister *what?*"

"She's here."

"How did she get there? She told me she had no money."

Hmm. "That's an excellent question." I scream, "Iris! How did you get here?"

"How do you think I got here, genius?" Iris yells through the closed door. "I flew!"

"How did you pay for the ticket?"

"Mom left me her credit card in case of an emergency! So I bought a ticket over the Net!"

Let me get this straight. The plane ticket to Boston counts as an emergency, so she charges it to Janie. But the cab fare from the airport to my apartment does not, so she makes me pay. A preview of my life to come.

"She bought a ticket over the Net with Janie's credit card," I tell Sam. "But we're veering off the subject."

"I didn't tell your sister to move in. I told her that Biggy Bear and I made up and that we're talking about moving in together."

They just got back together last night! He must have done some serious groveling. "Talking? Just talking? So does this mean you're not moving out right away?"

"Well...not yet."

Aha! There is hope. When a guy says not yet, he means never. "So, like never?"

"No, not never." Do I detect impatience in Sam's voice? "As soon as we can find someone else to take over my lease, I'm out. I don't want to screw you over."

"If you don't want to screw me over, don't move out. Don't you think you're being a little hasty with this decision?"

"I'm sorry, Jack. But aren't you happy for me? We're back together! We're talking about taking a vacation somewhere to celebrate. Maybe the Bahamas? We were on the Net late last night, looking for a cheapie ticket."

"Congratulations," I say sarcastically. I know I'm being a bitch, but I can't help it. Okay, fine. "I'm happy for you," I tell her, and hang up.

I need to take a shower. I'm disgusting. My eyes are sticky. I hate when I don't get washed before going to bed. My makeup is probably all over my pillow. The message button is flashing. How many phone calls did I sleep through this morning, exactly?

Iris. Iris. Wendy ("Call me back—it's urgent!"). Iris. Iris. My dad ("Happy New Year, Fern!") Iris.

First I search the house again. Under the couch? Nope. In the closet? Nope. Where the hell is my wallet?

This is the second time I've lost my wallet. The first time was at Penn. It was during exams and Wendy and I were going to the library to study. I decided to leave my wallet at home because of the signs posted all over the book stacks: "Thieves lurk here. Keep an eye on your valuables." So I, very responsibly I might add, left my wallet on the kitchen table, and we went to the library. Four hours later, we returned to find the door slightly ajar. Strange, at first it didn't register in my brain that someone broke in. I thought the landlord had changed our locks. Wendy pushed in the door, and then it hit me that we'd been robbed.

I started screaming not to go in. What if someone was still there? But Wendy was already inside looking around. The TV was still there. The VCR, too. I ran into my room. Computer? Check. Printer? Check. Stereo? Check. So we assumed nothing had been taken. All is well, we thought, until two hours later when I couldn't find my *Madonna: The Immaculate Collection*. So not only did the idiot steal only CDs, but they picked the two worst collections in Philadelphia. Collectively, Wendy and I owned two *Chicago's Greatest Hits,* two *Air Supply's Greatest Hits,* one *Here Come the Hits* (funky 80s mix), one *Pretty in Pink,* and one *The Spice Girls.* Inexplicably, they left behind *Cyndi Lauper's Greatest Hits.*

The next morning I realized the CD bandit had also taken my wallet from the kitchen table. When I told my dad, he confidently replied it was a good thing he had told me to photocopy everything in my wallet, in case.

A good thing. It was a good thing he *told* me.

And it's a good thing I learned from the experience and started making copies in case it ever happened again.

A good thing.

Damn.

Now the song ''Time After Time'' keeps playing in my head.

A bad thing.

I call Wendy.

''Happy New Year!'' she says cheerfully. ''I'm glad it's you. I made a New Year's resolution.''

''What is it?''

''I'm quitting my job.''

''What?''

''I'm going to Europe.''

''Wen…that's so not you.''

''It is now.''

''For how long?''

''I don't know. I bought an open-ended ticket.''

An open-ended ticket! What if she never comes back? What if she moves to Paris and I have to take French lessons just to communicate with her? ''You already bought a ticket?''

''Last night. I was playing around on the computer and I bought it on the Net.''

Boy, the Net must have been pretty busy last night. Everyone seems to have been buying tickets. "They made you stay at work on New Year's Eve?"

"They didn't make me do anything," she answers a bit too defensively. "I wanted to finish something."

"Do you really have it in you to take off just like that?"

Pause. "I'm not sure. But I really want to. I want to be happy. And I'm not. All I do is work and sleep. And talk to Bubbe. It's not a life."

"So just get your own place. You don't have to go across the world."

"But I want to! I want to do something crazy. Want to come?"

No. Yes! "To Europe? I can't go to Europe."

"Why not? I am."

"Because...I have a job, an apartment." An apartment soon to be minus one roommate. "And Iris is here."

"Iris? She's visiting?"

"Long story. Where are you flying to?"

"Heathrow."

Ah, London. "That's not fair. You know I've always wanted to go to London."

"So come."

"I can't. When are you going?"

"The beginning of February."

"In one month? You can't leave so soon! What if I have an emergency? How will I know where to find you if you're off gallivanting somewhere in Europe?"

"So come!"

"Get real, Wen. I can't just leave. I told you, I have a job."

"So do I."

"And I lost my wallet."

"Again?"

"What again? It was stolen last time." Wendy has this crazy theory that I "fabricated" the stolen wallet story and actually left it at the chocolate bar vending machine at the library.

"If you say so. Where did you lose it?"

"If I knew where, it wouldn't be lost, would it?"

"False. You could know where you last saw it."

"At the bar last night."

"You'd better cancel your cards right away."

"What a pain in the ass."

"You have to do it right away. Don't procrastinate."

But what if I find it?

Buzz.

"Someone's buzzing from downstairs. Hold on."

It had better not be another family member coming to visit. Please, please, please, let it not be Janie coming here to fetch Iris. Not that I want my sister to stay. I just can't deal with Janie right now. Maybe it's Andrew. I seem to remember him saying something about checking up on me today.

"Who is it?"

"Jeremy."

Omigod. What is he doing here in Boston? What is he doing at my apartment? I can't open the door smelling like this. I don't want to see him. "Come up," I say and buzz him in. Why did I do that? He can't see me like this. I'm dirty. He can't smell me like this. Do I have time to shower before he comes up? I have about three minutes before he's upstairs.

The intercom buzzes again. "What apartment are you?"

"Five-oh-eight."

I'm amazed he even remembered the building. The last time he saw the place was when we came to Boston to check it out together. Before he deserted me and ruined everything. Two minutes and forty seconds left.

When the knock appears on my door, three minutes and eleven seconds later (the elevator must have been stuck in the basement again—I usually hate when that happens, but now I'm thrilled that I had the extra time—my teeth are brushed, my face is washed, my jeans and sweater are on, I'm sprayed with perfume (no time for a dab on each arm, only for one all-encompassing spray), and my hair is tucked under the Red Sox hat he bought me. I hope he appreciates the gesture. I hope he remembers giving it to me.

Omigod. Jeremy's here. Why is Jeremy here?

Knock, knock. I open the door. He's standing in front of me, wearing a black leather jacket, faded blue jeans, and the black boots we bought together last spring. Why does he always smell so good?

"Hi," he says, trying to maintain eye contact.

"Hi." Don't look him in the eye; don't look him in the eye. I have to stay mad at him. He's seeing Crystal Werner. He's sleeping with Crystal Werner. He used at least seven condoms with Crystal Werner. "And you're here because...?" This question is getting old.

"Can we talk?"

I'm confused. "Can we talk?" is a question that usually precedes a breakup. We're already broken up. "I don't want to talk."

"Please? Let me come inside."

"No."

"Please. I miss you."

Ah. The three words every jilted woman longs to hear besides "I love you," or "(insert name) marry me," or "I'm a jerk," or "Use my Visa."

He misses me.

"Please?"

And he's saying please.... "Okay. We can talk. But Iris is here."

"She's in for the holidays?"

"Not exactly."

"Come to my place."

So he has a place already. "I'm not going to your place." Does he think I'm going to fall back into his arms, just like that? Don't I at least merit groveling?

"Why do you have a picture of naked people on your wall?" He is referring to Tim's Christmas present, which is hanging above the couch in the living room. There's no more wall space in my room.

"It was a present."

"It's weird."

"So don't look at it." Is this why he came here? To annoy me?

"I'm sorry," he says, gently touching my arm. "Only I'm talented enough to piss you off when I'm trying to suck up. Will you come to the Public Garden with me?"

A garden? How cute is that? "But it's winter."

"It's nice out. I'll keep you warm. Please?"

"Okay."

What's wrong with me?

We're sitting by the swan pond, which presently is swanless due to the season. He takes off his coat so that we can sit on it. Kind of sweet, actually.

Is it possible he's changed?

He doesn't even care that he's cold. He's thinking only about me.

It's possible.

He puts his hand on my knee. "I'm sorry about Crystal."

Yeah, me, too. "Is it over?"

"Yes. I promise."

I'm kind of curious about the details of their relationship, but I'm probably better off not knowing. I don't *want* to know. But— did she dump him? Maybe he dumped her. But what if she dumped him? Do I really want to be with someone else's dumpee? What if he just wants to be with me because I live here and she doesn't?

I run my fingers over his hand. I notice he's been taking care of his nails. They're so square, as if he's had a manicure.

He leans over and kisses me. I kiss him back. The familiar feel of his mouth feels nice. I guess we're getting back together.

He wants to show me his apartment, so I go. He's rented a small one-bedroom on Charles. I recognize the gray couch and wall units from his old place at Penn. Boxes are scattered all over the floor.

"The place is cute," I remark. He takes my jacket and hangs it up on what appears to be a new purchase—a coat stand. Appears to be a new purchase because the bottom is still sitting in a long rectangular box.

"Thanks. My mom found it for me."

"That was nice of her. When did you move in?"

"Two days ago." He runs the tips of fingers against my cheek, letting them linger on the back of my neck. We kiss. And keep kissing. "Want to christen the bedroom?" he pulls back and asks.

Am I really ready to take him back?

His hand traces lines up my back.

"Is it okay if I shower first?"

"Let me get you a towel." He pulls out a gray fluffy towel from the linen closet and wraps it around my shoulders. I used to love when he did that. We'd shower together and then he'd get out while I stayed warm under the water spray. A few moments later, I'd come out and he'd wrap the towel around my body, kissing me lightly on the lips.

The mirror in the bathroom has a row of round halogen lights on either side. Pretty fancy for a guy's apartment. The sun shines through the horizontal plastic blinds, casting prison bars across the floor's pale blue tiles. What does he have in the cabinet? I slowly open the mirrored door so that it doesn't make any noise. I see a small white box. Is that a condom box? Does he keep condoms in the bathroom? Has he already had sex in the shower? Would I be christening the bedroom but not the apartment, since he's already had sex with some girl behind the navy blue shower curtain that matches the bath rug?

Wait a minute. Let's give the guy a chance. He could have bought a box here in Boston, hoping, dreaming, et cetera, that he'd be able to use them with me. How many condoms come in a box again? Ten? Or is it twelve? Who figures out these things? Why not fifteen, or twenty, or one for each day of the month? What is the marketing strategy behind packaging condoms?

If there are any missing, I'm leaving.

Oh. The white box is full of vitamins.

I close the cabinet and turn on the water. Too cold. I turn the faucet knob to the left. Too hot. I hate not being able to find the exact line between hot and cold. I turn the shower on, or try to. I hate when this happens, too. I can't figure out how to get the shower part going. Why is it so hard to start the shower? There it is. The water is hot as I step onto a prison bar and reach for the soap. He has Dove. I have a feeling his mother came and set up the entire apartment before he got here.

Hmm. He's been here for two days. What did he do on New Year's Eve? If he's so crazy about me, why didn't he call me? Was he at Orgasm? I didn't see him at Orgasm. Did I see him at Orgasm? Did he see me at Orgasm? Did he see me sitting by myself at the bar? Maybe he saw me with Andrew. Maybe he saw me with leave with Andrew and is now afraid I'm getting on with my life, worried he'll lose his hold on me. Will he lose interest as soon as he feels comfortable again?

Here I am, a complete mass of confusion, standing under his Magic Massager showerhead, the hot water beating against my back. When did I become "the insecure girl?" When did I become the "searches-through-her-boyfriend's-cabinet-to-count-how-many-condoms-he-has girl?"

I can't breathe—there's too much steam in here. I turn off the water and step out of the stall. I have to figure out what I should do, what I should say, who I should be. I open the window and wrap myself in the fuzzy gray towel and sit down on the tiled floor. If I count to ten, maybe the steam will disappear and I'll be able to breathe again. One...two...three... If I count to ten, maybe by then the answers will come to me. Four...five...six...

Do my attempted romantic relationships fail because I'm destined to be with Jeremy? Or because I'm afraid to let myself like someone else, care about someone else, admit that Jeremy and I are over?

Am I in love? Or am I afraid of not being in love?

Seven...eight...nine. Ten.

Maybe we *are* meant to be together. The fact that we keep getting back together has to count for something.

"Jer?" I call out. "Come here for a second!"

"Hold on!" he yells from the living room. He opens the door. "It's too hot in here. Come out."

"It's too cold out there." I pull his arm and he comes inside, leaving the door open behind him. "Are you in love with me?"

He stares at me without answering. "I... How can I answer that? I just got here two days ago."

Wrong answer. "We've known each other for over three years. If you can't answer that now, you're never going to be able to."

His face turns red from the steam. "Are you in love with me?" he returns the question.

Maybe it doesn't matter that he doesn't say I love you. Maybe it doesn't matter that I'll always be monitoring the inventory in his condom box. Maybe this is as deep as it gets.

Maybe the only thing deep here is what I've been walking through these last few months. I'd need boots that go all the way up my thighs if I were to stay with Jeremy.

"I'm going home."

He watches me silently, and then leaves the bathroom. I put my clothes on and decide to take the subway. He doesn't try to stop me.

As I walk to the station, strands of my wet hair freeze into icicles. As soon as I get home, I'm taking a hot bath. Then I'm canceling my credit cards. Sometimes you just have to suck it up and cut your losses.

Chapter Eighteen

Can I Be Jo-Jo?

When I get home, Sam and Iris are sitting together on the couch, watching *Law and Order.*

"Hi," they say in unison.

"Hi."

I join them under the afghan. "Anyone call?"

"Yeah." Iris says. "Andrew."

My heart stops for a second and then resumes. "What did he say?"

"I don't know. He hung up pretty quickly."

"Huh? Why did he hang up?"

"He wasn't very thrilled that you went out with Jeremy."

"Why did you tell him I went out with Jeremy?"

"Oh, was it supposed to be a secret?"

Shouldn't sisters have radar for this type of thing? "How did you know I went out with Jeremy, anyway?" Wasn't she barricaded in my room when I left?

"Because after you yelled that you were leaving, I came out to get food, but you didn't have any, so I decided to order a pizza on Janie, but the phone was off the hook with Wendy on it. Apparently you forgot about her. That wasn't very nice, Jack. And she doesn't approve of Jer. Do you know she's going to London?"

Shit! Shit! Shit! My sister is in town for less than three hours and already she's turned my life upside down. I have to call Andrew right now. I run into my room and close the door. His machine picks up.

I try again an hour later and leave another message.

He doesn't call back.

By the next morning he still hasn't called back.

"What do I do?" I ask Sam.

"He probably has call display. Try him from my cell."

It works. "Hello?" he says.

"It's me."

"Yeah."

"Nothing happened with Jeremy."

"It doesn't matter."

It doesn't matter? "Obviously it does or you wouldn't be so pissed off."

"Maybe I'm pissed off because I think you're a bit pathetic."

Ouch. That was a bit uncalled for. "Why am I pathetic?"

"Because even though you say you want nothing to do with him, as soon as he whistles, you go running."

"That's not true. I didn't go running." Here again is the problem with lying. What's the point when the words sound hollow even to me?

"Your sister said he knocked on your door and you left with him. I'd call that running, wouldn't you?"

"What do you expect? I had to give him a chance to explain. But nothing happened! We are *not* getting back together."

"Whatever you say. My bet is that you two are back together before Valentine's Day."

"I told you, it's not going to happen."

"Okay. Sure. Take care." He hangs up.

The next morning the phone wakes us up. By "us," I mean me and Iris's sprawled-across-both-sides-of-the-bed body. How can such a little person take up so much space?

"Hello?" Maybe it's Andrew. Maybe he's realized that his unfair accusations were cruel and unjust.

"Jacquelyn, is that you?" It's Janie. A hysterical-sounding Janie.

I contemplate telling her she has the wrong number, but mumble yes by mistake.

"Iris is missing!" she exclaims. "I just got home and yesterday's paper is still sitting outside the door and the place is a mess. I think she's been kidnapped."

I'm awake. "Relax, she's here."

"She's in Boston? Why is she in Boston?"

"She wasn't too impressed with your emigration plan."

"Why didn't you call us so we wouldn't worry?"

I'm not quite sure why I didn't call. I didn't even think about it. I guess that was pretty irresponsible. If Iris were a plant she'd probably be all shriveled up by now for lack of being watered. "I didn't think. I'm sorry."

"You have to send her back to us right now."

"She's not a package I can send by Federal Express. Hold on a sec. When's your return flight?" I ask Iris.

"My ticket is one way. Don't you pay attention? I'm not leaving."

"Apparently she's not leaving," I say to Janie.

"Let me speak to her."

"She wants to talk to you." I hold out the phone.

"I'm not talking to her."

"Take it."

"No."

"Pick up the phone, Iris!" Janie screams through the receiver. Iris shakes her head.

I pick up the phone again. "She's in the shower."

"Don't lie."

"She's mad at you. She doesn't want to move to Arizona."

"Why not? It's a beautiful state."

"Because she's sixteen. And right now her friends are very important to her. She's moved a million times in the past ten years, and I think she's getting a little tired of it."

"Unfortunately, she's not the one who gets to make the decisions."

"Don't you think you're being unfair? To make her move in middle of the year?"

"What do you mean in the middle of the year? We still have to sell the house. That will take a couple of months at least, and then I'll stay with her until she finishes her junior year."

"I'm going to be a loser in my senior year!" Iris sobs.

"I hear her! She's not in the shower!"

I shoot Iris a look and continue negotiating with Janie. "So you're willing to wait until summer?"

"Yes, of course!"

I turn to my sobbing sister. "Why are you being such a baby?"

She grabs the phone. "I hate you! I won't have anyone to talk to all summer! And all senior year! I don't want to move again! I'd rather live with Jackie. She, at least, loves me. She, at least, cares about my happiness." She slams down the phone.

Her therapy bills are going to cost a fortune.

"Please can I live with you? Please?" she begs.

I do feel for her. Really. But what can I do? "I can't take care of you."

"I'm sixteen. I don't need to be taken care of. And what else are you going to do? Sam's moving out soon, and you hate to be alone."

"What do you think, the apartment is free? I already told you, I can't cover both rents."

"What if I drop out of school to work?"

"Yeah, that's what I want you do, drop out of school. Are you crazy? It's only one year, Iris. Then you're off to college. Can't you tough it out?"

She turns around and starts to cry into the pillow. I remember her first day of school in Boston. I was still on summer break from college, but junior high had already started. I was sitting in Janie's car, waiting to hear all the events of the day. She had been so excited, so nervous, that morning when she'd chosen just the right outfit: her Calvin Klein's and a midriff-peeking tank top.

"So how was it?" Janie asked tentatively.

Iris burst into tears and said, "No one talked to me the whole day. I had to eat lunch in the bathroom so I wouldn't have to sit by myself in the cafeteria."

It kills me when she cries. I look at her sobbing head and sigh. "What if you stay with me for the summer? Will you agree to move with Janie later?" I can't believe I said that. My sister stay with me the whole summer? Have I lost my mind? Why don't I just swallow a bottle of pills? The result will be the same. Janie once said that if Iris had been the firstborn, she would have remained an only child. By the end of the summer, I suspect she *will* be an only child.

She stops crying. "You'd let me stay with you for the summer?"

"Maybe. But you'd have to cover your own rent. And pay for your own food. So you'd have to get a job. And you'd have a curfew."

"I don't have a curfew at home."

"You should. I had a curfew. You have to follow my rules, and if you don't, you'll be on the first plane to Phoenix."

"Are you being serious? You'd let me live here?"

"For the summer. Only."

I call Janie back and fill her in on the new plan.

"You can't even take care of a turtle. How can you take care of a teenager?"

"I was ten, and the turtle escaped. It wasn't my fault."

"I don't think it's a good idea."

"Why not? It'll give us a chance to bond. We hardly ever get to spend time together. Pleasepleaseplease?"

"Well…I'll have to discuss it with her father. But maybe it's not such a terrible idea after all. It'll give me the chance to move in peace."

We were as good as in. At least I won't have to live by myself. Iris will move in from July until the end of August, and by then I should have a real roommate lined up. I might even have a serious boyfriend. Maybe even Andrew. He could move in at the beginning of September…

* * *

Two days later I drop Iris off at the airport and head straight to Andrew's. He refuses to talk to me on the phone, fine, but he can't just throw me out of his house, can he? I hope he's home. What a pain in the ass to go all the way to Cambridge and find he's not even there.

I park the car and ring his doorbell. He opens the door, wearing sweatpants, a white T-shirt, a baseball hat, and a look that says he's not happy to see me.

"Hi," I say.

"What are you doing here?"

"I want to talk to you."

He sighs. "Come in."

I follow him down the hall. I keep my coat on because he hasn't told me to take it off.

"Sit down." He motions to the coach.

I sit and decide to launch right into it. "I'm sorry. You were right."

"About what?"

"I've been pathetic. I thought I wanted Jeremy, but I don't. I figured it all out. I know what I want." And here it goes. "I want you."

"No, you don't."

"Yes, I do."

"No. You don't. You think you do, but you don't."

Is he trying to annoy me? "Okay, Freud, you tell me. What do I want?"

"You want a boyfriend."

"So?"

"So I don't want to be with someone who wants a boyfriend. I want to be with someone who wants to be with me."

This makes no sense. "But I want *you* to be my boyfriend."

"Look, I don't want to be with you just because you want to have a boyfriend. What part of that sentence don't you understand?" He pulls off his cap, runs his fingers through his hair, and places the it back on his head. "I like you. I like you a lot.

You're smart, you're beautiful, you're funny. I like who you are. I like me with you.''

"And I like *me* with *you*." So where's the problem here? Seems like a match, no?

"But I know that if we start dating, we'll screw it up. You're not over Jeremy yet. You can't be."

"I know I don't want to be with him. Isn't that enough?"

"No. I don't want to be the rebound guy."

"But you're not!"

"You need to be on your own for a while. If we're ever going to have a relationship, I need to know it's you I'm relating to. How can I know you if you don't really know yourself? And how can you know yourself if you've never really been alone with yourself?''

I think he's been watching too much *Oprah*. Is he suggesting I go off to Thailand to find myself? Look what happened to Jer: he came back an asshole. Actually, he was always an asshole. I know, I know, Andrew is right. A person can't hop from one serious relationship right into another. But be on my own? I hate being on my own. The whole point is to *not* be on my own. "For how long?"

"That's something you have to figure out for yourself."

"A month?" I can do a month.

"I don't know, Jack."

"Two months?" I can do two months.

"Maybe a year."

A year? Is he on crack? A year on my own? My face must turn white at the suggestion, because he laughs and puts his hand on my shoulder. "It's not that long."

I brush him away. "What are you going to do, get back together with Jess?"

"No, I broke up with Jess because we didn't click. I don't know why we didn't, but we didn't. You and I click. But now isn't the right time."

"I liked you better when you were a nihilist."

He shrugs.

"I think I'm going to go," I say and walk to the door. "I guess I'll be speaking to you in about a year, then." I hate this. I hate him. Now I have to look for a roommate. Now I have to look for a boyfriend.

"Jackie, wait. I don't want you to leave angry. For now, we can at least be friends."

"More friends I don't need." This has been the worst week ever. But I'm not going to cry. I haven't cried since New York. "Goodbye." I leave the apartment, slamming the door behind me.

I don't feel like talking much when I get home. I sit on the couch and turn on the TV. Maybe I'll never talk again. Maybe I'll become some sort of huge freak, and news stations will camp outside the apartment. The entire country will wonder what's wrong with me. Andrew will see me on TV and feel terrible for making me be by myself, and Sam will feel too bad to move out.

"Are you okay?" Sam asks.

I nod.

"Are you sure?"

I nod again.

I hate my life. I really do. And I have to go back to work tomorrow, where once again the focal point of my existence lies in the placement of semicolons. What's the point of them, anyway? Why can't sentences blend together into one long, convoluted unpunctuated idea, just like my pathetic life?

"I'm going to Marc's," Sam tells me. "I'll be back tomorrow."

I nod. What does it matter anyway?

Twenty minutes later I hear her key on the lock again. She's back. What did she forget? The handcuffs?

"I changed my mind. I went to the store and bought cookie dough ice cream, facial masks, and a pedicure set. Wanna have a makeover?"

I burst into tears.

"I think he's full of shit," she says fifteen minutes later from under a mud-drenched face. "What guy tells a girl she needs time to be alone? It's too bad—I thought he might take over my lease."

"What kind of person has a crazy idea like that?"

"One with an overzealous imagination. So what do you want to do about the apartment?"

"I don't know."

"Maybe Natalie will want to move in."

Could I live with Nat? She's been dropping hints lately. I think she's getting tired of living at home. "I guess. Maybe." As long as she leaves her calorie-counter in Beacon Hill.

After *Law and Order* (Sam's no longer addicted to *Beautiful Bride*), I call Wendy from bed.

"So come with me."

"I can't just come."

"Why not?"

Good question. "Well first of all, I can't afford it."

"You have no money put away?"

Hmm. "I have my therapy money. But it's supposed to go toward a CD player for my car."

"You don't have any CDs!"

"Yes I do! I've bought a couple since the robbery."

"How many?"

"Two. But I was I was planning to buy more with whatever I have left after I buy the player."

"You can buy a first-class ticket with the money you've been swindling! I'll talk you through buying it over the Net."

"There's more to buy than just the ticket. I have to eat in Europe. Baguettes don't grow on trees. And what about hotels?"

"We'll stay in youth hostels. We'll camp out on the highways. We'll wait tables. We'll sell costume jewelry in Hyde Park."

"You're an investment banker! What investment banker quits her job to sell costume jewelry?"

"I'll lend you the money. I made an absurd bonus last year."

"I can't borrow money from you." My mind is whirling. I

also got a small bonus for Christmas. Small but not entirely insignificant.

"So you won't borrow money from me. But you'll come? Say you'll come."

Can I really do this? Just take off? "You're leaving February first. That's too early for me. Sam won't mind—she can move into Marc's place, but we have to give the landlord two months' notice."

"So meet me in March. I'll tour a bit alone first. Where do you want to go?"

"Paris. And then the south of France. And then Italy. I want to take one of those leaning pictures in Pisa."

"So you're in?"

"Maybe. Yes. I think. Okay."

Why should I hang around here? I don't have a boyfriend, I soon won't have a roommate, and I'm stuck in a dead-end job.

Iris is going to kill me.

When I walk into work the next morning, I notice red balloons tied all around Helen's cubicle along with a big red banner that says, "Congratulations!"

What's going on? Did her dissertation get nominated for a Pulitzer? I will not gratify her by asking what has occurred.

I hate this office. I hate this grammar-obsessed world. I am going to resign immediately. I head toward Shauna's desk. "I need to talk to you about something."

"Sure," she says. "What's up?"

"I..." Suddenly a chorus of "For she's a jolly good fellow" interrupts my announcement. I can't take not knowing anymore. "What's going on?"

"Oh, didn't you hear?" Obviously not or I wouldn't be asking.

"We're publishing Helen's book!"

"What book?"

"Helen wrote a romance novel for *Love and Lust* and we're going to publish it!"

Helen wrote a novel? "When did Helen write a novel?"

"A couple of months ago."

"What's it called?"

"*The Millionaire Takes a Bride*. I guess it's about a millionaire who gets married."

Brilliant deduction, Shauna.

Wait a second. I edited *The Millionaire Takes a Bride*. There were sex scenes in it. Helen wrote sex scenes? Helen's had sex?

I storm over to Helen's desk.

"You wrote *The Millionaire Takes a Bride*?"

"Oh, good, Jackie, I'm glad you're here because—"

"Why didn't you tell me? I edited it for you!"

"I didn't want you to know it was mine. I wanted you to remain objective."

"But why did you ask for *my* help, since this was a personal project? Julie has a lot more experience." And you know I can't stand you, you comma-crazy co-worker.

Helen thinks about this for a second. "I wanted it to be polished, but not too polished."

"Gee, thanks." Bitch.

"Your editorial comments have been far more valuable to me than your copyediting."

I soften a bit. "Really?"

"I'm serious. I could never have published the book without your help. Thank you."

How was I tricked into involuntarily helping Helen fulfill her dreams? "You're welcome. And congratulations."

"Actually, there's more. I'm quitting my job to pursue writing full-time."

What? No more Helen? Yay! I'd be dancing for joy if I wasn't off to Europe anyway.

"And I'm going to recommend you for my position. I know how much you appreciate commas and punctuation, but you have an excellent eye for substantive editing. And my recommendation carries a lot of weight."

I stare at her openmouthed. Has the world gone mad? Helen is a romance writer? Helen is recommending me for her job?

What do I do? What about Europe? If I take this job, I may never again have the opportunity to find myself. I could remain lost forever. People will stop me in the street and ask, "How are you?" and I'll answer, "How should I know how I am when I don't even know where I am? Can't you see I'm lost?"

I thank her and bury myself in my cubicle. I desperately need to speak to someone about this, and while Wendy normally receives all my crisis-related phone calls, I have a feeling her opinion might be slightly biased.

I call Janie. Thank God she's home.

"What do I do?" I ask her.

"When I was about to graduate, my philosophy professor asked me what I was planning to do with my life. I told him I was getting married. He said I was too young, that I should go to Europe instead and find a lover."

"So...you're saying I should go?"

"I'm saying you're only young once. How often can you just pick up and take off?"

Hmm. According to you, all the time. "But what about Iris? She's supposed to stay with me this summer."

"You let me worry about Iris. Right now, you have to do what's best for you. Europe! How exciting!"

Something tells me that once I leave Boston, I'm never coming back. Not to live, anyway. Am I ready to leave Boston for good? I'll probably end up in New York. On the other hand, if I stay here, I will be in constant fear of running into Jeremy or Andrew. And what about a roommate? Do I want to spend the next year counting calories in a flowery spiraled notebook?

"I have a good feeling about this," Janie says. Janie has a thing about her "good feelings." She claims to have limited psychic powers. Maybe that's why I inherited only limited insight. "Maybe we should move to London, too," she says.

I call my dad and he pretty much says what I expect him to say, that running off to Europe would be irresponsible. "You're acting like your mother," he says. "Unable to see anything through." I'm not sure if he's referring to my half-completed master's degree or to their marriage. Am I really like that? Am I a quitter? I tell him I have to go.

What do I do? I need guidance. I need help. I need answers...I need a *real* psychic. Now there's an idea. Jo-Jo! I need Jo-Jo, world-renowned psychic and cosmetician (she also sidelines in hair replacement and acrylic nails). How can I call Jo-Jo? I look around the office for the newspaper. Where is Jo-Jo? Her hotline has mysteriously disappeared from the classifieds. But look—this one looks just as good. "P.P.I.A. Professional Psychic International Association—As Seen On TV!" Hmm. Unlike their competitors, these psychics are certified by an independent review board. That's encouraging. And the ad promises that their psychics will answer all my questions. "About love. About money. About destiny. And the first two minutes are Absolutely Free (followed by a charge of only $5.99 per minute, minimum 1 minute)!"

I dial the 900 number. I *so* can't charge this to work. Luckily, I have a credit card. My newly replaced credit card. I'm most definitely going to regret this at the end of the month.

"Welcome to the National Association of Professional Psychics," says a syrupy recorded woman's voice. "The certified psychic hotline. You must be over eighteen to continue. At the tone your first free two minutes will begin."

Beep. I set the timer on my digital clock.

"Hello... If...you...know...the...extension...of...the...psychic...you...wish...to...speak...to...please...type...in...the...extension...number...now."

Shouldn't they know the extension I want?

Lengthy pause. "Otherwise...please...hold."

Pause. Ring. Ring. Ring.

Finally, I meet Lewis.

"Hello," says Lewis with a Southern drawl. Not what I expected, but who am I to question the paranormal? "What is your name and birthday?" Hey! Shouldn't he know this, too?

I tell him anyway, and wait for the unraveling of my future.

"You are a generous person by nature," he says, sounding as

if he's reading from a computer screen. "You would give the shirt off your back to someone in need. You will have romance and security. You love young children. The coming week will be very good. You will have good news."

"Sorry?" I interrupt. I'm trying to be sly and test to see if he's just a recording. "I didn't hear that. Can you repeat that?"

He ignores me and continues. "You have excellent communication with someone in your life." Obviously not you, Lewis. "Within thirty days, all your problems will be solved. You will do some traveling. Possibly you will move. Maybe to another city. Maybe to another state. You may not actually move, or may not have the opportunity to move, but if you do, your life will be enriched."

What are you talking about, Lewis?

"You're life is at a crossroad."

Very true. Good job, Lewis!

"Something will happen concerning transportation."

An airplane? Will I be getting on an airplane?

"A new car is coming into your life." A new car? Will it have a CD player? Who does he think he is—a game show host?

"What kind of car?" I ask.

"You will be happy with your new car. March first is your lucky day. Any time within eighty days of this date, before or later, you might receive good news." That means anytime from now 'til June.

I make an attempt to interrupt again. "Will I be promoted?" I look at the timer. Six minutes and thirteen seconds. "And while I have you on the line, can you tell me if I'll ever get married? Will Andrew ever want to be with me? Will Jeremy miss me? Will I meet someone else? Will I forget about Jeremy? Will I forget about Andrew? Will—"

"I see romance in your life."

"I edit romance novels, of course there's romance in my life! Is there sex? I'd like to have sex again, one day soon. Is there an Andrew in the picture? Hello? Are you following? Are you there?"

"I see much romance. I see a cowboy."

A cowboy? He sees a cowboy? The timer now shows just over seven minutes. I know I should hang up, but I have to know more. I need to know more! Tell me more!

I ask about my health ("Very good health") and if I'll be rich ("Very, very rich") and eight and a half minutes later I realize I'm still asking questions. So I say thank you very much and he says to call again soon. Yeah, right. I've just paid the college tuition for all his kids. What more does he want? For me to put them through medical school?

I hang up, realizing I never asked my intended question.

Forget Europe. Forget my promotion. I'm going to be a psychic. Can I be Jo-Jo? I want to be Jo-Jo. Maybe I am Jo-Jo. Please call me at 1-900-New-Jojo. And have your Visa card ready.

At 2:30, Shauna pops her head over my cubicle. "Jackie, are you busy now? Leanne and I would like to talk to you." Leanne is the senior editor of *True Love*.

This is it. Decision time.

Chapter Nineteen

Happily Ever After—Kind Of

It's a day of passion, roses, and candy-grams. A day of romantic potential. A day that can be traced back to one of three roots: the ancient Roman festival Lupercalia, where young men whipped young women to increase their fertility, or one of the two different Christian martyrs named Valentine.

Happy VD, one and all.

"Would you like a drink and some peanuts?" the airline stewardess asks.

The thing is, I'm not really a salt person. "Do you have any cookies?"

"Plain oatmeal okay?"

Boooo. If they're buying oatmeal, couldn't they have at least thrown in some chocolate chips? Why not take the tiny extra step to bring people joy? Except lactose-intolerant people. They'd probably be happier with plain, run-of-the-mill oatmeal.

"Whatever you have, I guess. And some coffee, please."

She gives me the cookie, coffee in a takeout cup, and a mini package of cinnamon hearts to celebrate V-Day.

I think back to when I was in grade school. I used to make the cards myself out of red construction paper (Janie refused to give in to the so-called greeting-card company conspiracy) and send them to all the kids in my class. Well...not to everyone. I never did send one to the boy in second grade who covered his nose with one hand and picked it with the other. Or to the smelly girl who sat behind me and used to have "accidents." Hmm. I wonder if watching the rest of the class spreading and counting our valentines across our desks had anything to do with his assault conviction and her attempted suicide?

Damn communist holiday. It divides the haves from the havenots. Marc brought over two dozen long-stemmed red roses last night. I've never received roses on Valentine's Day. Around February twelfth, Jeremy used to declare himself a conscientious objector to the holiday's crass commercialism.

Cheapskate.

I'm stuck smack in the middle of a row of five seats. Two businessmen are in their thirties are sitting to the left of me, and a mom and her daughter are sitting on my right. Too bad Wendy left so much earlier. At least she's meeting me at Heathrow, because otherwise I'd never find my way to the hostel. I'd get lost on the tube for sure. I love that word. Tube. Yay! I'm going on the tube! First we're stopping in London for a few days, and then off to Paris, then down to the south of France, then to Florence, and then to Venice. Oh, and to Milan, as well. The original *The Kiss* is in Milan, which will be pretty cool to see up close. But first I have to kill five more hours. Luckily I brought a lot of reading material, ten potential *True Love* manuscripts.

I'm using up my entire vacation for the year all in one shot, but I figure it's worth it. I'm going to Europe!

I made the right decision, I think. Thankfully, Helen agreed to stay on at work until I get back. Love that Helen! Sam's thrilled I've decided to remain in Boston after all. Now that she finally has a female friend, she doesn't want to lose me. I told her she could move out a couple of months early, since Iris will be spending the summer with me and splitting the rent. Who knows after that? By that time I could be married, right? If not, there's always Nat. Maybe she'll move in with me after the summer.

And maybe not. It might be good for me to live on my own for a while, if I can afford it. I'm going to be slightly richer with my new job (yay!), although slightly more in debt because of this trip. Oh, well. That's what Visa is for. They're awful nice, those Visa guys. They never mind lending you money. I'm not putting the whole trip on the plastic, though. Just the ticket. My

Christmas bonus and therapy money will go toward making sure I enjoy all the food and wine Europe has to offer.

And there's my train money, too. Since they were not able to return my luggage, due to it having been consumed by flames, I got to claim everything I lost. Unfortunately, umm, my two pairs of high black leather boots were in the bag. And, um, lots of CDs, including *Chicago's Greatest Hits, Air Supply's Greatest Hits, Here Come the Hits, Pretty in Pink,* and *The Spice Girls.* It was all very unfortunate.

In the end, my dad didn't object to my going away, not after I made certain compromises. For instance, at first I said I was intending to move overseas forever, so when I finally told them I was going only for a few weeks, he was relieved. I guess everything depends on the way it's framed. And I told my stepmom that it was time, sigh, for me to, sigh, fix my spirit and mend my soul. And that I thought traveling to Europe would do the trick. And complement the therapy. She and Oprah thought it was a terrific idea.

The last few days have been a complete blur. Sam, Nat, and I went to Orgasm last night. Unfortunately, Andrew wasn't there. It was nice to have a girls' night out, of course, but I'm looking forward to a vacation from Nat. This is what she said: "Jack, if Jeremy was seeing someone, would you want to know?"

What kind of question was that? Of course I wouldn't want to know! I don't want him to be dating anyone. But naturally, as soon as Nat brought up the possibility of his seeing someone else, I had to know. I needed to know. I would explode if I didn't know immediately.

"Whatever. I don't really care," I said casually.

"Remember my friend Amber?"

"What? He's seeing Amber?"

"Well, not *seeing* Amber. They've only gone out a couple of times."

"But Jeremy hates dentists!"

This piece of information left a bad taste in my mouth, like a fluoride treatment. It's not that I don't want Jeremy to be happy.

Okay, so I don't want him to be happy. My mind will be in a much more serene state if I believe he's sitting in his apartment, alone, counting his condoms. Oh, wait. That's me. I'm the condom counter. At least I've stopped wishing he'd die a slow and excruciatingly painful death.

I called Andrew when I got home. It was around one in the morning, but I needed to tell him I was going away.

He answered on the third ring, half asleep. "Hello?"

Wow. I hope my sleep-voice sounds that sexy.

"Hi. It's me."

"Jackie. Hi."

"Hi."

"I haven't heard from you in a while."

Forty-one days, but who's counting? "I haven't heard from you, either," I returned. "I'm just calling to say hi." I experienced a brief moment of Iris-Kyle déjà vu. "And to tell you I'm going to London tomorrow."

"You are? Vacation or work?"

"Vacation. I'm meeting Wendy."

"I heard she quit the bank. I'm still in shock."

"Everyone is."

"She's really planning to stay indefinitely?"

"Yup."

"I hope she finds what she's looking for.... Jack?"

"Yeah?"

"Call me when you get home."

Sam and Marc drove me to the airport. We were twenty minutes late leaving the apartment because I had no idea where my passport was. When I was about to succumb to complete hysteria, Sam found it under my bed, which doesn't make any sense at all because how could it get under my bed? But it was, and Sam found it buried under an old sweatshirt, right there next to my missing wallet. And then she made Marc carry my backpack for me, which was nice, but I'm still not sure how I'm going to carry this thing on my back while I'm out country-hopping.

"What's that?" Marc said pointing to a white envelope lying on the floor under the mail slot. "It has your name on it, Jackie."

A bill? A note from the landlord? I stuffed it in my carry-on bag with the *True Love* manuscripts, one pair of underwear, contact stuff, a toothbrush, a bikini, a sundress, and my high black boots replacement, my fabulous new I-may-be-the-footwear-of-a-backpacker-but-I'm-still-sexy-and-stylish sandals. It's probably too cold to wear open-toe shoes, but they're so cute! And then off we went to the airport in Marc's two-door Civic. I had to endure a half hour of Sessie telling Biggy about all the changes his apartment would be undergoing once she moved in.

Uh-oh. I have to go the bathroom. Who should I make get up? The couple or the mom and her daughter? Never mind. The line's too long. Maybe I should start reading *The Sheik's Bride*. I reach into my carry-on and pull out the manuscript along with the five possible covers I get to choose from.

The sheik is quite hot. Are there sheiks in Europe? This sheik actually looks more Italian than Arabic. He looks very Italian. Omigod. He looks like Lorenzo. He *is* Lorenzo. An actor, my ass! He's a cover model! That's where I recognize him from! He's on the cover of half my books! He really should fix his tooth, though. Maybe I'll refer him to Amber.

On second thought, maybe I won't. Am I allowed to go to cover shoots?

I reach into my knapsack for some gum to pop my ears. But wait, what's this? I pull out the white envelope. It's slightly bulky. Is this the type of thing the British Airways check-in people were referring to when they asked if anyone had given me an unidentified package to take on the plane? Am I a terrorist?

I open the envelope and pull out what appears to be a Valentine's Day card. On the cover is a big strawberry. The inside says "Have a berry happy Valentine's Day." In blue pen it says, "Is it a year yet? Come home soon. Love, Andrew." A pack of sour berries is responsible for the bulkiness.

Love, Andrew? Does he always sign his cards like that, or did he do it intentionally? Does "Is it a year yet?" refer to when we can start dating or when we can start speaking again? How cute is that berry pun! And how sweet is it that he came all the way from Cambridge just to drop the card at my place! But the sweetest thing of all is that he remembered how much I like sour berries.

Is he just being nice? Does he like me or does he *like* me? He didn't sign the card "Like, Andrew." He signed it "Love, Andrew." So maybe he does *like* me, right?

Stop. Stop right there. I will not waste what could potentially be the best three weeks in the history of womankind by pining. I must keep my concentration capacity intact so that I can meet all types of sexy Lorenzos. (Speaking of Tae Kwon Do, Master NanChu said I'm almost ready to test for my yellow belt. Yay! Only seventeen classes left!) Or maybe I'll meet a British bookstore owner in Notting Hill. Maybe I'll meet a prince. How old is Prince William now? An experienced older woman might do him some good. I'll settle for a Duke. Duchess Jackie. Duchess Jacquelyn. Lady Fern Jacquelyn of Back Bay. Are their sheiks in London?

A voice comes over the intercom. "Today's holiday movies are *Sleepless in Seattle* and *When Harry Met Sally.*"

Yay!

The man sitting next to me turns to his business partner. "What holiday?" he asks.

He didn't have to include the sour berries. If he just wanted to be friends, he would have just sent the card, right?